Saints of the New Irish Kitchen

A NOVEL

SEAN GLEASON

Newcastlewest Books

Newcastlewest Books

First Edition: December 2015

ISBN: 978-0-9967131-0-8

The characters and events in this book are fictitious. Any similarity
to real persons, living or dead, is coincidental and not intended by
the author.

www. newcastlewestbooks.com

This book is dedicated to my sister, whose persistence has been an inspiration

Saints of the New Irish Kitchen

ONE

Just like Paris, Martie didn't see sabotage coming up behind her. Someone spread lies about her and got away with it because she didn't look over her shoulder, too focused on the road ahead. It was a cut-throat business and she should have learned from experience but it happened again. Just like Paris, she was too stunned to open her mouth and counter the claim that she was going in a different direction. She had been so sure, so confident that the financing for her own restaurant was in place. So certain, and the next thing she knew she was meeting her replacement. Never again. Standing in front of the 'Help Wanted' sign, Martie vowed to turn it all around and crush anyone who stood in her way.

If it meant starting over from the bottom, going back to the line, she would start at the bottom. And she would be ruthless. No more being nice. Where did that get her, but where she was, at a restaurant that was scheduled to open in less than a week but was not even close to meeting the deadline. Maybe it was a mistake, to apply. Maybe the place would never open and she was wasting precious time. Maybe she would be turned down for being overqualified like she had been at every other place she'd tried for the past two months. And maybe not. Martie walked around the ladder leaning against the wall, where an electrician was tussling with a light fixture. She was nearly impaled by a falling screwdriver.

"Hey, watch it," the electrician said. "Can't you read the sign?"

A strip of yellow caution tape barred her way. Looking up, she noticed a banner draped over the entryway. "Sign? 'Grand Opening', that sign?" she asked. "Not grand, or not opening?"

"The sign on the f-ing door, the one that says not to use the door. The door behind the caution tape. That door," he said. He reached for a drill while holding up the fixture but his arms were too short for the job. The lamp came away and swung from a thin wire while the bright yellow tape across the doorway parted, to flutter on the spring breeze. Martie turned her head away before the end snapped in her eye.

What had been grunts muffled by the door exploded into a full-scale screaming match that was more profanity than useful words. Threats and curses flew, accusations of slave-driving countered by assertions of sabotage. The dangling light fixture swung like a pendulum in the spring breeze, scraping away at the freshly painted facade. A combatant in dust-coated jeans took note of the damage and yanked the lamp down. Standing in the open doorway, he shook it as if he meant to club his adversaries.

"Everyone's being careful, Mac? Everyone's being careful? This is what you call careful? All this care is bankrupting me, for Christ's sake." He marched back outside to confront the electrician, who was too busy tugging at wire nuts to pay the madman much attention. "Hey, Riordan, you lose something?"

"Thanks, Mr. McKechnie," Riordan said, returning to his task as if nothing out of the ordinary was happening. "You done for the day?"

"For the day? I'm done for the fucking rest of my life," McKechnie said. Turning to Martie, he barked, "You want something?"

"Just curious," Martie said. She canted her head towards the sign in the window. "You must be the man I should talk to."

"Yeah, lucky me." He looked her over and the hint of a smile creased his cheek. "Come on back."

Sawdust drifted from his brown hair and settled on his shoulders, adding a touch of red oak to the grey haze of plaster and stone. His right hand looked swollen, as if he had punched something. Or someone. "You might want to ice your knuckles," Martie said.

"No big deal," McKechnie said. "Air compressor fell on it."

4

The front door opened into a small entry that was common in the Midwest, a spot to trap the cold air in winter and keep a draft out of the restaurant. Martie pulled on the handle of the inner door and took note of its etched glass inserts, partially hidden by a large sign. It was easy to read, even backwards. Big letters scrawled with a thick black marker declared that no one was to use the door until further notice. It was signed by Brendan McKechnie, President, McKechnie Construction. She almost crashed into the ladder, and the painter standing on it, that blocked the way.

"Are you sure it's not broken?" Martie said as she skirted the hazard.

Piles of debris created an obstacle course from the foyer to the bar room, a clear indication that the pub was not close to meeting the opening day deadline. A hostess stand stood forlorn and alone, out of place in a small forest of plastic sheeting that covered what Martie guessed were stacks of chairs. A group of carpenters were putting their backs into shifting pieces of an antique bar into place. An older man, probably the foreman, filled a nail gun but paused in his chore to give McKechnie a look that was not anger, but pure mockery. He made a show of connecting the hose to the air gun and McKechnie swore under his breath.

"The kitchen is state of the art. Come take a look," McKechnie said.

"Thank you, I'd like to see it," Martie said.

"But I can't take the credit. I'm following the advice of a restaurant consultant," he said. "Did I introduce myself? Brendan McKechnie. Proud owner of McKechnie's Pub."

She had heard of Brendan McKechnie from her former employer, a force in the local restaurant industry, who regaled his culinary staff with tales of a clueless building contractor who thought he could be a restaurateur because he watched the Food Network. An idea took shape in Martie's mind. If she played it right, she could be back where she wanted to be in no time. She would have to be cold-blooded, calculating, and as callous as the bastard who ruined her plans, but she had to do what was necessary to salvage her future. There would be one less restaurant in town before she was finished, and it would not be hers going under.

He steered her to the left, and Martie slowed her pace. Something about the room's layout felt very familiar, with a small stage tucked into the corner near the front window. When she reached the back she saw a pair of snugs exactly where she expected them to be, but she could not have known they were there because she had never been in the place before.

The kitchen doors opened on a corridor, and Martie was certain that if she kept walking straight ahead she would find herself in a dining room half–paneled in oak, with walls an earthy tone of green. A shiver crept up her spine.

With confidence that was all for show, she pushed the swinging door with her hip and entered a kitchen in absolute anarchy. A battle for control was being waged between three cooks, a sure sign that the pub was not going to open on time, if ever. With Brendan's hand growing puffier by the minute, she ignored the shouting and snatched a towel from one of the warriors. She headed towards the ice machine, realizing that she knew where it was because she had sketched out the kitchen plan for her ex-boss when he asked her to design her ideal kitchen. So he had used her again, made her think she was doing all that work for herself when he only intended to sell her plan to someone else and keep all the profit. Never again.

While she settled the ice onto Brendan's knuckles, Martie gave the kitchen a quick glance. She could make it hers, and establish a base of operations that would be unassailable, but could she get that far before the reunion? The baby she had given up for adoption was expecting to meet a birth mother who had climbed to the top of the cooking industry, and to get back to where she was when he first contacted her, she would have to get Brendan wedged firmly under her thumb.

She had skill and knowledge, but there were other chefs out there who were hungry for acclaim. Martie had something else that Brendan needed, and needed desperately, or so her sources said. Without an influx of cash, the place might not open. And Martie had the money, a lifetime's worth of scrimping and saving so she could open her own place. Brendan was going to be in her debt, and once she had him pinned, the restaurant was as good as hers.

TWO

Pans rattled on the burners and a pair of cooks faced off in a culinary battle, each vowing to show the other how to cook chicken. The rest of the line cooks stood off to one side, not sure which camp to join. A third contestant for the role of head chef demanded mirepoix, but no one raised a knife to the pile of celery and carrots on the cutting board.

"I think I need a drink," Brendan said, examining his injury.

"Are you sure? Do you want to get that x-rayed or anything?" Martie asked. A plate crashed to the floor and a shouting match erupted. "Too many cooks, right?"

Brendan shrugged. "I figured they could sort it out."

"If they don't stab each other to death first. I wouldn't count on any of them knowing enough to make a peanut butter sandwich." Martie glanced at his hand. "Still pretty swollen. Can you make a fist?"

The sound of air hammers cut through the cacophony of battle. Martie followed Brendan back to the bar, where the carpenters were nailing trim around the bar back while a crew of painters followed on their heels, filling the holes with putty. A sharp prick of deja vu made her shudder. Even the bar itself was familiar, with a century's worth of Guinness rubbed into its finish.

"Might as well pull off the molding and crate up everything," Brendan mumbled. "This is all headed to foreclosure."

Stacked in the far corner was a forest of marble-topped tables that brought to mind Bewley's Oriental Cafe in Dublin, where she once lingered over coffee with fellow prep cooks, dreaming of culinary glory. She made a circuit of the room, taking in the scene. A shaft of sunlight sparkled on the etched glass of the front door, a lovely work of art featuring twining ivy and shamrocks. This was the first time she had seen it, she was certain. Then there was the bank of French doors separating the bar room from the patio. Poking her head through an open door, she realized that the patio was not at all familiar, just an area that looked like every other outdoor dining venue. It was common to use French doors in a restaurant, to give a room some spatial flexibility, and there were probably hundreds of establishments that had banks of French doors. Her imagination was getting the best of her. The notion that she had been in this place before was the result of stress and low blood sugar, not reality.

Brendan waved a weak, defeated farewell to the laborers as they stowed their tools, the bar installed with such skill that it seemed to have always been there. The empty liquor shelves were out of place, and Martie had an urge to put a few bottles out, to set the stage and imagine how the place was going to look in a few more days, when she was running it. She peered over the edge of the bar and found a trap door in the floor that led down to a storage room. Someone was rattling around in the basement, another worker finishing up, but she didn't feel comfortable enough to climb down the ladder and help herself. Not yet, at any rate.

"Can I ask you a huge favor? Could you hang out a minute, until I make sure I can move my hand?" Brendan asked. "Might need a ride to the hospital if I can't grip the steering wheel."

A turn to the left, to enter the waiting area for the dining room, and Martie gasped in shock. She had been here before. Not here, of course, in this new building, but in another place exactly like it. The wood paneled wall and the stairs that climbed to the second floor had been copied, down to the millimeter. The fireplace with its glass fishing floats from the beach at Spanish Point, the upholstered armchairs drawn up to the hearth, it was the pub in Miltown Malbay where they stayed last summer. Separate rooms. Separate planets would have been a better idea.

Walking up the stairs brought it all back, the fierce argument followed by a lapse in judgment that was beyond stupid. She entered the office, too disoriented to sit still, while Brendan stretched out on an old sofa. The lace curtains hanging in the windows were identical to the ones that hung in her room above the Miltown pub, although the accommodations were not replicated in Brendan's version. What if he had been there at the music festival and overheard everything, all those everythings she could not fully recall because she drank herself blind to erase the misery and ended up in bed with a man she'd only just met. She could not dare comment on the similarity or say a word about Miltown Malbay.

She walked around the room as if she could outrun the memories, concentrating instead on the empty bookshelves that would soon hold her collection of cookbooks. The bare walls would be decorated with her awards and souvenirs of a lifetime spent behind a stove. On the desk, a roll of blueprints balanced on a stack of bills, some stamped with a large, very red "Past Due" notice. There was a way to get where she wanted to go. It was right there in front of her.

"How are you feeling?" she asked.

"Numb," he said, only to launch into an unbidden confession. He wanted to own an authentic pub, bigger and better than the old pub, even before it was remodeled into a 1980's eyesore. Without explaining what old pub he meant, he moved on, cursing at himself, at his over-reaching, at his drive, at his dreams of grandeur. A man in a deep financial pit would take any help he could get to climb out, and he wouldn't be too particular about the cost. She was in the right place at the right time, the luck of the Irish befalling the daughter of Irish immigrants who had yet to forgive her sin.

While Brendan rattled on about the outrageous shipping costs for Irish antiques, Martie picked over the pile of jewel cases that littered the desk. "Mary Black. A beautiful voice. Are you a fan?" she asked, holding up an autographed liner note.

"That CD, a friend gave it to me," Brendan said. "He got us in backstage after a concert, introduced me and I'm standing there like an eejit with my mouth hanging open and she's asking who to sign the autograph for. Couldn't remember my name for a minute."

To change the mood, Martie popped the disc into the computer and a woman's voice soared through the room. She turned down the volume and took a seat behind the desk, ready to engage in the sort of give and take that was needed to iron out an arrangement that suited her needs. Brendan, however, wasn't ready to move on.

"You know, I'd rather sit through a public bankruptcy than tell him I'm broke," Brendan said. "All success, all the time, that's what he thinks of me, living the good life. Until now. Sure, I took my dad's business and built it up. Big mover and shaker in construction, that was me. Now the Midas touch is gone and I'm just another failure, another rags to riches and back to rags story. How did I let it happen, that's what I can't for the life of me figure out."

In response, Martie murmured a response to suggest that she was still listening when she had tuned him out. Her attention was snagged by a framed photograph that was partially covered by a blueprint. With the back of her hand, she wiped away the dirt and studied the black and white image of two men. They stood side-by-side, as if propping one another up. An infant in a christening robe was crushed against one man's chest, held tight in the firm grip of a father who was determined to protect his offspring from a harsh world. There was no way to know if the picture was a family heirloom or something picked up at an antique store for next to nothing.

"So she calls this my midlife crisis bar and grill," Brendan said. "What does she know? I mean, she grew up in Port Clinton and never had it rough."

"She doesn't know what you're looking for, you mean?" Martie said. Now who was he talking about? She should be paying attention, picking up on clues that would help her negotiate their deal.

"Please God, send a fire to burn this all down before I have to listen to how her brother would have helped and I told you so and Jesus Christ, the whining."

Martie let him talk, to air his grievances while she started organizing things. She found a copy of her resume in her tote bag, next to the note pad that she kept handy in case an idea appeared. For the sake of having everything in order, she put the resume on the desk for Brendan to peruse later, as if it would ever be necessary. A sliver of paper fell to the floor, the remnant of the sheet she had torn from the notepad the week before when a possible job fell through and she ripped out the menu ideas with a fury. She would not toss out another scribbled note. If she had to step on a few toes, she would step without mercy. Martie Smurfit was headed back to the top.

THREE

On and on Brendan rattled, detailing the many problems that had popped up during construction, only to veer off on a tangent that involved his girlfriend and her lack of support. A retort came to her, a witticism about having problems with girlfriends herself, but this was not the place for that much soul-baring. This was not the time for soul-baring, to be specific. Her baby had been adopted by hard-core Catholics and who knew what the boy thought of unconventional lifestyles? Martie did not want anything to leak out that might endanger the planned reunion, and if it meant hiding her sexual orientation, it was the price to pay. In her own time, and in her own way, she would break the news. Until then, her private life had to remain private.

It was more important to focus on Brendan and his issues, because a rocky relationship could create problems and derail the take-over. Martie understood that she could end up worse off, with some unexpected incident taking ownership in a wrong direction, but hadn't her entire career involved leaping such hurdles? She would just have to do it again. A woman didn't become an executive chef by giving up when things got hot. Hoping for enough information to guide her, she let Brendan ramble, but once he started in on his father and meeting the old man's expectations, she decided it was time to go. She was a chef, not a psychiatrist.

At the bottom of the stairs, Brendan took her elbow, as if he had found a rapt audience and he didn't want her to leave. He guided her to the wall in the waiting area where old photos had been hung as a distraction to waiting customers. Brendan flipped some switches behind the hostess stand and the overhead lights came on, to shine on the gallery. Here was his family, his childhood, his ancestors, and he pointed to the picture hanging at eye level, a blurry image of unruly boys making rabbit ears behind each other's heads.

"This one's me," Brendan said, indicating a scruffy kid with dirty jeans and an arm wrapped around a companion's neck in a half-Nelson. He moved his finger and touched the glass above the face of the boy in the head lock. "And this is Paddy. He's a singer now. Ever hear of Paddy Dunne?"

Martie stared at the younger face of last summer's one night stand, too stunned to speak. She understood where the plan for the pub had come from, why it had all seemed so painfully familiar. Within the grain of the photo was the memory of an impulsive act that might yet cost her the one relationship she truly valued. For a single afternoon she had been the rebellious teenager she had worked so hard to leave behind, the fool who only hurt herself when she lashed out. She had yet to find the words to explain to Manon. She could not mention a thing to Brendan, about the person and place they shared. It was a night to be erased from all human memory.

She gave the rest of the pictures a cursory glance while her mind churned. Not a word about Miltown would escape her lips, and so her secret would be safe. As for Paddy revealing a thing, Martie knew of his fear of flying and a general refusal to go anywhere he could not reach by car or ferry. He was far away in Ireland, forever and always. Not a word about Miltown, but at the same time she could never let Brendan snap her picture to show his old friend. She would have to avoid him, the man who owned the kitchen she was about to take over. How was she supposed to do that?

"You're in some kind of pain," she said. "Are you sure you're not hurt more than you're letting on?"

"The hand? It's good. Better than my head, which has been hurting for months. Stress," he said.

Even though Martie wanted to escape from his monologue of grief, she had to inspect the dining room. Behind the gallery wall was another snug, situated to separate the noisy waiting area from the main dining room and create a subdued atmosphere. She tested the dark green upholstery of the bench, judging it comfortable but not so plush that the patrons would sit for hours and tie up the table. Brendan slid into the seat across from her.

"Like I was saying, this is not my midlife crisis," he said. Technically, not a midlife crisis because Brendan was on the sunny side of forty, but he was definitely engaging in some risky behavior. "I work my ass off, I give her my undivided attention when I have free time, and all I ask in return is a place to go on a Saturday night for a beer with the guys. What's wrong with that?"

"Nothing," Martie said. She had been working in restaurants since she was fifteen, and she had never once gone out on a Saturday night unless it was after work. If someone had the chance to do normal things like regular people did, what was the harm? Her financial future depended on that kind of activity.

"The cost over-runs," he said. "I'm tapped out. The staff, their salaries alone, and who knows how long I'm supposed to keep paying them? How am I ever going to open this place?"

"It will open on time," she said.

"You sound pretty confident."

She would be fair, splitting the profits equally, once they were partners. Too bad for him that the investment wasn't fifty-fifty, but her reputation counted for more than all the cash she was going to sink into the venture. Brendan was in no position to accept anything other than her terms. "I am confident," she said.

"Just, confidence? That's it?" he asked. Brendan sat up a little straighter, shoulders set, ready to lean into the grindstone once again. "That's the best advice I've had in weeks. Thanks for listening to me. Sometimes, you know, a disinterested third party, fresh point of view."

"But I'm very interested," Martie said.

"I hope you'll come again," he said.

"You bet I will." Martie scanned the snug, admiring the heavy drapes that suggested an intimate and private setting. In Ireland, the snugs were designed for the ladies so that they could drink without being seen.

And just like in Irish pubs, there was a sliding door that opened on the back of the bar, for discreet liquor dispensing. "Does this thing work?"

Without waiting for an answer, Martie knocked and the partition opened with the slightest squeak. She almost jumped out of her skin.

"Bless me father, for I am dry. It's been twenty-four hours since my last drink," the stranger said in a thick Ulster brogue. "Des O'Hare, plumber and master dispenser of God's own gift to mankind."

With a practiced hand, he drew a pint while chatting about his experiences in his family's pub. With every word he uttered, Martie heard the sound of money dropping into the till. She had the perfect bartender, a man with an easy grace and a trove of anecdotes to amuse the clients. Perfect, until Des mentioned the political boundary that had divided the O'Hare clan, with one side in Lifford and the other in Strabane. Flashing a proud grin, he reached through the door and handed Brendan the pint, the brown foam limned with a shamrock. Martie looked closely at his large hand, the strong fingers, the power gathering in a fist. Maybe this particular Irishman wasn't quite so perfect as she had thought.

"The beer's flowing and the bar's ready to open," Des said. "We've done it, finished it all in time for the big day."

Des asked if Martie wanted a pint herself, and when she turned down the offer, he slide the partition back. She sat back to get a feel for the atmosphere in the snug and Brendan took her pose as an invitation to rattle on about Des O'Hare. The plumber was a hard-working man with more kids than he could easily afford. It was Des who talked Brendan into giving him the job; it was Des who pointed out the importance of a genuine Irishman behind the bar if the pub was to have the proper atmosphere. It was Des who reminded him that pouring Guinness was an art and the pub needed an artist, who just happened to be Des O'Hare. Brendan drooped in his seat, his head resting against the hard wood of the snug wall.

He took a careful sip, as if verifying authenticity of the stout. She took advantage of every break in the conversation to ask questions, to tease out the information needed to formulate a workable plan. Before long, she knew who was handling the construction loan at the bank, even though she had to waste fifteen minutes in listening to Brendan's experiences with a restaurant expert who Martie once considered a friend and now looked on as a bitter rival.

While Des polished the bar, Martie toured the barroom with Brendan on her heels. One by one, he checked the locks on the French doors, sighing as if he would never open them again. "Dress rehearsal tomorrow?" Des asked, and Brendan's shoulders slumped down around his knees.

"There's no time to lose, that's for sure," Martie said.

"We schedule a dress rehearsal for the bastard and then he calls the day before to tell me he's not coming," Brendan said. "I hired a chef, one of the best in Dublin, and now? I've got no one."

"There's always kinks to be worked out," Martie said. "Look on the bright side. The bar is ready to open up right now."

"Bright side?" Brendan countered. "My liquor license is a Class 2. That's—"

"Sixty percent food, forty percent liquor," Martie broke in. "There will never be a violation here, I guarantee you."

Ready or not, Martie had to turn the kitchen completely around, get control, rattle a few skulls and whip the staff into shape. All in a matter of days. Excusing herself for a minute, not wanting Brendan to follow her, she made for the ladies room but ducked into the kitchen. She grabbed a sauté pan from the shelf and slammed it against the steel counter top with the power of an executive chef who could make or break a career.

"Now that I have your attention," she said. "You're working for me. You got a problem with it, then leave. Ten a.m. tomorrow. Not ten minutes after. Any questions?"

"We were told," the heavily tattooed man said, only to be elbowed by a colleague who told him to shut it. A mumbled chorus of 'yes, chef' indicated that the message had been received.

Brendan was talking to Des when she got back to the bar, having the sort of conversation that a man on the verge of bankruptcy did not want to have with an employee who was elaborating on all the great things that he would be doing with his second paycheck. Martie extended her hand in farewell. Brendan winced, forgetting that his right hand had met an air compressor and lost.

"Working man's hands," he said.

Martie displayed her palms, always scrubbed clean, often red and chapped. "Working woman's hands," she said. "See you soon, Des."

At the front door, Brendan poked his head out and announced that the electrician had finished the lighting and the exit was safe. He must have noticed that she was checking out the holy water font that stood near the hostess stand. It was a beautiful piece of carved marble, suitably Irish with Celtic crosses carved on the pedestal.

"The Augustinians had to get rid of it," he said. "The junkies were using it to wash their needles. I figured it would be a great conversation piece, and I'd fill the bowl with after-dinner mints. A buddy of mine, he owns a hospital supply place and he sterilized it for me."

Before she got sick at the thought of her guests dipping their fingers into some HIV-tainted block of stone, Martie stepped out of the front door and took another look at the facade. The brushed copper lamps cast a soft glow on the authentic colors of Ireland, and Martie had to sniff back a tear of joy. Brendan didn't stand a chance. She wouldn't let this fall through her hands.

FOUR

All the liquid assets had been liquefied and were now dried up, but Brendan would never ask Chip for a dime. He would march up and down the street, proclaiming his failure, before he let Bonnie's brother meddle in the pub. Bonnie had pushed the idea, pushed it hard, but Brendan did not want partners. Instead he turned to his more reliable sources, leaning on clients to pay past due bills or pleading for an early draw on the office complex in Buffalo Trace. Whatever he could scrape together had to be put into the construction company accounts, to pay back loans he had given himself to cover bills at the restaurant. He had woven a financial web so tangled that it would take his accountant ten years to unravel it. Not a problem if he could dig himself out of the hole by then.

Flat broke, but life went on, a life that required Brendan to return to McKechnie's and deal with the final blows. Just yesterday, hoping to salvage something, he turned to his primary source of restaurant management expertise but it had failed him when he was most in need of Michael DeCecco's wisdom. Unaware of the brotherhood of restaurant owners in town, Brendan had never intended to loot the man's staff, even if DeCecco had strongly implied the very thing.

"A line cook, two busboys, a dishwasher," Michael had ticked off his losses. "My executive chef decides to go into teaching. Might as well close shop myself, and forget about opening my bistro."

All that and more, and just because Brendan had asked how to find a good chef. Not even top notch, but adequate would do. Michael found it hilarious. "You want to open a restaurant?" the highly regarded chef had said. "You better know how to cook, my friend."

Good advice, but it came too late to save Brendan's skin. Cook? If there was a book about boiling water for dummies, that would be too advanced for him. The conversation he'd had with the woman who happened to be passing the other day when he smashed his hand had lifted his spirits. Beautiful blue eyes, nice figure, and if it wasn't for Bonnie he would have asked the woman for her phone number. If it wasn't for Des working on the beer lines in the cellar, he would have tried to hook up with her, but that was how his luck was running.

The positive outlook he had the night before had collided with reality in the morning. After sleeping on it, Brendan realized that he had spent a fortune and brewed up nothing more than a toxic stew of ambition and dreams. He was chasing after the life he knew from his uncle's pub in Ireland, but thought he could stir in the determination he learned from his father and create the perfect blend. No, he sure as hell did not know how to cook and he had concocted a recipe that was doomed to fail. Like an over-confident idiot he had not known when to quit, and all he had to show for the investment was a pub that wouldn't be, where he would tell the people he had hired that they were fired, and their final paychecks were sure to bounce. The odds of selling the place and breaking even were slim and none.

Before he reached the entrance, he heard static and crackling from the patio speakers. With so many other things to worry about, Brendan had forgotten about the guy that Chip, the professional media guru, had scheduled to install the computer-controlled sound system. Quickening the pace, almost jogging past the make-believe *An Post* office, Brendan reached for the handle of the front door.

Out of clear air, a loud voice boomed, "Talk to Joe," and a group of people began to applaud and cheer. All the French doors along the patio were wide open, spewing sound into the summer afternoon.

A swell of Irish fiddles screeched and was abruptly subdued. The front door opened of its own accord as another jackeen chirped, "Hello, and you're very welcome to Liveline."

"Hello, and you're very welcome to McKechnie's."

His eyes not yet adjusted to the dim light of the foyer, Brendan could not see who was talking to him. Gradually, the room grow less dim and he was shocked to discover that the person holding the door open and greeting him was one of his employees. Standing next to the holy water font, his jaw growing slack, Brendan came face to face with Aidan Murtaugh. Red haired, blue-eyed and suitably freckled, the lad had the map of Ireland on his face and the brogue of Kildare on his tongue.

"Who are these people?" Brendan lifted a weak arm to indicate the dozen men standing around the bar.

"We've put on our best face," Aidan grumbled. "Open the doors, she says. We're not ready, says I, but does she listen? Feckin' madness. And open them again. And again. Madness."

Eyes accustomed to the light, Brendan scanned the bar room, up one side and down the other, seeing more with every pass. Most, but not all, of the men at the bar were his employees, Mac and the rest of the lads who had earned the right to christen the place. Three side tables were in use by a loose amalgam of office workers, ties askew and jackets off, women's stiletto-clad feet delicately resting on the chair rails.

The voice of Joe Duffy, presenter of RTE's *Liveline*, cut off as abruptly as it had before, replaced by the driving electric guitar of *Wicklow Hills*. The office crowd applauded and cheered again, suggesting that the pints on the table were not the first of the afternoon. The loudest shouts came from the tradesmen of McKechnie Construction, taking pride in a job well done. Brendan had no idea who had opened the doors and given the orders to start pouring.

Like a mouse fleeing the house cat, April scurried by, her white shirt straining to contain the plastic surgeon's bounty. Within seconds, she dashed back to the top of the bar, hauling a large chalkboard that she took great care not to smudge with her heaving bosom. Brendan was amazed by the transformation, from slightly surly waitress whom he hired because she had big tits, to obedient and possibly frightened servant. Only the strain of fabric and physical attributes remained of the woman who had answered the help wanted ad. Someone had put the fear of God into her, or he was hallucinating. Surely it was the latter, because all of this, the bar and customers, could not be happening.

From the open doors, sounds of traffic and the growl of the Metra train punctuated the short blasts of music, talk radio and static. Mingled with the rhythm of Pierce Turner's Celtic soul and chattering human voices, the clink of glasses provided a backbeat that matched the pulsing in Brendan's brain. He was awake, he was here, and he had no idea what was going on or why it was happening. Somewhere along the line, he had missed a memo, forget to check his voice mail, or lost his mind.

At the top of the bar, April was unquestionably taking an order. It was Mac who was studying the scrawl on the board, pointing and nodding before spending a few moments discussing things with his crew. The meeting adjourned, Mac clapped his hands and rubbed them together with glee, and then he raised his glass and offered a toast to Mr. Brendan McKechnie, the esteemed proprietor. Mac was a great one for practical jokes, but the scope of this prank seemed to be too enormous, beyond his reach.

The office party joined in, to laud someone they had never met. Brendan felt the craic drifting in the air, seeping up through the floorboards and exuding from the marred finish of the old bar top. The camaraderie and good cheer of an Irish pub must have inoculated the wood of the pricey antique and spread throughout the room. Sliding along from bottom to top, Brendan made for the kitchen door, which popped open before he could get past Mac and the lads.

"She's a right aul' bitch," Emer said as she hurried past him on her way to the dining room.

"Ah, she's grand," her sister Eilìs countered, rushing off to the patio with a heavy tray balanced on her right shoulder.

Wedges of fresh soda bread and steamy plates of meat and potatoes left a mouth-watering trail in her wake. Food was being prepared, meals were being served, but this was more than Brendan expected of the disorganized group he had last seen a few days ago. Mac grabbed his arm before he could investigate, to find out who was behind this full-blown performance.

A cold pint slid down the bar while the carpenters slapped Brendan's back, ebullient congratulations for a job well done. Taking a sip, and then another gulp, he decided that he had fallen into some sort of twilight zone, a dimension of sound, a land of both shadow and substance.

Brendan downed the pint and the empty glass was quickly replaced. He chugged half of the fresh beer, staring in amazement at the scene before him.

From the speakers in the ceiling came another song that was more stops, starts and static than music. One more quick swig, and Brendan broke away from the party and made for his office, where someone was playing around with the sound system. He reached the hostess stand and noticed clusters of people milling about, faces aglow with anticipation, as if they had reached the promised land. Business people in summer suits greeted him but he couldn't waste a minute with pleasantries. A pair of men who resembled prizefighters, but dressed in Key West style, stuck out their hands as Brendan raced by, babbling good cheer intermixed with a financial offer that Mr. McKechnie wouldn't want to pass up, but this was no time for glad-handing or finagling a reprieve from foreclosure.

A fresh-faced teenager was fiddling with a volume control dial as he tapped his foot to the Wolfe Tones, pleased with his ability to copy from a CD to the computer and then have the music actually play. Scattered across the desk were jewel cases, some open and empty, others in piles of three or four. A few were Brendan's, Mary Black and Clannad and Paddy Dunne's most recent releases, but there were several that were not the sort of music he listened to, or had ever owned. The sort of music that was too obscure for iTunes.

"These from Chip?" he asked the technician. Because if they were, they were going in the garbage and every song from every one of these discs would be erased at once from the computer hard drive. He did not need Chip inserting his musical tastes in McKechnie's.

"Wasn't me," the kid said. "Ask your partner."

Stopping to listen, Brendan discovered all the clues that he needed, floating through the air in Irish sound waves. He would apologize to Mac, because clearly the man had set up a brilliant prank to repay the months of verbal abuse and long hours. Recruiting who knew how many others, Mac surely toiled for days, even weeks, to bring everything together in a phenomenally clever hoax. The mournful ballad wailed through the speakers, Kevin Barry gave his young life for the cause of liberty, and Brendan had to applaud the lead carpenter's audacity. While the Wolfe Tones sang of Kevin's tragic demise, the defeated boss charged back to the bar, to buy Mac a pint and tell him he was a genius. Never again would Brendan drive his crew so relentlessly.

Everything was becoming clear to him. The phone call from Dublin was part of the set-up, making him think that he had a restaurant but no chef, giving him sleepless nights and stressful days. He would go down to the kitchen and find the Michelin-star-earning chef toiling away, and the boys would have a long laugh. They could all sing a rousing chorus of *Kevin Barry* together, mending fences over a beer. Brendan's worries were not quite over, but his financial ruin was no longer assured, or at least not quite so imminent.

From his spot at the bar, Mac was leading the sing-along, crooning to the tables of office workers who were attempting to learn the refrain. They were the best of friends, one big party, and Brendan felt every care and worry slide off his shoulders. To rig up such an elaborate scheme, Mac must have been furious with him. He would join the fun, but he would take Mac aside and grovel because the carpenter had earned a novena's worth of grovel.

After taking a bow, Mac returned to the table where his son-in-law sat at his right hand. A sea of jovial grins slid into somber frowns as April set up a tray stand. Right behind her a busboy appeared, carrying a heavy tray that he deposited on the stand with the smoothest of moves. Using a corner of her long apron to lift the hot plates, April distributed the food without a word, looking nervous.

Brendan was about to march into the kitchen, to welcome the chef and laugh over the hoax, when he had to stop and rub his eyes. Walking through the swinging door, taking a place at April's side, was the woman who made him the ice bag, dressed in chef's whites. The kitchen door flew open again and a very irate young man charged out. He stomped to a spot directly across the table from her, glaring like a cornered lion. Brendan reached towards the bar and a glass of beer was nestled into his hand. Watching the impossible scene, he took a sip, as if he could make sense of it all with more alcohol in his system.

In unison, the diners picked up their cutlery and examined their plates. Brendan approached the table, only to pause when he sensed the searing heat of a fierce battle being waged over the heads of his employees. From a safe distance, he sniffed at the aroma of boiled bacon and cabbage and recalled Aunt Eleanor's dining room on a Saturday night. A glance at the composition of the plates told him that this was not the work of the Irish chef he had originally hired. Neither did the smells match those he recalled from his last trip to Dublin. The dinner service could not be Mac's messing. This was no prank. What it was Brendan could not begin to guess.

Six mouths chewed; six men pondered the flavors like wise judges. Mac laid aside his fork and the other five men followed his lead. He picked up a basket, took a steaming wedge of soda bread, and passed the basket to his left. The process was repeated for the butter, yellow and pure Irish, nestled in a white porcelain ramekin like a spring daisy. Six knives flashed, the butter melted into a golden sheen, and every man sampled and chewed with deep thought. The glaring man eyed every eater, folding his hands across his chest and letting a smug sneer creep across his face.

"Lovely," Mac said. The sneer left the young man's face and the murderous look returned. "Ah, lad, and didn't we tell you there's no fruit in soda bread?"

Enraged, the man ripped the cap off his head and flung it to the floor as if he could throw it through the boards and halfway to the center of the earth. "I quit," he bellowed.

"Bye," the ice-bag lady said. She smiled, but not warmly, and slipped her hands into her pants pockets. She rocked back on her heels, waiting for someone else to make the next move.

"As good as home, Martie," Mac said. "None of that seed nonsense, like weevils in the loaf."

Having lost some obscure contest, the vanquished party stormed out of the restaurant, wishing Aidan good luck as the manager held the door open. His heart beginning to pound in anxiety, Brendan feared that all this was not Mac's doing at all. It was Michael DeCecco, the restaurant king of Moraine Hills, getting even by driving away McKechnie's employees. The kitchen was filled with traitors, and Martie was the ringleader. The sounds of happy diners went unheard as Brendan pondered his next move, to find some way to salvage the last threads that held up his enterprise. His inexperience and lack of knowledge were to blame, leaving him vulnerable to sabotage. His eyes wide open, he had walked into the trap.

Martie sidled over towards Mac, her head a beacon of cheer in an outlandish scarf that had all the marks of a 1950's souvenir of Ireland. She put two more plates on the table, pork medallions and venison pate, asking the diners for their honest assessment. She meant to poison McKechnie's key employees, to destroy the construction company while bringing down the pub. To make matters worse, Brendan had told Martie his life story, supplying her with enough ammunition to blow his world to pieces. His complete destruction was now playing out before him.

"About time you got here," Martie said. Her smile was warm, full of welcome, *cead mile failte*, like a snake ready to strike with a venomous bite. As quickly as she had come, she was gone.

"Will you look at that," Mac said. "Here I'm saying how odd, a woman in the kitchen, and isn't it a woman in the kitchen at home?"

"You're sexist," an office girl called out.

"That's shocking," Mac retorted. "Fifty-six years of age, and she thinks I'm sexy. Ah. lads, the girls today. Shocking, it is. I'm a married man, so, and lead me not into temptation."

Mumbling under her breath, April hurried to the tables of office workers while the busboy hung the chalkboard on the wall where it was visible throughout the bar room. McKechnie's name was written in green, the thick letters edged in gold to match the sign outside. Someone with European penmanship, all swirls and loops, had written out a menu on the board. There were no paper menus in sight, a marked Continental touch that Brendan had not thought of before. In truth, he had not figured out very much as far as the restaurant details were concerned. Tables being served, hot food coming out of the kitchen; this did not look exactly like a plot to bring down the McKechnie empire. Things looked more like a restaurant being opened by someone who knew the business, the very industry he knew nothing about. Without question, he had just crossed over into the twilight zone.

The dregs of Brendan's beer had grown warm by the time he returned to the top of the bar, still trying to understand all that he had just witnessed. Des was in place, pulling pints as fast as his arm could move, pouring wine and mixing cocktails while answering the door to the snug. The room was filling up nicely, and with a very mixed crowd, blue and white collars mingling comfortably. Even the pastel-attired gentlemen were enjoying a pint, although they seemed to be keeping to themselves. Brendan didn't know that his place was going to open, but these people must have been waiting, checking the doors or waiting in line for days, eager to be the first customer.

"Madness," Des said. "Open the doors, we'll be slow. Jesus, if this is slow, the fast'll kill me."

April was frazzled, scarcely able to keep pace with the demands of too many tables and one pair of legs. Food poisoning was eliminated as a possible outcome. This many people taken ill would upset the entire restaurant industry in Moraine Hills, and even DeCecco's ire would not extend into his own pocket. Brendan did not know the food business, but he knew about business, and he had to think like a businessman to get to the bottom of this.

Half-listening to the painter who was arguing over a correction on the punch list, Brendan examined the entire scenario. Employees working meant hours of wages to be paid. Serving food meant bills from suppliers. If DeCecco meant to get even with McKechnie, he might be manipulating the finances, adding costs on top of past due bills. At the same time, he could be using the pub to train people that he would hire for his new spot, gaining experienced servers and cooks at Brendan's expense. When all the paychecks bounced, every one of the people working here would storm out and head around the corner, seeking employment that paid.

"Part time should do," Des was carrying on, only parts of his monologue heard as he stood near Brendan, depositing a cluster of glasses on April's tray.

That was the last thing that he needed, more people and more salaries. As he considered his situation, Brendan began to see the logic to DeCecco's plot. A rival had sent Martie and Brendan never thought to ask who she was before he spilled his guts, a bit too dazzled by her blue eyes to think with his brain. He fell for the gag, jumped in with both feet. No one ever got the better of Brendan McKechnie, and he was not going to let DeCecco wipe him out so easily.

"Would you be willing?" Des asked on another trip past Brendan.

"Yeah, yeah, yeah," Brendan brushed off the question. He wanted answers and there was one employee who would be on his side. Aidan had been vetted by Aunt Eleanor's cousin's son, a tenuous connection but the only one that led back to the family in Miltown.

Craning his neck to find Aidan, Brendan caught sight of a man sitting at the bottom of the bar, dressed in a suit coat that looked like an authentic Armani. The gentleman eyed Brendan, taking his measure in return. On the surface, the stranger appeared to be a successful businessman with a sense of GQ style. His hands gave him away. Thick fingers, strong, rested comfortably on a glass that looked too small for such a large fist. It was the hand of a bricklayer or a boxer. When Des went over to talk to him, an Ulster burr buzzed over the noise, a brogue that pricked up Brendan's ears. Out of a habit he had learned at his uncle's place, his stomach tensed.

The Troubles were never far from anyone's mind in Miltown Malbay, the danger of men from the north with their bombs and their bullets, and Brendan carried that fear with him from childhood.

Making for the hostess stand, Brendan was stopped by the Armani-wearing guest who grabbed his arm. Brendan flinched, expecting trouble. "I've plenty of experience," the man said.

"I can vouch for that," Des said. "My cousin, Ger O'Hare. Crossed over the River Foyle every weekend to tend bar with me as a lad. Had to travel to a different country to find work, isn't that so, Ger."

Able to relax, Brendan shook Ger's hand, but he had no time for chatter. The pub's existence was at stake if Brendan did not regain control. While he was glad to hear the man's verbal resume, there were more important things to worry about. Later, after he had sorted everything out, they could have a long chat, but only if the salvaging operation proceeded at once.

FIVE

Martie had his arm when he was only steps away from a very harried Aidan, who was preoccupied with seating a party who claimed that they knew the owner. There was no time to verify the truth of the statement, not when Martie forcibly guided him to a table near the back of the dining room.

"Sorry for the rush," she said, pushing him into a chair. With a snap of her wrist, she unfurled the white napkin and draped it across his lap. Her sleeve smelled of grilled meat and maybe cinnamon, an aphrodisiac to a hungry man. Until this very moment, he had not noticed that he was famished.

"Look, I've got to ask you," he began, but she was gone, constantly in a hurry.

Turning to call her back, Brendan found that the table in the far corner, next to the antique pine dresser, was hosting a rowdy group of men who looked every bit as tough as Des and his relations. More than loud, they were bordering on crude, snapping fingers at Eilìs to get her attention when she was obviously busy with another party.

Her customers were ordering drinks, asking about wine and specifying vintages. Brendan recognized one of the group as the labor union's shop steward, a very important person who was due the best service and undivided attention. Mike waved at Brendan; they knew each other well from the job sites. "You've got a winner here," he said, two thumbs up.

Smiling like a fool, Brendan waved back, nodding to Mike's wife who looked every inch the former showgirl that she was. She turned to her friends, pleased with the acclaim that came her way because she knew, indirectly, the illustrious proprietor of this first-class establishment. By next week, she could be talking to the same group, discussing the downfall of Brendan McKechnie, the bankrupt construction magnate who thought he could run a restaurant, hubris on legs.

Emer put two plates in front of him, her eyes flicking nervously at Martie, who was also serving two dishes. A delicious aroma of pork and apples drifted into Brendan's nose, mingling with the scent of chives, lamb and butter. All four entrees were beautifully presented, peas not dropped on a plate but placed with care. Sauce, meat, garnish; he was served a still life worthy of Monet.

"Perfect, good job," Martie said, drawing a relieved smile from Emer. The waitress dashed off, while Martie launched into a monologue of restaurant-speak, describing the food in terms that Brendan did not understand. What questions he might have had were answered in one bite of veal drizzled with a rich wine reduction. If he needed any further proof of his incompetence in the dining industry, it was laying out before him. When he first thought of building a pub, he had never thought to offer fine dining instead of grub. Right now, he was too hungry to think about the costs of the materials that went into the cuisine, the costs that would sink him that much faster. All he knew was that the food was outstanding, and this was what he really wanted all along even though he did not know it when he started the project.

Enough food to feed a large family was arrayed on the table, but Martie did not give him time to finish anything. As Eilìs walked by, the barely touched entree was whisked away, to be replaced by a generous helping of fish and chips. One chip later, Martie pulled the plate, leaving only the bits of fish that Brendan had managed to spear with his fork.

"Hey, hey, you," a man's coarse voice resounded through the back of the room. "Hey, little girl."

Martie's spiel ended abruptly. The person snapping his fingers at Eilìs had big hands, like the Ulsterman at the bar. All four of the men at the table had the look of thugs, wise guys, and not the sort of person that Brendan would expect in an Irish pub.

"She has a name, Sal," Martie said. Her tone was peevish, not the best way to address such a meeting. After praying for fire to release him from the coming debacle, Brendan feared that God would answer his prayers after all. Men named Sal, with fingers that could lock around one's neck like a vice, were not to be treated shabbily.

"We're dying of thirst over here," Sal said, holding aloft an empty wine bottle.

"It's always about you," Martie said. "Men. All the same."

The party of thugs erupted in laughter and Brendan could hear the wood paneling crackling as flames licked the wainscoting. For a woman who had little to say the other day, she was talking too much now. In case it was his last meal, Brendan gulped down the remnants of colcannon that he scraped off his fork. He could not remember if he had let the fire insurance lapse, or if he had reached an agreement with his agent to pay the premium next month. There was time to polish off the duck breast, if he did not chew too much, a few minutes of culinary pleasure before the end. Brendan had experience with men like Sal, men who made their money by promising to not block the cement trucks or send the ironworkers off on a wildcat strike. When crossed, they could be brutal, or so it was said. He did not wish to find out how true the rumors were.

Hooking Eilìs' elbow, Martie brought her to the table. "Gentlemen, this is Eilìs," she announced. "You take care of her and she'll take good care of you."

"Pleased to meet you," Sal said. "That's all I'm asking, you know? Take care of me and mine."

"Don't I always take care of you, darling?" Martie said.

"That's what we're shooting for," Brendan said, jumping into the conversation with a poor choice of words. As if he needed to protect his womenfolk, he got up and stood between Martie and Sal. Without missing a beat, Martie introduced the proud owner of McKechnie's to Sal Lardino.

Hastily wiping his mouth, Sal rose and offered his hand. He was pleasant, behind an agreeable smile, but Brendan felt the brute strength in the man's grip. Maybe he was making a threat, or maybe he was only making conversation, but Sal noted that Brendan had done a bang-up job on a relative's house in Burr Oak Village, where McKechnie Construction had built a subdivision of luxury homes a few years back. If the quality of that one project could save the pub, Brendan was grateful for the Lord's grace. He did not want to lose the pub, not when he felt that he had a chance, a very tiny chance, to recoup his investment.

Dinner was over. As much as he wanted to sit back down and enjoy the food, Martie dragged him out of the dining room while instructing Eilìs on the finer points of customer care when the customer was a regular. Brendan wondered what constituted a regular patron, when he knew that the place could not have been open for more than three days. Sal and company were to be given dessert on the house, but they were getting the apple tarts that were slated for the soup kitchen because the crusts were not perfect. Something for nothing, Brendan thought, making the customer feel special while building goodwill. It was good business, in any business. But if DeCecco was using Martie to undermine him, why would she be concerned with goodwill?

He followed her to the foot of the stairs, the meek lamb following the shepherd who knew every intimate detail of his pathetic life. When he started babbling the other night, she should have stopped him, told him that she was a chef and not a shrink. Now Brendan was in a bind, positioned for some serious blackmail. He was out of his league in this business, with little hope of moving up to the majors. A new thought flashed in his mind, that DeCecco coveted the pub and meant to steal it out from under his nose, using Martie's trove of information to turn the screws. Brendan could not quite believe that he had allowed this to happen, when he was too smart to be fooled.

"Don't worry about them," Martie said. She was prepared to deal with a novice, but Brendan was thoroughly clueless. Even his banker was a push-over, seduced into silent agreement by a cottage pie and bread pudding with whisky sauce. Martie knew every food lover within fifty miles and she wasn't afraid to use her knowledge in devious ways, if it got her where she needed to go. The money she secretly sank into the operation was for Brendan's good as well, and what man would ask why she was being so charitable when his mouth was stuffed with tender chicken in a rich gravy? The banker never questioned her motives, and she ticked off another win for her side.

To appease Brendan's curiosity, and to keep him from bungling the operation, she briefed him on Sal, who was said to have some tenuous links to organized crime. Whether any of the stories Martie had heard were true made no difference, not when she had come to know Sal as she advanced in her career with stints at some of the leading restaurants in Chicago. He looked dangerous, but underneath the threatening physique beat the heart of a trend-chaser who pursued fads with intensity and drive. The finest restaurant, the most fashionable night club, the latest hot spot were all the places that Sal could be found, flaunting his wealth with the panache of a commodities broker. Did his great-uncle really operate a casino in his suburban home, and had he inherited the business from another relative who owned a chain of speakeasies? The way that Sal tried so hard to be accepted by the well-heeled citizens of Port Clinton gave credence to the gossip, but he was not so different from anyone else who came up from nothing and discovered that all their money was too new to let them slip into the tonier set.

With Brendan on her heels, Martie walked through the noisy bar, delighted to find that the place was packed. Des bellowed out from behind the bar, calling to her to come over and meet his cousin. The newest employee of McKechnie's Pub was behaving exactly the way Martie wanted a bartender to behave. Ger flirted with the women and joked easily with the men, creating the right atmosphere. As she shook his hand, Martie thanked him for taking the job she had not expected to be in need of filling so quickly. His grip was strong, with the sort of confidence she expected from a bouncer. Something in the glint in Ger's eye told her that he would use charm first, but would not hesitate to use his fists if necessary. It was always better to handle the belligerent drunks in-house where possible, to keep things quiet.

Martie's eye was drawn to two men who had Ger's attention as well. They were hard to miss, in pale pinks and creams, and one of them had a pastel yellow sweater draped over his shoulders. Looking like they just dropped in from the Bahamas, the customers reminded her of men who came from poverty and didn't know how to appear prosperous without flash. She didn't like the way that Ger glared at them from the corner of his eye, and she didn't like the feeling that was sprouting in her mind. She knew next to nothing about her bartenders beyond what they told her. How could she tell if they were involved in Ireland's version of the Mafia? A fresh worry sprouted in her brain.

To escape the distractions of the bar, with its music, chatter and flowing beer, Martie took Brendan's arm and pulled him up to the office. Dead tired after so many long days, she flopped onto the sofa which she had covered with an old afghan, the crest of Ireland's four provinces woven in Donegal wool. Brendan paused for a moment, not sure where he was supposed to go, as if the sofa was his territory and she had taken over his corner of the world. With no other option, he was left to drop into the chair behind the desk, where he began to browse the collection of CDs that she had brought in to decorate the rooms with music.

"Mick Flannery," Brendan said, holding up a jewel case. "Paddy did a duet with him in Dublin. One of those intimate little places that feel like someone's living room."

They had a hundred things to review, but musical memories was not one of them. Martie had figured Brendan for the highly involved type, maybe a micromanager, and she was relieved that he did not come in during the warm-ups. He gave every sign of being more of a delegator, someone who would let her do her thing without interference. A wise man, in that case. The partnership agreement was that much closer to being signed. Just in case she was wrong, however, she had to involve him in some small projects. Let him feel that he had a role, no matter how insignificant, and he was less likely to resent her prominent role. Mingling with customers was usually safe, especially when it was the so-called owner at the front of the house. She would ease him into his role, however, and make it look like his idea.

"I saw him at the Cork Opera House. He's a brilliant songwriter, in my opinion," she said. The concert was a memory from another era, the age of blackness. For so long, Martie had been lost, and for all she knew she might still be lost. Trying to be who her parents wanted her to be, but pulled by something inside her that she still questioned. Getting pregnant at fifteen had not proved her heart wrong or her mother right. Experimenting with drugs, drinking, sleeping around, none of it had answered a single question. Her time in Ireland was a bleak period that hurt to recall.

"So, Friday?" Brendan asked.

"Ready or not, we are officially open for business," she said. "You did a good job in hiring the staff. They're on top of things."

"Not me. I have to be honest with you. Let's start off, from here on in, and be honest with each other," he said. Like a true civil engineer, he arranged the CD cases in neat, even stacks, aligned in a grid pattern. "Aidan pretty much took charge."

"That's what restaurant managers do," she said. "Are you sure that your bartenders are legal?"

"Des? I sponsored him to come over. It's still rough, along the border where he's from. No jobs to speak of. A bunch of my foremen, my

32

dad sponsored them. There was a time, back in the eighties, nineties, when guys would show up at the office with a letter from my uncle Donal, looking for a job. Everyone coming to America, looking for a job and a decent place to raise their kids."

"When we talked the other day," Martie began. Brendan flinched, as if he was very uncomfortable. He wanted honesty, and she would give it to him. "You really don't have any idea what you've gotten into, have you?"

A pub like his uncle's, success; he was into that. What he lacked were the details, the knowledge he needed to get where he wanted to go. He admitted that, at this point, proving Bonnie wrong was his chief motivating factor, avoiding her 'I told you so' chant at all costs. He had thrown more money at the pub, determined to the point of illogical blindness, until he had sunk into debt and stood to lose more than the restaurant. Martie nodded as he spoke, realizing that Brendan was depending on her, and not just to run the kitchen. Put up a building, decorate the interior, and that was as much as he could accomplish on his own. It was up to her to turn a building into a destination, an attraction that generated profits.

"We got off to a wrong start. People talked to me and I didn't pay attention so it's my fault. But it's all good, right? We're on the same page," Brendan said. "The craic going ninety, the best service, great food. It's like there's two halves, you know? We're matched, you know what I mean? And what a miracle, right, that you just happened to stop by the other day."

Brendan's grey eyes glowed, as if the intensity of his emotions was lighting him up inside. They were going to get along just fine, Martie believed, because Brendan needed her talent and her confidence, and he liked her. If she had to make a guess, she would say that Brendan McKechnie liked her a lot. She smiled at him, the poor man already wrapping himself around her little finger, submissive to her every action. They were going to get along beautifully. As long as she could maintain the myth he created in his testosterone-fueled brain.

"So, are you comfortable with Des and Ger?" she asked.

"What about your friends, the garlic snappers?" he said.

"Jumping to conclusions, there, Brendan. You assume that their ethnic heritage automatically makes them criminals," she said. "Looks are very deceiving. Which is why I encourage the police to stop in, spend their dinner break at the bar with a free meal. If they need a cold glass of water, I want them to get it here. Take care of them and they will take care of us."

"You know how to play the game, I take it."

"At the risk of sounding conceited, I would say that I have mastered the game." she said. He must not have read her resume, which she took as further proof of his incompetence. "I'll bet you've played the same game yourself."

"There's some things the same in every business," he said. "But I have to admit, there's a lot of differences. More than I expected, I guess."

Humbled by his confession, Brendan turned his attention to the computer and clicked through the set lists. Every now and then he made a comment under his breath, a puzzled tone as he encountered performers he had never heard of, or music he could not categorize. Martie ran through the artists with him as a courtesy, to let him feel a part of what she had done without him, but she did not have time to waste on the inconsequential. "Now, the menu," she said, getting down to business.

Before he could respond, his cell phone rang. "Bonnie," he sighed. He sounded as if the call caught him in the middle of a marathon, he was that exhausted. He grumbled and growled, complaining that she had interrupted an important meeting at the pub. Business had to come first, and she had to understand. Everything else he said was a variation on the same theme. By the time Brendan hung up the phone, he had not resolved anything. Martie heard the sort of disagreement that could give her trouble at some point if she didn't stay on top of things. One disgruntled female could upend her entire plan. Manon had been disgruntled after Martie turned down her offer of a restaurant partnership. Did the disgruntlement extend so far as sabotage? Martie rubbed the thought from her temples and focused her mind on business.

"The bar menu will be limited, mostly the classic dishes that people expect to find in an Irish pub. The dining room will feature New Irish cuisine. More continental. Haute cuisine, a French influence. No one is doing it around here. I'll be breaking new ground." Martie slipped off her clogs and put her feet up. Any chance she got, she put her feet up. Flexing her toes, she watched the shamrocks wiggle on her lucky socks that had never failed her.

"Whatever you want. The place is yours," he said, stating the obvious. "We can both agree that I don't know jack about the restaurant business."

"Can't argue with you there."

"We trust each other, don't we? I mean, well, I, um, can I trust you?" Brendan leaned forward, as if he were pleading.

Getting to her feet, Martie offered her hand and they shook on the deal. "We're both up to our ears in this, Brendan. This is personal for me, and I will not let it fail. I'm trusting you, too, that you won't screw me over."

He held her hand and looked into her eyes until she pulled her hand away, uncomfortable with his moony gaze. She turned his attention back to the music and the songs that Des particularly liked, the songs of The Troubles and the old rebel ballads. There were a few of Paddy Dunne's renditions in support of the hunger strikes, the prisoners in Long Kesh and the suffering Irish of the London ghettos. "Where do you shop, the Sinn Fein Bookstore?" Brendan asked.

"*Tiocfaidh àr là*," she said, giving him a sly wink. Too much time had been wasted already. Martie jumped into her shoes and ran down the stairs, back to the kitchen that was still not performing up to her standards.

Brid's Nut Cake

1 pint flour

1/2 dozen eggs

1 wine glass whiskey

1 wine glass lemon extract

1 tbsp baking powder heaping not level like Americans do

sweet milk to make a batter

1 cup chopped walnuts

1 1/2 cups sugar

1/2 lb salted butter

mace & nutmeg

SIX

Last night was rough, and Brendan was still in trouble on the home front. Missing dinner was one thing, but not answering the phone was another, and Bonnie had ripped him a new one. To make matters worse, he did not eat the warmed over dinner she had prepared, but tuna noodle casserole could not compare to the delicacies he had sampled at the pub. The way that Bonnie had sniffed him, like a bloodhound, had been funny, and she was furious at him for laughing. No sweet scents of perfume or freshly-showered guilt, but he had reeked of sawdust, sweat and some late night beers with Mac and the crew. Most likely, she was more angry that her pet theory had been disproved, that he had not been with another woman, so she let fly about the drinking instead. Any excuse would do for Bonnie.

Alcohol had not quieted his nerves and he had slept lightly, mulling over the personnel that had been hired with little thought. There were no guarantees that Des was only a plumber, and Ger could have just gotten out of prison for as much as Brendan knew. There was no way that Martie was anything less than legitimate. When they shook hands, and what soft, warm hands she had, there had been a slight tremor, a sign that she was just as tense about the pub as he was. Sink or swim, they would go together.

Turning off onto the exit for the airport, he shook his head. It was funny how things often fell into his lap. First, it was Martie when he needed a chef, and then a couple of men who said they were from Belfast had asked to meet with him to talk over investments. They looked like a gay couple, but who was he to judge? They must have faced fierce discrimination in Northern Ireland, where intolerance was genetically coded into the Free Presbyterians. This was America, where a man's private life was private and money was money. Judging by the way Ger inspected every single twenty-dollar bill that the men used to pay their bar tab, they were possessed of legal tender and that was exactly what Brendan needed to get his newborn enterprise off of life support.

As his eyes adjusted to the gloom of the parking garage, Brendan had second thoughts about his surprise. Martie was a huge Paddy Dunne fan, and he hadn't told her about the performance because he wanted to enjoy the stunned look on her face when Paddy strolled in and bellied up to the bar. What if Martie were to faint, or get so flustered that she couldn't cook? Would it have been better to prepare her, to set up a private get-together with the singer so that she could concentrate on work and not be distracted? And should he have told her that he was meeting with his banker to beg for an extension on his home equity loan while pleading for a third mortgage to cover the payroll at the restaurant? The fact that McKechnie Construction had only enough cash on hand to meet expenses meant Mac was getting paid, but the pub had nothing in the bank. What good would it do, to tell that to Martie? Honesty, he had said, and he was being less than honest with her now.

While he stood at Arrivals, Brendan let the smile creep across his lips. Waiting for Paddy and the other members of Shift/Move, he recalled some of the good memories, funny incidents that centered on one pub or another. Most of Brendan's fondest recollections of summers in Miltown revolved around the Dunne boys, Paddy in particular. Not even impending doom could alter the anticipation of seeing an old friend, hearing him sing and listening to his stories. This weekend would be like a vacation from stress, a temporary reprieve until all the wheels finally fell off.

"McKechnie, ye bollix," Paddy bellowed from across the echoing room. One of the last to clear customs, Brendan suspected that Paddy's political leanings had followed him across the water. Always outspoken, the Irish singer had never made any apologies for supporting socialist causes and Irish unity. "Brawling already, are you? Look at the state of you."

Hugs, back slaps and handshakes went all around as Brendan turned his bruised knuckles into a long, drawn out joke. He renewed old friendships with Liam and Rory, whom he had known as boys in Miltown. Back then, they were inseparable. Over the years they had drifted apart, but tight bonds could never be fully broken. Even though Brendan hadn't seen them for at least two years, he found that Rory was almost unchanged, his locks still long, although thinned and streaked with grey. It was Liam who had mellowed, exuding the gravity and dignity of a musical elder statesman.

"I'd forgotten why I hated flying," Paddy said. He tugged at his suitcase and let Brendan pick up the guitar case. "Jesus. Pumped full of Ambien or I'd never set foot in that winged coffin. Tinned kippers for eight hours, and at my age. "

"Your man had his eyes closed for seven out of the eight," Liam added.

"Got enough energy left for a quick tour?" Brendan asked. "First time in Chicago. Come on, let me give you a look around."

"Did you read my mind?" Rory said. "Coming in, we flew over the lake, and I says to the lads, wouldn't it be grand to see the city itself?"

With pride of ownership, Brendan motored east on the Kennedy, letting his passengers take in the view. From the hotels near the airport through the bungalow belt, Rory watched the scenery change, soaking up the sights with the eager eye of a lifetime student. Paddy tapped out a tune with his fingertips on the dashboard.

"Even if I thanked you before," Brendan said, "I'm thanking you again. I know what it means, you flying over."

With his head turned to face the side window, Paddy grunted, lost in thought. "It's me should be thanking you," he said. "I've missed you these past months."

"Will you be back for Willie Week this year?" Liam asked. The annual music festival had drawn the McKechnie clan back to Miltown every July, until Brendan got too wrapped up in his pub project to travel.

"Depends," Brendan said. Brake lights ahead warned of an afternoon traffic jam at the junction. "You buying me a plane ticket, Liam?"

"Ah, all you Yanks are as rich as kings," Liam said. "Expensive project, so, your pub?"

"Approaching my eyeballs and sinking fast," Brendan admitted. "Pray God I find a way out."

"We'll pass the hat for you," Rory said. "And never was a cause more worthy."

Coming up to the Ohio Street exit, the conversation lagged. Unusual for a normally gregarious man, Paddy was rather subdued, his head turned to watch the city of Chicago pass the window. "Dublin'll never be a high rise town," he said.

"There's no beauty in them," Liam said. "Heartless. Cold. And the property crash put paid to the developer's dreams."

"But there's a certain drama," Rory said. "Looming up on the horizon and then getting taller as you get closer. Did I read somewhere that there's observation decks in the tallest ones?"

"How about a pint ninety-five stories up?" Brendan suggested.

An awkward pause filled the car, crowding out the chilled air. Liam cleared his throat and Paddy finally turned his head. "A nice cuppa'd be grand," he said. "I don't know if it's day or night, so, with the jet lag."

"Didn't I tell you that your clock setting notion was a nonsense?" Rory said. "Our man here sets his clock to Chicago time two days ago and he's living at half-past lost."

"Ah, now, and haven't I been a good boy?" Paddy said. "Eating yogurt and lettuce and going to Mass and saying my prayers."

"The Christian Brothers would be proud of you," Brendan said.

"Some of what they beat into me must have taken hold," Paddy said.

Brendan pulled into a non-descript parking garage off Rush Street, a very comfortable walking distance for three men who had been confined to an airplane for half a day. They followed his lead to the exit, but within the space of a few feet from the garage, his guests slowed their steps to a halt. It was entirely unintentional, but the juxtaposition of the old water works and the sleek marble skin of the Water Tower mall were startling to country boys. The guided tour went off on a tangent to encompass Mrs. O'Leary's cow and the fire that gutted the city but could not reduce the water tower to ash, the patter delivered as they walked through the crowd on Michigan Avenue.

"It's feckin' madness," Paddy said. "Shops and then more shops. Even Dublin's gone over to this, covering up the greens with concrete."

"America's taking over the world," Brendan said. "A bloodless coup."

Wandering past the high-end shops that lined the street, Rory spoke of the matching storefronts that were all the rage in Dalkey and Dundrum. Comparisons between modern Ireland and the States were made while the quartet rode the elevator to the top of the Hancock Building, ears popping in the rapid ascent. Brendan was relieved to learn that, even though Miltown had gotten bigger over the years, relatively little had changed in the west of Ireland. The Celtic Tiger had grazed Miltown but it had molded Dublin into a city that looked like every other city, a sorry fact that left Paddy grumbling.

Irish brogues were enough to charm the maitre d' to seat the party next to the window facing south, far above the city that stretched out from the lake to the western horizon. Long shadows dipped fingers into the blue water of Lake Michigan, where late afternoon sailors glided into the harbor. The beauty of Chicago held them all spellbound, speechless as they absorbed the sights from cloud height.

"Sparkling water," Paddy ordered his beverage. Brendan stared at him, shocked, oblivious to the waiter. "And could I trouble you for a wedge of lime?"

"Water? Paddy? Are you all right??" Brendan asked when he found his tongue.

"Brendan, my boy, I'm an alcoholic and I'll be so until the day I die," Paddy said.

"Came close enough to that," Rory said. He flashed a look of warning, or was it a reproach?

SEVEN

Three beers and a glass of water were placed on the table, the water free of charge for the designated driver. Brendan hesitated to put the glass of beer to his lips, feeling self-conscious in the harsh light of Paddy's confession. So much of his relationship with the singer revolved around the pub, the sessions at Uncle Donal's place in Miltown, all awash in liquor with Paddy leading the way to the bar. Never had he thought of his old friend as a boozer. Brendan saw him as a sociable drinker, a bon vivant whose shyness floated away in a few pints and a gin and tonic. The idea that Patrick Dunne was an alcoholic did not square with the carefully constructed box that Brendan had crafted around the man.

"I should have told you the truth about my health problems long ago, but," Paddy paused. He squeezed the lime wedge into his water, rubbing the rind across the rim before dropping the fruit into the glass. "Didn't want you to think less of me, so."

"It's not a crime to have a drinking problem," Brendan said.

"No, it's the curse of the Irish people," Rory said.

"Sounds like Aislinn finally got to you," Brendan said. As much as drinking was a part of his fondest memories, so too did Aislinn's tears figure into the picture. Paddy's wife had begged and pleaded for nearly fifteen years, her entreaties forming a final note to Willie Week, like the master of ceremony's farewell.

"The heart attack put a scare into me," Paddy said.

"The delirium tremens as well," Liam added. "Sure, the song you wrote about it is light-hearted, but I sat with you through most of it and it wasn't so pleasant, son."

"Everything together is what changed me," Paddy continued. "I was possessed of an unquenchable thirst, Brendan, and if the occasional line of cocaine should fall my way, so much the better. Wasn't it all great fun, I'd think to myself. Fooling myself."

"And I'm ashamed to say that I gave up on himself and walked away," Rory said. With that one simple sentence, the break-up of Shift/Move was explained. A group of friends who had forged a new direction for Celtic rock, the three men sitting there looking out over Chicago had been torn apart by Paddy's love of the bottle. On the heels of a new found sobriety, the group was coming back, the same gang who had torn through Miltown on long summer evenings all those years ago. What Brendan had expected was not what arrived, and he didn't know if he was disappointed or glad of the changes.

"You're not saying this is a reunion, are you?" Brendan asked, aware of an unexpected possibility. After Friday night's performances, the word would spread and Saturday would feature a packed house, a chance to recoup some of his losses in one evening. It would cost him nothing more than the price of bed and board, with the rest of the expenses being donated by Paddy as a pub-warming gift. A little promotion and he could guarantee that full house, the answer to his fervent prayers.

"What we had back then, it was grand," Liam said. "After Paddy here pulled himself together, we'd pass an evening at the house with a few tunes. The old fire was back, better than before."

"Sober, you mean, and there's no need to tread lightly," Paddy said. "No one could make me see reason; I had to find it myself. The regrets, Brendan. I missed so much."

"Not everyone gets a second chance," Brendan said. "I'm glad you're feeling better. Christ, am I dense. When I heard about your heart attack, I figured it was a genetic thing. You know, your dad was young."

"Could have been a part of it, but if I'd looked after myself," Paddy wondered aloud. He sipped his water, gazing out of the window. "So, where's Chicago's famous kelly green river?"

Changing the subject changed the mood, which had been verging on the morose. As the glasses were drained, Brendan made plans to show the group around the city in the short span of time that was available. Too uncomfortable with Paddy's frank admissions, Brendan avoided ordering a second round. Observing the stifled yawns of his guests, he suggested that they move on, head for the hotel and a comfortable bed. He had heard about all he could process in one evening, news that was wholly unexpected, some good, some bad.

"What I'd like right now," Rory said, "is a fry. Truth be told, I'm starving."

"Let's have a look at your place," Liam said. "I'll not sleep until I've set my eyes on the only thing that's kept you from Ireland these past two years."

"She's a seductive mistress, the public house," Paddy joked. Brendan heard an implication, a figment of his imagination that Bonnie had planted there.

Through an endless line of homes, apartments and warehouses, Brendan pointed out the sights from the expressway. Urban sprawl had invaded Dublin as well, and all three visitors kept up a steady conversation about the ugliness outside of the car's windows and the damage done to their homeland, where a rush to catch up with the rest of the world had left ghost estates in its wake. Brendan understood exactly what they meant, having seen the cold face of prosperity gaze upon his mother's once poor homeland. His cousin's construction business had flourished during the boom years, only to collapse when the good times ended. Emigration had once again become Ireland's leading export.

The pub's parking lot was full, an unexpected situation in the middle of the week. A Wednesday should be a quiet dining night, but McKechnie's was quickly becoming the place to be, even when most people would be home in bed, getting ready for the next work day. Brendan escorted the trio through the patio where the umbrellas had been closed up for the night, pausing for Liam's accolades over reproducing every small detail of the Miltown pub's original facade. At the front door, Brendan reached for the handle but Aidan was at the ready, pushing it open and standing aside to admit the guests.

"Sweet Jesus," the manager whispered.

"Is this Mrs. O'Cleary's nephew?" Paddy said, his usual gregarious personality called forth. "Your auntie sends her best, lad, and don't be missing Mass on the Sunday."

Dumbfounded, Aidan shook Paddy's hand while Brendan made introductions. After taking one step into the foyer, Paddy turned and went back out, to theatrically examine the street, north to south, before staring at the building like a man who was lost. "Sure and I thought I was in Miltown for a minute, so," he said.

"It's brilliant," Liam said. "How did you do it? Put your grandfather's old Morris Minor out front and I'd swear I was eight years old again."

Drawn to the stage, Paddy wandered into the barroom, mounting the three steps to the platform as if twenty years had fallen from his frame. He moved the chairs and rearranged the small tables until he had the set-up to his liking. A glass crashed to the floor, the clicks of splinters echoing over the crowd noise. "Sweet Jesus I'm hallucinating," Des said.

"Paddy Dunne," a sound of shocked admiration drifted around the bar. Liam caught Paddy's arm and directed his attention to the framed photo on the wall next to the stage, in which a group of boys aped for the camera.

"Will you look at this," Liam bellowed. "I look like a feckin' eejit in short trousers."

"You were trying to bash my skull with that hurley," Rory accused his old friend. "Waving it over me, and me with a bare head. Ah, wasn't my mammy fond of the razor? I had to go to England to grow hair."

A crowd of rough and tumble boys had been captured in the photograph, evoking a time of simplicity, innocence and little money. Just outside the French doors of the pub, the background of that very picture was reproduced with every detail intact, and now the central characters were back, but they were grown men, their youthful innocence cast aside. For a brief second, Brendan feared that it was all a big, expensive mistake.

Taking seats at an empty table, Paddy and Brendan exchanged brief glances of wicked complicity. No one was expecting Paddy Dunne and he relished the surprise and the subtle stares of the few patrons who knew of him. Despite his shy nature, he liked the attention while craving privacy at the same time, torn by a mental dilemma that had no solution. One time, Paddy might have sought the answer at the bottom of a glass, but those days were done. Brendan was already feeling the loss.

"April, four fries," Brendan called out.

"Ah now, Brendan," Paddy sighed, ogling April's ample curves. "Sure and isn't everything bigger in America."

Sniggering and nudging like school boys, the group reflected the image that hung on the wall behind them. With forced control, Brendan spoke in what he assumed was his normal business voice, asking April to send Martie around. The alcohol from his first beer tickled his brain and created a wave of giggles that he could not suppress. He felt that the four little boys in the photograph were still there, locked up inside, and he had only to find the right key to set them free.

With a tea pot in her hand, Eilìs appeared in a cloud of timid silence. To a man, the party flipped over their cups, signaling their thirst to a young woman who could only gape like a stunned trout at the gaggle of musical legends. "Go on, now," Liam said. "We'd all love a cuppa. Please. Before my head falls to the table."

"Miss Eilìs McGivern, may I present," Brendan began, but the girl ran off after slopping the tea into Paddy's cup. In two seconds, she was back, dragging an unbelieving Emer by the arm.

"Sweet Jesus, it's himself, indeed," Emer gasped. She held out a pen and one of her order slips. "For my mammy. Could you sign it, Mr. Dunne? Back home. Roscommon town."

"I've many a fond memory of Roscommon," Paddy said as he inked his name. "And more than enough times forgotten and lost."

"I made the tea," Eilìs mumbled. Her silly grin had yet to leave her face, beaming away as she poured tea without taking her eyes off the musicians.

"It's grand," Liam said. "Stand a spoon in it, so. Even the tea at Dublin Airport's gone weak."

Rory rubbed at his eyes, the effect of living on Irish time in Chicago. He shared an anecdote, as if it were a cure for jet lag, describing a recent concert in Galway, where Paddy's son played the bodhràn with his father for the first time in public. Underneath the chuckles and the laughs about a broken guitar string and the lady in the front row, Brendan picked up on a hazy sentiment. It seemed that Rory was implying something significant about the boy's drumming. What else had Brendan missed in the past couple of years, when he was too consumed with his pub to give his old friends a thought?

46

"Nice of you to join us," Martie said. Underneath her smile was a weariness that hinted at long hours in a hot kitchen. He would make a greater effort to help out, put in more time and maybe learn how to cook a few simple things to ease the burden. In the meantime, he had a contribution to the partnership that no one else could match.

"Found a couple of stragglers at the airport," Brendan joked. "Gentlemen, may I present Martie Smurfit, head chef of McKechnie's Pub."

Martie's jaw dropped. She looked at Paddy, who was more clear-eyed than ever, his face less bloated, and blinked as if she could not believe what she was seeing. "He never flies," she mumbled. "Only travels by ferry. Ireland and England. How? No. It can't..."

"Sure you've found the way to my old heart," Liam said. He dipped a corner of soda bread into a pool of egg yolk. "If I wasn't already married, I'd be on my knee proposing."

She squeezed her eyes shut and opened them wide, her face not reflecting the great joy that Brendan expected. Amazed, most likely, and he would have to give her some time to recover from the shock before they discussed how best to handle the opening weekend. A flush crept up from her neck and he was not so sure that she was not about to faint. "Best fry this side of Spanish Point," he said. She did not seem to hear him.

An avalanche of compliments rolled down from Irish mouths, although Paddy was on the quiet side. He spoke to Brendan, lauded the food to the rest of his merry band, but he couldn't bring himself to say a word directly to Martie. It was not shyness, but a hesitancy that felt more like Paddy did not want to intrude on Brendan's territory. Could there be any greater sign of male bonding than backing off and leaving the field open to a friend? Rather than flirt like he usually did, Paddy was retreating into the background so that Brendan had Martie's full attention. Of course Paddy was in the dark about Brendan's current relationship status because Brendan had been too busy to stay in touch. Still, it was a thoughtful gesture.

"Okay. I have to get back to the kitchen," Martie said.

Before Brendan could stop her, she was gone, without saying a word to Paddy. Liam and Rory watched her go and then turned to Brendan, grinning like the imps they once were. "Jesus, Mary and Holy St. Joseph does your luck never end?" Rory asked.

"She works for me, that's it," Brendan said, but he couldn't help puffing up a little, playing the alpha male. "I'm in a relationship with someone else. A serious relationship."

"Sure you are," Liam said.

"Something wrong with the black pudding, Paddy?" Brendan asked. The singer was pushing bits of sausage around on the plate as if he found something amiss but was too polite to say anything.

"Everything is grand, so," Paddy said. "I think it's the Ambien. My head feels foggy."

"Did your Martie spend any time in Ireland?" Liam asked. "How authentic is your menu?"

Brendan had yet to review her resume, nor did he need to. Everywhere he went, people congratulated him on landing one of the most accomplished chefs around. Clients who dined out often knew all about her, and it took all his acting skills to appear as if he were fully aware of her impressive credentials. "She started in Dublin and then trained in Paris. I think she worked in New York City, all over Chicago," he said. "And she has relatives, grandparents I think, in Clare, so, yes, I'd say her food is authentic. New Irish cuisine authentic."

"Very posh," Rory said.

"Someone in her family is musical," Brendan said. "I wonder if she's ever gone to Willie Week. I'll have to ask her."

"Do you think it's possible?" Paddy asked, his gaze fixed on the beans he was placing on a piece of bread, one bean at a time.

"I guess," Brendan said. "Do you think she saw you sing there? Fishing for some compliments, old son?"

Paddy stirred a spoonful of sugar into his tea, deep in thought. "You've re-created your uncle's pub. It's like being there almost. But for the food. Sorry to say, but your aunt never made anything so grand as this."

Basking in the approval, Brendan scanned the room that was filled with paying customers. As a contractor, he had seen his family name slapped on construction sites across the region. He was known in the industry, an important player. The pub, however, was the one place where he felt as if he had accomplished something real, something special. He could only imagine that Paddy felt the same way about his performances, those moments when the singer connected to the audience and shared an emotion. In Brendan's mind, he was sharing the best memories of his childhood with those who sat at the tables in his namesake restaurant. The pub, for all the blood and sweat he'd poured into it, was richly rewarding.

"Accommodations up the stairs?" Liam asked.

"This is a replica of McKechnie's in Miltown Malbay in all ways but that," Brendan said. "I've booked you rooms in a hotel not too far from here. And those rooms, I promise, are much nicer. Newer mattresses where you won't sink into the hole in the middle and never get out."

Driving to the hotel in Deerhaven, Brendan was on top of the world. The very people whose opinion mattered were pleased with his pub, more than impressed with the food and awed by Martie's physical attributes. The lads teased him endlessly as he drove through darkened streets, innuendo flavored with a dash of envy for a single man who was free to explore those same attributes. Not that Brendan thought of himself as single, considering he had been living with Bonnie for nearly two years. More like engaged, or in a committed relationship. For all he knew, Martie was married. They had yet to talk about their private lives.

With his guests safely tucked in for the night, he debated between going home or returning to the pub. Why not go back and receive the accolades of his staff? Bonnie would assume he was drinking the night away and would not expect him back at a decent hour. This was his night to enjoy what he had created, a genuine Irish pub that was a sanctuary from the stress of his Type A life. At home, he was the ATM on legs, dispensing cash as if it was his only function. At McKechnie's, he was the publican. He was the man who brought Paddy Dunne, Rory Callahan and Liam Carty to America. He was the man who gave Martie something unique and rare in a grand display of his appreciation for her brilliance. They were partners, to rise or fall together, and he wanted her to know that he would not let her down.

EIGHT

Dinner service was a disaster. At the end of the evening, Martie sat at a table with Aidan and a shot of whiskey, trying to calm her nerves and regain focus. The afternoon in Miltown Malbay kept pushing to the front of her mind, however, crowding out rational thought. One time she got blind drunk, one time, and expounded on her journey from teen mom to culinary success. The father of her child was fighting over her refusal to meet the boy, her lover was pushing her to commit, she questioned her sexual orientation. She had shamed her parents, been banished from home, and Paddy had been sympathetic. Falling down, oblivious drunk, but sympathetic.

What if Brendan was old school, like her immigrant parents? She had two strikes against her, in that case. He could fire her because she was a lesbian but claim her cooking style was all wrong for his place of business and there was no proving him otherwise. He might see her as reckless for getting pregnant in high school and then watch her every move. If he lost trust in her, she would lose the control she needed to realize her dream.

One scenario after another played out in her head, painting an increasingly more bleak picture. What if Paddy repeated even half of what she had told him, right before she invited him to her room? She had seen the look in Brendan's eye. She knew what he was thinking. Would she have to stoop that low, to trade sex for job security? Never. And how would she explain it to Manon, who was bound to find out once the story drifted into the river of gossip that ran through the restaurant kitchens of Moraine Hills. Where would Martie go if her entire life was torn apart? She was not going anywhere. She would have to get out of it, somehow or other.

Her hands shook as she examined the set of Brendan's shoulders when he strutted in, took note of his attitude when he greeted Des. She could not tell if she had been discussed by the quartet. The tension wound tighter in her gut and then snapped. "What were you thinking, to pull a stunt like that without telling me?" she asked. "Do you think I can snap my fingers and the coolers will magically be filled? We're going to run out of food, for God's sake."

"Did they bring a sound man?" Aidan asked. "Do I need to find someone to light the stage?"

"How about musicians?" Martie asked. "The last time I saw Shift/ Move they had a fiddler, keyboards. And a sound mixer."

"Oh." Brendan took to observing his feet, as if his jubilation was crushed somewhere under his shoe. Abruptly, his head lifted. "That kid who works for my brother-in-law. He's worked the mixer at Ravinia."

Not a word or a sly grin directed at her. Could she be so blessed? Had Paddy forgotten an afternoon that was less than memorable? Not that she was shocked, having plenty of experience with alcoholics who made promises that were forgotten when the booze wore off. A slight twinge of relief pulsed through her tight shoulders. She was safe, most likely, if she avoided running into Paddy at all costs, to keep his recollections from gathering. Concentrate on her job, that was the best solution, and make it through the weekend with her secret intact. "First thing tomorrow, you get on it," Martie said. She hunted through the paperwork on the table and found a pen, using it to write a phone number on a bar napkin. "Here, Aidan, hire the Celtic Airs for a back-up band."

While the manager hurried off to make the call, Brendan took his seat at the table and shuffled a few papers without looking at the contents. "I thought, I don't know, I guess I was thinking that you'd like the surprise."

"Exactly, Brendan, you don't know," Martie said. There was no surprise she liked less than the one that fell on her that evening. "Can you picture the reviews if we run out of food? Out of beer? We'd be crucified before we'd even got started."

"Didn't think of that," he said, his finger tracing a vein in the marble table top.

"Are we together on this?"

"You know we are." He met her gaze with warm grey eyes that were empty of any knowledge of her past.

"Look, I'm not snapping at you. It's been a long day and I shouldn't take it out on you." She put her hand on his arm, to reassure him. Without being blunt, she had to make him see that he should do nothing without going through her first. "And thank you. I'm really and truly grateful that you arranged something so spectacular. But we're business people first, okay?"

All he needed to reconnect with her was a compliment. His mood brightened, and Brendan began to spin yarns of his childhood, the summers in Miltown. He told the saga of Dermot and Donal McKechnie, sons of Irish immigrants, who married the Moore sisters of Miltown Malbay. Multitasking, Martie listened with one ear and went on filling out order sheets, commenting on the golden life that Brendan led while ensuring that enough cod was on hand for a Friday special. At last, the beer percolated through his kidneys and he had to break off his reverie.

"Des is over the moon," Aidan said, returning to the seat that Brendan had vacated. "We'll be packed on Friday, and all word of mouth."

"I don't like the looks of those two over there," Martie said. She tilted her head toward the middle of the bar, where a couple of stragglers were finishing late night pints.

Soft pastels might be suitable for the season, but no one from the Midwest would drape a pink cotton sweater over his shoulders. She had seen the same couple in the bar from the minute the doors were opened, perched on the same seats every night since. The man with the bleached blond hair tips was Eurotrash gangster, like the drug kingpins who made their fortunes in the U.K. and their homes in sunny Spain. His companion was utterly nondescript, calling attention to his presence by a nervous shifting of his eyes, as if he were casing the bar.

"Not much chance of a fight from that sort," Aidan said. "Wouldn't want to soil their British hands. They're maybe born in Ireland but their hearts are sporting Union Jacks, if you get my meaning."

Behind the bar, Des was conducting his own form of interrogation, polishing glasses and making conversation. Anyone looking for a position as a regular at this pub would have to pass the suitability test, and Martie was confident that Des would ban anyone who was looking for a brawl. Religion would make no difference, but loyalty to one soccer team over another might be a concern, given the propensity for the British hooligan to cause mayhem. Something in the back of Martie's mind flashed, a warning perhaps. She could not pinpoint the reason, but she had a feeling the pair were involved in crime of some sort.

Martie sent a quick text to Manon, to let her know she was working late and a planned dinner had to be cancelled. She hashed out some seating capacity issues with Aidan, to see if it was possible to move furniture and add an extra table or two, but she could not take her eye off the couple at the bar. Using an empty tea cup as an excuse, she walked towards the bus pan and canted her head towards the odd couple. Ger shrugged his shoulders. So he hadn't figured them out either, despite the fact that they'd practically taken up residence. Her senses were tingling, but maybe it was just exhaustion. Martie fell back into her chair and kicked off her clogs.

"Go on home, Aidan," she said. "You've put in too many hours. Rest up for the weekend."

"Thanks, I will. Can I have a word, before I go," the manager said. "About April."

For most of the evening, Aidan had been 'Ah, now, April'-ing while the waitress aired her complaints. For a girl who dreamed of being discovered by Hollywood, she displayed a flair for melodrama but she was not a great actress. All of April's whining revolved around Martie's stringent expectations. All of Aidan's sympathy revolved around bedding April, a highly unlikely scenario. Years in the kitchens of Moraine Hills had taught Martie that the town was full of waitresses like April, looking to cash in on their good looks with a wealthy husband. While Aidan was not dirt poor, he was not sugar daddy material.

"Here's the deal," Martie said. She leaned forward to share a confidence. "One day she'll wake up and she'll be my age and the men won't be falling all over her. And you know what, Aidan? She'll have nothing. No house, no family, no savings. I'm not going to stand by and let her throw her life away for something that she'll never find in a bar. April's bright and she's capable. I'm going to stay on her until she makes something of herself. There's good money to be made in this business, but you have to treat it as a job and not like a singles mixer."

Harsh words, but Martie could back them up with facts, with names of women who thought they could score and ended up as a discarded mistress with little to show for the effort. Being an employer meant more than providing work; she believed that she had a duty to serve as nanny or mentor as the situation dictated. She knew the restaurant industry, she had years of experience, and she would share her knowledge with her crew while sheltering them under a protective wing. The sort of success that Martie wanted required an equally focused crew, everyone on the same page, dedicating their working lives to McKechnie's. If April did not care to join the program, the door was not locked and the young lady was free to go.

"Time, gentlemen" spelled the closing of another day and sent the last few patrons to the front door. While Martie lingered over her paperwork, the bartenders and busboys did a final clean-up before they, too, called out their good-byes. Brendan drifted back to the table and sat down, to regale her with tales of Miltown summers that he probably had been telling for years. She let him ramble on, her mind wandering to one particular Miltown summer and one particular night, until she snapped her thoughts back to the situation at hand.

She needed to know more about Brendan than he knew about himself if she was to keep the upper hand in their relationship. Sooner rather than later, they would have to talk finances, making the partnership legal. Sinking all her savings into a shaky business was risky, but she was confident that Brendan would never balk at making her a full partner once she showed what she could do when given a chance. Right now, while he laughed over his father's boldness in talking to Miltown's parish priest as if they were equals, he did not know that he owed Martie over a quarter of a million dollars, or his signature on a partnership agreement. He couldn't possibly repay the debt if she called it in tomorrow, and she could blackmail him if she had to. Martie had him just where she wanted him, her position as secure as she could make it.

A very weary Jay Elizalde shuffled to the table, keen to go home but aware that his day was not quite over. He took the chair next to Martie, ready to review the menu plans for the grand opening. As sous chef, he was second in command, and if there was one thing the former Army Ranger understood, it was the chain of command and a respect for his superior officer. He also could count on Martie listening to his ideas and letting him experiment in the kitchen, giving him full credit for his successes. Which was more than Michael DeCecco ever did for her.

"The weekend from hell has just entered the ninth circle of hell," she said. "Every ex-pat in the Midwest is going to be here this weekend."

Brendan tried to explain Paddy Dunne's appeal, but his muddled conglomeration of Bob Dylan, Bruce Springsteen, Pearl Jam and Queens of the Stone Age did not clarify anything. Jay nodded and then stretched his neck, a sign that the shrapnel in his shoulder was giving him trouble. "I'm sure you'll be glad to hear that the Reserves booked some tables for Saturday lunch," he said.

"An early show would not be a wise move, I see," Brendan said. He painted Paddy as a dove of the first order, an outspoken and belligerent critic of war. Burly and strong, the singer could intimidate a heckler into submission, but Martie pictured a slightly different scenario in which a battle erupted pitting Paddy against the United States Army. A brawl could spell the end of McKechnie's. Reputation was everything in the restaurant business.

"Well done, Jay, we sure can use the business," Martie said. She appreciated his string-pulling, and she knew the price he paid to weave those ties. A boy with no direction had found his place, until his body was torn up by an improvised bomb planted on a dusty road in Iraq. With that, he lost what he had found in the Army, until a stint at a nearby cooking school had given him a new path to follow. Martie plucked him out of an associate degree program, gave him a push when he needed it, and he had returned the favor through unwavering devotion to her kitchen. She knew full well that she would be nowhere without people like Jay to do her bidding.

After the pub was closed, the kitchen staff sat down to an evening meal that consisted of dishes Martie planned to serve as specials while Shift/Move was drawing in a crowd over the weekend. Already the crew had their preferred spots, with Jay directly across from her and the line cooks arrayed between them. As soon as the hot plates were set in the middle of the round table, the pastry chef delivered a selection of sliced breads and took a seat at Martie's right hand. While Peaches said a short prayer, Martie paused to thank God for such a loyal staff. It was her name that made the papers, her name in the reviews and etched on the reward plaques, but she wouldn't have any of it on her own.

As each dish was presented, Martie explained the preparation. The plates were passed around the table, inspected and sniffed, before each cook sampled. Encouraged to join in, Brendan helped himself to a morsel of sea bass, looking very pleased that he had been included in the chosen circle. He could have been the geeky line cook when he copied the kid's technique of running his nose over the herb-encrusted pork. They settled down to eat, chatting about the events of the day and the events of their lives outside of work. Out of his element, Brendan was silent, respectful, and clearly in awe of Martie. It was lovely, to be paired with someone who truly appreciated her talents and would not interfere with her plans. She could not have latched on to a better partner, the moneyman who would give her all the space she needed to finally have her own place, financed by someone else.

"I just realized," Brendan said when the table grew quiet. "I build a house, and it's different from the other house I built. You guys, you cook something, and you've got to make it the same way every time. My success comes from not repeating myself, and your success comes from doing it again and again without change. I've got to hand it to you. I don't think I could do that."

The stares were somewhat blank, as if a moron had stepped into a philosopher's den and dared to open his mouth. Martie quickly switched topics, returning to the upcoming grand opening and the madhouse that would be McKechnie's on Friday and Saturday nights. To bring Brendan into the group, she turned to him to explain to the cooks what he had organized. As long as he felt that he was a part of things, getting a gentle ego stroking from time to time, he would be highly manageable.

"You probably don't know him," Brendan began. He paused and smiled at Martie. Finally, he noticed that she had programmed the sound system to play Shift/Move and Paddy Dunne during the meeting, setting the stage. With a wave of his hand, he indicated the music that was softly drifting out of the speakers tucked into the ceiling. A genuine recording artist, the toast of Ireland, was going to perform as a gift to his old friend. As expected, the cooks listened attentively and nodded politely, but the news meant little to them beyond the increased work load and pressure they would face. The kitchen crew never heard the music; they were too busy working while the band played.

Martie scheduled another meeting for the following day at half-past two, a meeting that would be repeated every day until she was satisfied with kitchen operations. Once business was settled, the cooks bussed their tables and drifted off to the kitchen, heading for home. Brendan held the door for Martie as they left together, locking it behind him and then bouncing the key in his hand. Close to midnight, the streets of Moraine Hills were deserted, the quiet lending an intimacy to their walk.

"Guess I should get you one of these," he said.

"Got it already," she said.

She was entitled to more than a key, and Brendan decided that this was as good a time as any to fill her in on the day's activities. A meeting with Ed at the bank had gone splendidly, even if Brendan was confused by Ed's carefree attitude. The banker assured his old friend that he had nothing to worry about, the payroll was taken care of, Brendan was in the best hands, and Ed just chuckled over Brendan's heartfelt pleading for more time. The golden touch was still intact, and Brendan wanted Martie to know how lucky he was, how successful the pub would be. In a roundabout way, he wanted to dig up something about Martie, to figure out what it would take to make her stick around. He knew enough about business to protect the top employees, to make them happy and content.

"You've been to Miltown?" He made inane conversation as they walked to the far corner of the parking lot.

"Me and a million other people," she said. "What was it like there before Willie Week became a big deal?"

Given an opening, Brendan grabbed the opportunity to relate his favorite stories and funny little quips about summers in a sleepy Irish hamlet. He wanted Martie to see how close he was to Paddy, but without boasting about his influence on the man. In all likelihood, Paddy would have ended his days as a bank clerk if Brendan hadn't been there to push him out of Miltown and convince him to have faith in his talent. He kept that thought to himself and described the origin of one of the photographs that hung near the stage.

"He has a drinking problem," Martie said. "It's sad to see in someone so talented. Have you ever considered talking to him, getting him some help?"

"He's on the wagon."

Her eyebrows arched in surprise. "That's great. Good for him. So it can be done. It is possible to quit if you put your mind to it."

She stopped next to her car, the last one left in the employee lot. He thought that executive chefs pulled in close to six figures, but she was driving a cheap, small, fuel-efficient coffee pot. Had everyone been mistaken when they warned him about the big salary she would command? If not, then where did all the money go? Not to expensive designer clothes or pricey jewelry, from what he had seen. He might have made a mistake in taking her on when he knew nothing about her private life.

"You don't, uh, you don't have a drinking problem, do you?" he asked. "Sorry. That came out wrong. If you needed help, you'd come to me, wouldn't you?"

For a minute, she only looked at him, a slight smile at the corner of her mouth. "No problem with over-consumption on my part," she said. "That's all we can truly control, ourselves. I mean, you can't run someone's life, can you? You give them the space they need and if it's meant to be, they'll come around."

When she offered to drive him to his car, he accepted because he wanted to spend a few more minutes with her. Dropping him off in front of the pub, she gave him a short lecture about everyone, him included, using the employee lot and saving the nearby spots for the customers. Her manner was playful, so light-hearted that he phoned her as soon as he got behind the wheel of his Suburban. Winding through the deserted streets of Moraine Hills, he followed behind her to be sure that she arrived home safely, chatting away. The headlights of their cars created a circle of light that glided along Indian Trail Road, driveway reflectors winking back at them as the convoy slipped north.

The blinking turn signal startled him, his mind elsewhere even though Martie told him that she was taking a right. Pulling to a stop at the curb in front of her house, he watched her car ease into the garage. As the door came down, Martie waved good-bye, shutting him out of her life until tomorrow. Still he could not let go, continuing to talk to her as she unlocked the door, kicked off her shoes, and wished him good night about three times.

The front window went dark and the house itself seemed to have gone to sleep while he lingered, puzzled by the lack of affluence. Martie's home was on the far edge of Shields, a small suburb that was considered affordable by the blue-collar set, an area unknown to the wealthy people they worked for. Not rundown, but her place could use a coat of paint. Here was a house that needed the skills that he possessed, to give back to Martie with his special talents. New windows, a different door, he could improve the look of her home as a way of thanking her for saving his hide.

Back on the road home, he thought of his house, the castle that he never asked for. Martie's place was closer to his ideal, a small cottage that needed only a layer of stucco to look more Old World. Even her front yard reminded him of an Irish landscape, filled with different shrubs and flowers that were on the verge of running riot. What he really wanted in his life before St. Patrick called him home was more like what Martie already had. They were more compatible than he had believed at first. Soulmates, he thought, a term he once found ridiculous. Not so ridiculous after all.

NINE

In the hour between the last lunch and the first cocktail, the pub was quiet. Louis from the sound system company was already at work, adjusting the stage lights with the cheerful energy of a man who was in love with his job. He had his territory staked out, the mixer set up against a back wall with a good view of the stage. The board was his own, an elaborate piece of equipment that fit in with McKechnie's audio devices because, he boasted, he had set it up that way.

An older woman who worked the lunch shift greeted the party as she poured out strong tea and served a platter of scones. As comforting as the food was her voice, maternal and warm, suggesting that her customers were sitting at grandmother's kitchen table. She had been previously employed by Michael DeCecco, and made no apologies for leaving her job and the suggestive antics of a famous chef with a big ego who hit on every young thing who walked in the door. In her anecdotes Brendan heard the stern morality that governed his childhood, a morality that always blamed the woman while the man skated.

"Jesus, I can't eat another thing," Liam groaned.

"I better try one," Brendan said. "In case there's a test later."

Their tea party was interrupted by the arrival of the session musicians, the Celtic Airs. The apparent leader was Kevin, while the second in command was Denny, who seemed to be the road manager as well, burdened as he was by a dolly loaded with equipment cases. They quickly unpacked their instruments and all five musicians began to tune up without a word, as if this was standard operating procedure. Their language was music, unspoken, and Brendan sat back to watch a scene that was reproduced countless times at countless venues in County Clare. The image was a reproduction from Willie Week, the famous musical festival that centered in Miltown Malbay for seven days in July, transported to America but not changed by the journey.

To a man, this was dead serious business, with Paddy or Liam calling out a song that might be played over the weekend. Paddy strummed the opening bars and carefully listened to the new arrivals as they followed and then carried along. Denny, the piper, switched to concertina and displayed a dexterity that was rarely seen in an average pub. As the first customers began to straggle into the bar, the musical group grew more and more cohesive, trading riffs and licks as if competing to outdo one another. Brendan had not seen two uilleann pipers do battle since Willie Week six years past, as two men who were unquestionable masters of their instrument played to a draw.

Taking a seat at the bottom of the bar, Brendan tucked into a corner where he could watch the stage and the front door. Des had left his copy of *The Irish Times*, along with the local rag, and Brendan thumbed through the papers to unwind after a very long day. While scanning an article about Martha Smurfit cooking for a charity fundraiser, he thought about calling in to see if the construction company had fallen apart in his absence. He read the sheet more carefully, and then ripped it out of the paper. Before he could damage it with spilled beer or smudges, he brought the page to the office to keep it safe until he could get it to a frame shop. This was exactly the sort of thing that should be hanging in the foyer, where people waiting for tables could be assured that McKechnie's was worth the wait.

He stopped in the banquet room upstairs to straighten up the mess. Brendan had to have order and organization, and the haphazard arrangement of instrument cases and boxes of sheet music annoyed him. Picking up a small briefcase, he spilled out Paddy's hand written chord progressions and a few CDs. Like Martie's music collection, he knew none of the names, but one title caught his eye. 'Recorded Live at Schulien's Tavern' gave Brendan a brilliant idea.

Des was on duty when Brendan returned. The place was getting busy again, vibrant with Paddy and the lads rehearsing while bar patrons chatted. When Mac and his wife turned up, followed by O'Connor and his brood, Brendan jumped off his stool to welcome the first of the ex-pats who would create the irresistible atmosphere of McKechnie's. Customers would hear brogues of all four provinces, and spread the word that Irish people ate at Brendan's pub, a stamp of authenticity that tilted the odds in favor of success. Pushed into a deep recess, Brendan's fear of failure and bankruptcy was fading, buried under a sense that he was on his way to the top, and Martie was his lovely guide who knew how to avoid every pitfall.

At the bar, Brendan ordered drinks sent round to the band, but it was apparent that some of the musicians had already gotten started. Before he could assess the piper's sobriety, he was startled by a beefy hand touching his forearm. Brendan turned away from the stage and discovered that the pastel-attired gentleman he noticed the night before was trying to get his attention.

"I understand you're the landlord here," he said in his thick Belfast brogue. "Jim Gray, sir, pleased to make your acquaintance. And my associate, Graham Brown."

"What can I do for you?" Brendan replied, trying not to laugh. If ever there were phony names, Gray and Brown certainly made the cut. Considering the attitude towards homosexuality in Belfast, he was not surprised that a gay couple would hide behind a facade.

"You've a fine place here," Jim said. "The sort of place I've been looking for."

"It's not for sale," Brendan said.

Jim smiled while his colleague stared into his pint. "You misunderstand me. I'm a businessman such as yourself, and I'm looking about for some sound investment opportunities."

A partner would mean an infusion of cash that was very much needed. McKechnie's was no longer on life support, but the pub remained in critical condition. There was only so long that the bank would wait to be repaid. "What are you proposing?" Brendan asked. It could not hurt to listen, and it was just as easy to turn down an offer as it was to accept one.

The nondescript Graham Brown came alive. "A fine place like this must have been expensive to build."

"What it costs, it costs," Brendan said. "Cut corners and it shows. Thinking of building yourself, Mr. Gray?"

"Now, I had given it some thought at one time, back home." Jim lowered his voice and Brendan had to lean closer to hear. "Sectarianism. It's killing Belfast. Think poorly of me if you will, but, I gave up on the town myself. Like all the rest, I've come to America to try my hand."

"You can't serve all equal," Graham mumbled. "What's the point of adding to the divide? We're here to do what we wanted to do at home, but couldn't."

"Investing at first, to build up our capital," Jim continued. "We've saved up for this since we were lads. Here's our thoughts. We sink our nest egg into your place, and, after a time, when's it grown, we branch out. Put up another pub in another town and me and Graham here would look after it."

"Franchises, you mean?" Brendan asked.

With a jab at Brendan's shoulder, Jim indicated that his point was understood. To show that he meant business, he pulled a wad of paper money out of his pants pocket. "It's a matter of converting some Northern Bank notes into dollars. We don't know any bankers here, men we could work with. Discreet. Everything we ever had is in our pockets right now."

Ger wiped the bar until he had wiped his way to the trio. His ears actually seemed to prick up as he rubbed at a particularly stubborn spot that Brendan did not see. "Couple of pints here," Brendan said, sending Ger a few feet away to the taps. "Your proposal is interesting. I have to take it up with my, um, my, partner."

"Fair enough," Graham said, turning to his fresh glass of beer. Ger mopped up the minutest of droplets from the bar.

"Time's time," Jim said. "We're considering other ventures as well. How's tomorrow, early evening? We'll come to an agreement then, but remember, we'll be interviewing others as well, just to hedge our bets."

The business world moved swiftly, as Brendan knew from long experience. He thought for a moment, watching Ger slice limes into wedges. With the grand opening party planned for Friday, it was the worst possible day to arrange a meeting, but hesitation could be disastrous. Money offered today might be gone by Saturday, and Brendan needed the cash. There was no time, but he had to make time. Or close the doors. He would rather sell his soul to the devil than take money from Bonnie's brother or surrender to her defeatism. Besides, he had made promises to Martie, to not pull out, and he would find a way to get more investors for her sake.

With a buzz, Brendan's cell phone went off in his pocket. He quickly agreed to a meeting and raced off to the office to take the call. Bonnie was on the line, but he would not complain. She had been generous, turning him loose with his guests and letting him run free. Of course, she operated under the belief that Paddy, Liam and Rory did not chase women, they chased the next pint. Feeling on top of a world that was less shaky than it had been a week ago, he rested his feet on the desk and related his activities of the day. Bonnie babbled on and on about new shoes while he picked up the torn newsprint to re-read the article about Martie.

Not only had Martie cooked for a fundraiser, she was reported to be quite active in a cooking program at the junior college. A spokesperson for a battered women's shelter was quoted, praising the chef to the heavens for bringing hope to the shelter's residents through education. A thought flashed through his brain, that Martie was giving so much of her time because she owed the group something. Maybe she was once a battered woman. That would explain her hesitancy to talk about herself. His business brain kicked in when Bonnie mentioned the Boys and Girls Club, a reminder of the North Shore mania for volunteering. The ladies who decided where to eat dinner in a town filled with restaurants tended to support their own, and what better advertising could he have than a lengthy article about Martie's personal mania for volunteering? He had to post the newsprint in a prominent place, a piece of tasteful decor meant to impress and sway opinion.

"How's your friends?" Bonnie said. "Pickled or half in the bag?"

For a long time, Brendan had not been listening. "Off the drink," he said without thinking. "Hasn't had a drop."

"I'm not helping out on Friday if he's drunk," Bonnie said. "God, he was obnoxious the last time. I will not subject myself to his bullshit if he's not dead cold sober."

Of all the times for Paddy to give up drinking, this was not the best. Tempted to take her up on her offer to boycott McKechnie's, Brendan dreamed of having the pub all to himself, without Bonnie's interference. "Paddy's being here is going to give me a jump start like nothing else in the world. As far as I'm concerned, he's more than making up for anything he did in the past. But I'll understand if you don't come. Really, I won't mind. I won't say a word to you about it. I understand completely."

"Okay, then. I'll think about it."

"Whatever you want to do, it's up to you. No offense taken if you stay home Friday, I swear. Go out to dinner with the girls if you want. I'll be fine here on my own."

Rather than overdo his sales pitch, Brendan stopped before he came right out and asked her to steer clear of the pub. At some point during the grand opening, he could count on Bonnie to make a scene if she misunderstood some banter between him and Martie. God help him if she had it out with Martie over a friendly smile taken the wrong way. He'd be dead if he lost his cook.

TEN

The day's current crop of bills reminded him that he was on the edge and he did not need a push over the side. Tidying up his desk, he stacked the invoices, noticing that Paddy's sister Ann had finally asked for payment for the truckload of antiques that adorned the walls of McKechnie's Pub. He put her bill on top, vowing to pay it first, no matter what else might be more pressing. In the back of his mind, he realized that Bonnie had asked him to do something, but he had already forgotten, if he had even heard her clearly. Something to do with money, probably, when the last thing he needed was another expense to cover with non-existent income. He was about to call her back when he was distracted by the sound of a fierce verbal altercation.

Suppressed rage reached his ears, drifting up from the bottom of the stairs. "Look at the state of you," Martie hissed, keeping her voice down. "All your promises. All lies. Is this the way to thank me for trying to help you get on your feet?"

She stopped her tirade when she saw Brendan creeping down the stairs. Denny the set musician was on the receiving end of the verbal club, but he was not chastised by the battering. Instead, he flashed a smirk that smacked of defiance before he skulked away. "The music sounds great," Brendan said. He ran his hand along the edge of the holy water font. He had a pretty good idea why Martie had been so rough on the guy. "Can he still play?"

"He could play if he was passed out," she grumbled. "All that talent. Stupid."

"Let's leave it up to Paddy," Brendan said. "It's his show. Hell, he's been there."

"Been there, done that, and figured out that he was wasting his life."

"That about sums it up," Brendan said.

Martie shook her head, ready to move on. "We're in good shape for tomorrow. Not perfect, but we'll fake our way through."

Excited by her implication of stellar success, Brendan ran down a list of important people who would be attending the grand opening, insisting that Martie had to meet every one of them. He was extolling the wisdom of his attorney and golf partner when a familiar party walked by on their way out the door. Sal Lardino was holding court again, but with a different group, made up of women who bore a strong, though unfortunate, resemblance to himself. If he was entertaining his family, it must mean that McKechnie's was on the verge of becoming the latest must-dine establishment. The crowds would roll in soon enough. Keeping them rolling in was going to be the next trick.

Playing the role of proud owner, Brendan moved through the dining room greeting his customers, asking about the food and the service in the same way he had seen Michael DeCecco work a room. Even if all of this collapsed tomorrow, Brendan could walk away with a memory of those few minutes, where he was the star in the middle of his life's dream. He could brag to Martie about the pleasure he felt when he realized he had outdone his uncle, but he did not want her to think that he was competing. To succeed in America, the pub had to be bigger, the food had to be better and the atmosphere had to be larger. He was not in some sort of race, like he was in the construction business with its fierce competition. Would she understand his thinking, or was it foreign to someone whose success came from repetition so that everyone had the same experience?

Rehearsal went on, with Paddy oblivious to the noisy crowd that was surprised by the presence of an unadvertised live band. He sang a couple of requests for Mac and did a few bars of *The Enniskillen Dragoon* for Ger, but as the room filled he became more focused on practice, tuning out distractions. A shy request for an autograph broke the spell. Signing his name with a flourish, the musician marveled at the passage of time, two hours that had flown by like two minutes. He rubbed his right wrist, as if the tendons ached from years of over-use, and scheduled a final sound check with the Celtic Airs. Either he was unaware that one of them was intoxicated, or he was too polite to comment.

With a glass of sparkling water in his hand, Paddy slid onto the seat next to Brendan. "Did you ever have the feeling that you've been with someone before," the singer said. "But you don't know if you actually have?"

"Your man was in no fit state to remember where he was at," Rory said, "let alone recall where he'd been. That Denny fella remind you of yourself?"

"Ah, now, the man can play, and he'd pipe rings around you," Paddy said. "We'll mind him, keep him away from the drink. It breaks my heart to see so much talent drowned in alcohol."

"He's one of Martie's lost lambs," Brendan said.

"Martie's doing, so?" Liam said. "We'll have to keep him on, won't we?"

Rory rolled his eyes, but Brendan didn't catch the meaning. They sipped at another drink, reminisced over old times, and talked with Ger about the possibility of County Clare making any sort of mark in the All-Ireland hurling tournament. Unexpectedly, four Irish fries were delivered from the kitchen, sent around for tea, compliments of the chef. No one said another word about the overly-thirsty Celtic Air.

"Ready to turn in?" Brendan asked as they finished the last of the rashers.

Liam's sad eyes were pleading because he was far too polite to voice a protest and counter his host. When Brendan added a remark about old men needing their rest, Liam retorted, "Having the slag. You're a sly one, Brendan McKechnie."

Without telling them where they were going, Brendan drove south towards the city. Excited for his friend, Paddy was full of questions about the pub and the Moraine Hills restaurant market. It was a topic that Brendan could dive into, and he was running off at the mouth with every marketing tidbit that he had acquired during the past two years of planning and construction. Comparisons to the original pub in Miltown were made, with Paddy pondering the reaction of the locals to Martie's style of cooking. His thoughts sent Brendan on a lovely reverie, where he bought out his uncle and branched out, franchise-like, to Ireland. He saw himself waltzing into Uncle Donal's place with Martie on his arm, every eye on him, every heart beating with jealousy. The possibilities were as endless as the potential headaches.

One by one, the lads brought up one of Miltown's resident characters, placing each one in Brendan's bar, with the situations growing increasingly ridiculous and increasingly silly. Liam aped old Father McIlhennie, the parish priest who found Dermot McKechnie too high and mighty altogether, sitting down to a platter of lamb medallions in tarragon apricot sauce. His send-up had the party in stitches. They were laughing their heads off when Brendan slowed down, looking for a place to park.

"If you were a girl, I'd kiss you," Paddy shouted. He had caught sight of the large sign that glowed brightly at the corner, colors that spelled out 'Schulien's'.

"I'm full of surprises," Brendan said.

After living in the suburbs for so many years, Brendan had forgotten that people went out to clubs and restaurants late at night during the work week. The bar room was crowded, busier than any place was at that moment in Moraine Hills on a Thursday evening. The only seats available were close to the stage, hard by a speaker. Given no other options, he took what he could get and hoped that the music would not be so loud that conversation became a shouting session.

A woman on stage was hammering a dulcimer into submission while her partner strummed a twelve-string guitar. They concluded their song, a ballad that decried urban sprawl, and took a break. The guitarist took a long look at the new arrivals, as if he should recognize the members of the party but could not quite place the faces. Shift/Move was hardly a blip on Chicago's radar, and Brendan did not expect that anyone would recognize Paddy Dunne in a city that had more than enough talent of its own.

"They'll think you're the designated driver," Brendan said after Paddy expressed his fear of being pushed towards temptation. The risk of taking an alcoholic into a bar was only a danger if the other three members of the party gave in to a weakening of Paddy's resolve. Through this group effort, they could ease Paddy back into the treacherous outside world that he could not avoid if he was going to live a normal life. Being the one man at the table who never touched a drop could be glossed over by a label, a socially acceptable niche that acted as a deterrent to anyone who would try to force a drink on a weak man.

"You see, it's done here, the not drinking," Paddy said. "I've got to learn to live in the world with my addiction. You're a good man, Brendan, to help me through my troubles."

"Sure, and you don't have half the audience wanting to send you a round," Rory added.

"Give it time," Liam said. "We'll all have to wake up some day. Christ, go to Dublin and you'll not walk ten feet on a Friday night without some kid spewing on your shoes."

"Newfound prosperity for our island," Paddy said. "And the excess came right along behind."

Over beer and water they discussed modern Ireland, a land made rich by embracing technology and free market economics, and lately frightened by a falling economy. It was a country that had shaken off the dust of isolation in the span of Brendan's lifetime, never to return to its hiding place. Once upon a time, his American lifestyle had seemed exotic to his Irish friends, but now their children were making their way in a very European world. Underneath the anecdotes, Brendan could hear a longing for a place that had been left behind by the rat race, the old ways pushed aside in the name of progress.

Liam was aware of the mania for work, the drive to put in long hours, and Brendan felt called upon to defend his own penchant for a heavy load. "That's competition is all. If I don't put in the time, I lose out to the guy who's available. Come on, I still go on vacation."

"Now there's a grand holiday," Rory said. "Shall we go abroad this year? Ah, no, I think I'll start a new business for relaxation. You're mad about work, Brendan, if you'd rather build another building than spend a week or two back home."

"Can you fault the man?" Paddy said. "What was he to do with his evenings? How can he work around the clock without a business that's open at night?"

"Pity that sleep got in the way, so," Liam added to the sarcasm.

"Very funny," Brendan said. "I'm not the only one taking a nap in the office. You want a workaholic, talk to Martie."

"And how would you know where the woman sleeps?" Liam said. "Shocking, and you in a 'committed relationship.'"

Brendan could feel the blood rising in his cheeks, as if his secret longings were ready to burst forth from every pore. He had complained about Bonnie many times, told plenty to these same three men, but they had all been mellowed by alcohol at the time and not capable of remembering anything. Despite his hope that his confessions were perceived as so much hot air, Brendan could not shake the feeling that his negative attitude had remained behind, like background noise.

"Not all of us were blessed with a sweetheart like Aislinn," Brendan said to Paddy, the one who was laughing the loudest.

"I've got you there, son," Paddy said. "I don't have Aislinn anymore, either."

"What?"

Laughter became bitter as Paddy leaned across the table. "She left me last year, right before Willie Week. Do you not recall, how she always promised to go if I didn't give up the drink? How often did she say that? So, how often did I swear off the booze? This time she kept her promise when I broke mine."

Scanning the faces before him, Brendan searched for the truth that he found reflected in Rory's downcast eyes and Liam's nervous nonchalance. Paddy valued Brendan's respect, and to confess such a tragedy took a great deal of courage. Laid out on the small table, Paddy's shame was expressed for his friend to see, no veil to cover the humiliation. A sudden urge to blurt out a confession took hold of Brendan's tongue and he put his mouth to work in tasting the craft beer. He had experienced a momentary pang of jealousy, brought on by a wish that he, too, was a single man. Paddy had no cause to be embarrassed by an admission of failure.

"Jesus Christ," Brendan said. "Oh my God, I'm sorry for your troubles."

"So now I've kept my promise, off the drink, but it's come too late," Paddy said.

The duo returned to the stage, their amplified voices breaking into the conversation. The woman adjusted the strap of her guitar and fixed her eyes on the party that had grown subdued and gloomy. "We'd like to do a request for our host," she said. "This next song was first performed by Paddy Dunne."

"Christ Almighty, is that aul' bastard still alive?" Rory bellowed.

"Let's hear some Bob Dylan," Paddy rejoined, copying Brendan's Chicago twang to near perfection.

Not to be put off by heckling, the performers launched into their version of a Shift/Move classic, but they kept stealing glances at Paddy, as if they were not wholly convinced that he was not the man they took him for.

The mood lifted, by force of Paddy's will, and he laughed over his marital problems until they almost ceased to exist.

After a couple of hours of chat and music, Brendan switched to water, as much to keep Paddy company as to remain sober enough to drive home. The topic of their discussion shifted between Brendan's pub and life in modern Miltown, where Rory's dreams of big American cars and lots of money had come to fruition, but not quite as he had once pictured. The grasping that Brendan knew from America had arrived in Ireland, catching his friends off-guard because Brendan had never been able to explain it to them. What he had lived with all his life touched the lives of people who were unprepared for the consequences of the free market. What could he say, when he planted the seeds of urban sprawl in fertile farmland and reaped the profit while others had to put up with the traffic jams. There was money to be made, and Brendan made it, just like his cousin Daìthi had once prospered. Business had been good, but then the good times came crashing down and decent people were hurt. Men like Paddy reported the disappointments in song, but the rich men were not listening to his lyrics.

On the trip home, Paddy offered his thanks for the evening's entertainment. "That was a grand kip. Your man had that singer thinking he was Eric fucking Clapton."

Liam giggled, giddy with drink and good company. "Fair play to me. An honest man I was. Never signed an autograph."

"As honest as the day is long," Rory said, only to break into a chorus of laughter.

Watching Paddy from the corner of his eye, Brendan looked for a flinch or a spark that would reveal if the reformed alcoholic missed the pleasant buzz that a couple of pints delivered. Paddy was, as far as Brendan had ever seen, a fun-loving drunk, not given to brawling. Then again, a full-blown alcoholic might not feel that buzz in the same way, if he felt it at all. Satisfied by two, or maybe three, pints, Brendan could not imagine the unconquerable urge to have another, and then more, until the body shut down in a drunken stupor. Given that Paddy had fallen to that point, there could not be anything about drinking that he truly missed. It was a pure addiction, then, without logic.

"You should have told me," Brendan said after Liam and Rory dozed off in the back seat.

"At the time, I couldn't face my troubles," Paddy said. "She left a drunkard, you see? But I didn't believe that I was a drunkard, so how could she have left me?"

"What about later?"

"Later is now, my boy. The hardest part of my rehab has been telling you the truth. Bad enough to face them all at home, and the young ones who look up to me. Sure I'm a feckin' icon."

"I'd think that would be a misery."

"Now, it wasn't easy, coming clean. It was you thinking less of me, that's where I found the greatest fear."

"Patrick Dunne, if you ever believe that I'd think less of you for something so, well, Christ, do you think I'd turn my back on you if you announced that you had epilepsy or diabetes?"

"The drink is only a weakness."

"Weakness, my ass. It's a sickness."

"You're a good man, so, Brendan."

"Just a good friend, my man. I'd like to have you around a little longer."

On the verge of getting maudlin, Paddy lapsed into a comfortable silence that was broken by Liam's inebriated snorts. "Fucking jet lag," the sleeper mumbled, coming to.

"Ah, you're an old sot, falling asleep after a pint," Paddy said.

"Who's the old man, now?"

"Old, me? Just very well hydrated. How much further, Brendan? I need to take a slash."

Cod

julienne onions, sauté in butter to caramelize

POTATOES? brown in butter after cooking onions
salt & pepper

champagne instead of white wine – poach
deglaze pan with ~~vinegar~~ champagne vinegar

Sauce: lobster cream – use tarragon & parsley
tomatoes – talk Manon into growing striped Roma plums

ELEVEN

Work was his closest companion, but the demands of the construction business were unwelcome. Phone calls, estimates and job site inspections took up all of Brendan's morning when he wanted only to be at the pub, getting ready for the grand opening. Aidan had everything under control, Martie was on top of her game, but he longed to see it all unfold. He had not even had a chance to visit the kitchen yet, to watch Martie perform her culinary magic. Thinking of the scene, imaging Aunt Eleanor's little room behind the bar, he drove past the Deerhaven Inn with his head in a fog and had to go around the block to reach the entrance.

Liam and Rory were waiting in the lobby when he arrived, playing the role of chauffeur for the band that was scheduled for a sound check in less than thirty minutes. Paddy was nowhere to be found. No one actually suggested looking in the bar; they just moved to the room automatically. They were a gang, prepared to physically lift Paddy off a stool if he had slipped and broken his vow, but the darkened corner of the hotel lounge was deserted.

"He's been walking away the cravings," Rory recalled. "Christ, where the hell would he go?"

"Around to the shops?" Liam suggested. "He likes to bring back souvenirs for his children. Do you think he's after buying a gift or two?"

Together they drove the two blocks to the shopping district, where Brendan steered slowly around the square. Most of the stores catered to women, clothing boutiques or high-priced linens, and not the sort of place that Paddy would enter. They tried the side streets, popping into the coffee shop in the hope that the prodigal singer had only been in need of a cup of tea. A few ladies, all blond and slim, barely glanced at the frantic trio who made a circuit of the small tables and the seating area.

"No, he can't be," Rory said to Liam, half-whispering. The two Irishmen looked at Brendan, uncomfortable. "Could he have walked to the pub, do you think?"

McKechnie's was at least five miles away, not an impossible distance but long enough for a man with a weak heart. "Why would he go there?" Brendan said. "He won't get served there; they know he's off the drink."

Rory grinned. "It's not a drink that I had in mind. A lovely fry. Or a lovely ride."

"Oh, come on," Brendan said. "He walked five miles to get laid?"

"Back in the day, I would have walked further," Liam said.

"If ever a man loved liquor more than women," Brendan began.

"And without the drink now?" Liam cut in.

"If he gets lucky with April and her silicone tits, more power to him," Brendan said.

"Ah, you're feckin' blind," Rory said. "And deaf. He'll run off with your cook if you're not careful."

They were dead wrong about Paddy's intentions. Hadn't the man evaporated into the shadows when he met Martie? If anything, he was likely to be a good mate and talk up Brendan's many fine qualities so that Martie saw her boss in a rose-hued light. What if Martie got her hopes up, based on who knew what Paddy might tell her? He was in a committed relationship, not on the market. Brendan sprinted to his car and then scrolled through the contacts list on his phone as he turned the key in the ignition. "Aidan, is Paddy?" he blurted out. "Did he turn up?"

"He's been wandering," Aidan said. "Don't know where he's at right now. On the premises, I'm sure."

"Where's Martie?"

"Staff lunch. She just sliced up the new waiter. Josh." Aidan drew out the name with mockery. "Looking for easy money, he says to me when I offered the job. Ah, she's brilliant."

Sighing loudly, Brendan let his shoulders slump, not afraid to express his great relief. Paddy had walked and he had not keeled over dead. He was not spinning a web that would trap Brendan and all his hopes for his new venture. If everything else went as well, the pub was guaranteed to be the biggest success in restaurant history.

Rory ranted, a tirade that earned little more than a mumbled "Sorry, lads" from a man who was not listening with both ears. Paddy tested a bodhràn, put it down and picked up another guitar, as restless as a caged lion. He glued his eyes to the floor and strummed a chord, accepting without words the stress he had caused his band mates. As Liam noted, it was not too much to ask that Paddy inform them in future when he planned to wander off, especially those who were making a great effort to help him overcome a debilitating addiction.

"You're right, you're right," Paddy said. "But I feel like I'm in prison, watched every minute."

"You've earned it, old son," Liam said. "Until you show you're ready to be on your own, you'll have us in your back pocket. Is that clear?"

Right on time, the Celtic Airs turned up, ready for work. Denny was undeniably shaking, his hands steady enough to play but not perfectly still. The cure was another drink to calm the nerves, and then another when that wore off, and another until the performance suffered. Brendan was not going to let that happen. Apparently Martie was not going to let it happen either. As if she knew exactly when she needed to make an appearance, she showed up in the bar and told Des in no uncertain terms that there would be no alcohol served to the set musicians.

A nod and a grunt was Denny's greeting to her, as if the previous day's events had never been. "You're on your own. No more chances. I won't cover for you," she called to him across the room, and returned to the kitchen before he had a chance to answer.

The bar was empty and the dining room quiet when the band began to prepare for the night's performance. Kevin sawed a bow across the strings of his fiddle and twisted the tuning pegs, his ear in tune with perfect pitch. Denny pumped the bellows of his pipe, pausing to take a sip from a bottle of Evian water. Random notes arose like so many distinct voices, not harmonizing but carrying on individual monologues. Paddy strummed a riff, fingered a few chords, and shifted on a chair in search of a comfortable position.

"Aislinn called and I couldn't pick up," Paddy said in what sounded like a confession.

"There's a phone in my office upstairs," Brendan said. "Private, if that matters."

"Private or public, I don't know what to say," Paddy said.

"Start with hello and see what comes out of your mouth after that," Rory said. "We can practice without you for a bit. Go on, so. Take that first step."

Leaving Brendan to tape set lists to the floor in front of each musician's station, Paddy set off with shoulders hunched against the unknown that awaited him at the other end of a wireless connection. Liam opened the rehearsal with a song that would be released in July, to coincide with the beginning of Willie Week. As the last note sounded, Rory suggested they change the program to allow for audience requests, to make the performance more like a casual Sunday session than the usual concert. The venue was too intimate to do otherwise.

"Sounds good," Martie said as she crossed the room. Brendan watched her climb the stairs, never tiring of the view.

As Liam tuned his mandolin, he began to chuckle. "What time is it in Ireland, would you guess?"

Rory looked at his watch. "Not so late. Ten o'clock." He played a riff, the opening of an old traditional song. "If he's on the phone."

The piper must have been dehydrated, judging by the way he kept returning to a bottle of water. Brendan had heard that recovering alcoholics were prone to drink liquids to excess, as if they had to have something in their mouths that was wet. The way that Paddy downed water the previous night had proved the theory, where a hand wrapped around a glass was as necessary as breathing to survive a craving. He went to the bar and returned to the stage with a quart bottle of Ballygowen, pumped from St. Patrick's well in Limerick.

Making himself useful, Brendan volunteered to climb the stairs to the banquet room and retrieve a new string for the mandolin. He went back for a file of sheet music and listened for a minute as Shift/Move found harmony with the Celtic Airs, playing a new song for the first time. After a third trip, he began to wonder if Paddy was all right, or if something had happened to Aislinn. The office door was closed and Paddy had been gone for fifteen minutes.

As soon as he put his ear to the door, Brendan pulled away and raced back to the stage, regaining his composure as he handed the packet of picks to Liam. "How's that for service?" he said, attempting to make a joke. He was going to be sick. His legs were shaking, he could not believe what he had heard, he wanted to wipe the sounds out of his brain. He wanted it to be him in the office and Paddy in the bar room.

"Where's himself?" Rory asked. "Sorry, Brendan, but can you give him a shout?"

Back up he went, slowly passing the office door and wandering into the banquet room. Leaning against the wall, Brendan slid down until he was sitting on the floor, surrounded by instrument cases and sheet music. Paddy was not the same man he had known two years ago. Abruptly, he had twisted into some sort of ballooning ego on legs. Giving up drink had caused this transformation, Brendan was certain. A once humble singer was taking advantage of a star-struck woman with a kind heart, a victim of Paddy's conceit who would be used and discarded. Without doubt, Paddy could be a selfish human being. For years, he had seen to his lust for booze while his family sat at home to worry about his safety and his life. If Paddy had been loathe to confess his sins for fear of losing Brendan's respect, his fears were well-founded. As if he was seeing Paddy for the first time, Brendan was deeply disappointed, disillusioned and bitter.

The door opened and the sounds of voices crept around the corner to Brendan's ears. Too quiet to hear clearly, he could judge well enough that it was an Irish tongue dripping honey. "Don't tell herself," it sounded like. Don't tell Aislinn? How could any man be that callous, to try to win back his wife and then fuck another woman right after?

Waiting for silence, Brendan sat on the floor, the chaotic clutter of tables and chairs making fun of him. What he thought he had might not be in his possession. After years in the construction business, he knew that he had to fight his rivals, and whatever means necessary was fair. No one was going to ruin him, not the bank, not the Mafia goons in the dining room, and definitely not Paddy's libido.

Artificial good cheer pounded into him with every step, to radiate from his grinning face as he took a seat in front of the stage. "So, how's Aislinn?" Brendan asked.

"Didn't reach her," Paddy said. He was perfectly calm, a housecat licking a saucer of cream. "I'll give it another go before the gig."

"That'd be midnight," Liam noted.

"It's a feckin' spa up there," Paddy said. "Jacks like I've never seen."

The flippant humor about the men's toilets annoyed Brendan. Paddy's nonchalance was disgusting. Without a care in the world, Paddy called out a song title, as if he had pulled the tune out of the air. The group was surprisingly cohesive on *The Boys of Barr na Sraida*. Brendan switched seats, pulling up a stool at the bottom of the bar where he could lean his weary frame against the wall and stare directly at the photograph next to the stage. Pity that he had not bashed Paddy with the hurley when he had the chance, instead of convincing Katie O'Malley to accept a ride on the bar of Paddy's bike. Twelve years old, and Paddy was in love with the belle of Miltown who was mooning over the Yank lad and all that he represented. Brendan had given up Katie, but he was not going to let Martie go without a fight.

When she spotted Paddy heading for the office, Martie hid in the ladies' room until she heard him walk down the hall. Heart pounding, she listened for the door of the men's room to shut before dashing down the back stairs to the sanctuary of her kitchen. Eventually Paddy would go home and she would be free. "This too will end," she said.

"You are ready now to admit I am right?"

Manon Roche leaned against the door of the walk-in cooler, casting a dismissive glance at the kitchen. For longer than Martie cared to remember, Manon had been after her to form a partnership and open a restaurant that would feature Manon's cuisine and leave Martie as the second in command, the inferior position that would spell the end of her ambitions. Their last argument revolved around Manon being too bossy, too controlling, and the relationship had been strained for months.

"I thought you came to tell me you were wrong," Martie said.

"We need something to," Manon said, twining her fingers together to suggest an interweaving of two into one. "Before you are too old, chere, and you once wanted another baby. If not to work together, to make a family. After you see your son, you will change your mind. My brother, he is willing to help us."

"This is not the time," Martie said. "You just want me to get pregnant so I have to take time off and you know damn well this place would go under."

"I want you to stop running from me when you get close."

"Now you sound like Aunt Brid." The only relative who did not disown Martie had provided shelter in Dublin when her niece needed a home and a firm hand to set her life back on track. Martie found her footing in cooking, and Aunt Brid moved where Martie's career took her, from Dublin to Rome and then Paris. When Martie followed Manon to Chicago, Aunt Brid tagged along like a guardian angel.

"I miss her too, you know."

The normal volume of chattering cooks decreased, a sign that Martie's staff was tuning in to a private conversation. She tugged at Manon's arm and dragged her into the walk-in cooler, the only area that afforded some well-insulated privacy.

"Why can't you respect my intention to be my own boss and have my own place and cook what I want to cook?"

"Why isn't my dream enough for both of us?"

There was a time when Manon's pretty reveries might have been enough, back when Martie was a line cook in Paris and Manon was the chef de cuisine who began a seduction with a lesson in frenching a lamb chop. They were far from inseparable back in those days, when Martie was discovering herself while trying to make that person fit the Smurfit family mold. Maybe that was why Aunt Brid pushed her so hard, to keep climbing instead of settling for the comfort of some culinary base camp. To go all out and not be held back by emotional entanglements. For so many years, Martie's aunt had been there for her, and it hurt to realize that Aunt Brid had passed away less than a year before Martie achieved her dream.

Looking back to her days in Paris resurrected an unpleasant memory. It was on Manon's day off, and the owner of the bistro where they worked took Martie aside. A complaint had been lodged, he said, an accusation of sexual harassment. Inappropriate contact with one of the line cooks, but everyone in the kitchen knew he was having an affair with the sous chef. Not that Martie would reveal the details, especially because both parties were married to other people, but she had to defend herself. All she could do was claim that her unknown accuser was lying, about as feeble a defense as anyone could muster.

Someone had set her up, but Martie had yet to figure out who it had been. Who had the most to gain by removing her? She had been so conscientious, nose to the grindstone, and had never seen the end coming in such a cruel way. Without a trial, she was judged guilty and promptly fired. Replaying the weeks leading up to the incident brought back a spat that arose from Manon's jealousy over a harmless conversation. Martie chatted with a woman in a bar, just a little friendly banter, and Manon was furious. Was it possible? Was it Manon who got her fired, and forced her to become dependent on Manon's generosity? Would Manon go that far? Worse, had she pulled the same stunt with Michael DeCecco to derail Martie's career as a way to force her into accepting the partnership offer?

"I might crush your dream," Martie said. A knot formed in her gut. She thought she knew Manon well enough, but appearances could be deceiving. A person could be a skilled manipulator and hide behind whatever image suited their purpose. Somehow, it did not seem possible. Their history did not fit such a picture.

Manon shrugged in her Gallic fashion. "More than anything, I want you to be happy," she said. A quick kiss and she was out the door, as if she could leave the unpleasantness in the cooler. "You picked this location to be close to me. That's fine. When my dining room fills, I send the overflow to you. But they will be disappointed, chère, to find what? This new Irish food?"

"Pan-seared cod with lobster brandy cream?" Martie countered. "Quelle horreur."

"I came by to wish you all the best," she said. "After closing, come over. I'll open my best bottle of wine to toast your success."

"Do you mean it? Do you really want me to succeed?"

"Always. Even when you believed I was hurting you, I was helping you."

She watched Manon traipse down the alley, making for the back door of Le Grenouille at the far end of the block. It could have been Manon, acting out of misguided love. It could have been any number of other chefs who were envious of Martie's ability or the power she wielded in DeCecco's restaurant empire. Like a good stock, she needed to let things stew a little longer. Someone had sabotaged her career, and she had to uncover her enemy before they attacked again. And then? What would she do when she figured out who it was?

TWELVE

The music grated on a man's last nerve, with the repetition of eight bars over and over until Paddy had the lyrics down. Brendan drummed his fingers on the bar. "You've healed nicely," Ger said, pointing at the fading bruise on Brendan's knuckles. "Emer's queen for the day. Seems your man, that Italian fella, gave her a hundred by way of a tip. And it was genuine, the bill."

"Did you check it for blood stains?" Brendan said. "Probably payment on a gambling debt from an unwilling debtor."

"Ah, now," Ger said. With a sidelong glance, he took in Brendan's mood. "You can't go discriminating against a man if he's one thing or another. If he was to open a casino here, that's another matter, right?"

"No one's going to spoil this for me," Brendan vowed. He gulped down his beer. "No way. I worked my ass off for this and no one's going to take it away."

"Indeed not. Do you like my decorating touch, so?"

Under his elbow, Brendan found a stack of Irish newspapers, the dates as current as could be expected. The three latest rags all had stories about a recent arrest in an old bank robbery. It was a favorite topic of Des and Ger, who loved to puzzle over the perpetrators, convinced that the IRA had nothing at all, at all to do with the crime. They had managed to educate the regulars, so that everyone was playing detective over their pints.

"Nice touch," Brendan said.

A group of women came in, falling under the smooth spell of a polished restaurant manager who sported a warm and seductive smile. Twisting around on the barstool, Brendan watched Aidan meet, greet and seat the tea party that cooed over the decor. One of the guests laughed and declared the manager authentic before proclaiming the pub just as authentic, because she had been to Ireland, several times, and stayed exclusively at four-star accommodations.

"You'll make a success," Ger said. "Failure is not an option. What movie was that from?"

"The Gerald O'Hare story," Brendan said. "If the band asks for a round, don't forget that Paddy prefers sparkling to still."

"Fair play to him for giving it up."

Fair play to the amputee who learned to use a prosthesis, Brendan wanted to add. Fair play to the burn victim who stopped playing with matches. Fair play to all the cripples, the lame and infirm. Where was fair play to a man who had put up with Bonnie for three years? He was due his reward.

Using his best fist, Aidan was carefully lettering the chalkboard with the startling news which he read aloud as he wrote. "Tonight, Live Music, Paddy Dunne with Rory Callahan and Liam Carty. Grand Opening," he said slowly. "April says there's a post on Paddy's website announcing the show. Sure it's spread all over cyberspace by now."

"Free publicity. Can't complain at the price," Brendan said. His name graced the facade and he was ready to take them all on, the naysayers and the begrudgers and anyone who hoped he would fail. Paddy's gift, a live performance, was not costing money, but it was not truly free, not with the man's interference in the kitchen. The kitchen was everything, the heart of the pub and the most important aspect of McKechnie's salvation. To win the pub but lose Martie was no victory at all.

Ger descended through the trapdoor behind the bar, climbing down the creaking wooden steps to the liquor storage room. Brendan wandered over to the dining room to play host. The eight women who had the place to themselves were familiar, clones of Bonnie's friends who moved to the suburbs from the city when the babies came along. Being the restaurateur lost its luster and it was all he could do to bluff his way through a conversation. He escaped just as Eilìs delivered the stacked platter of cake slices and imported tea biscuits that formed the core of afternoon tea. The ladies could discuss Roddy Doyle's latest novel to their heart's content and he did not have to listen. He had more important things to figure out.

A full blown rehearsal was in progress on stage, where Louis the sound man was tweaking his equipment while the band made music. Aidan had a dozen worries to review with the boss, from the number of guests to the shortage of table linen. Brendan did not want to deal with the minor issues. He wanted to pop into the kitchen and talk to Martie, to find out if she needed anything more, from money to equipment to hot sex. Paddy had an expensive Aga range at his place in Miltown, and Brendan would buy one for Martie if she lusted after it. Everything top of the line, that was what he would provide if she would only stay. She would want for nothing, and have no reason to go elsewhere. If she needed to get laid, he was ready to drop his pants on command.

The after work crowd began to filter in, taking up their familiar positions at favorite tables. To a man, every one of the Irish immigrants who worked for McKechnie Construction showed up, and every one of them stared at the band with rapt admiration. Too humble to get close, they gathered at the top of the bar, chattering like schoolgirls in the presence of a rock and roll god. Des turned up behind the bar, taking credit for their incredible good luck.

"The lads are standing you to a pint," he said.

Lifting the full glass, Brendan toasted the carpenters, plumbers and joiners who made his business what it was. The band settled for a round of mineral water, which Paddy guzzled like a man fresh from a trek through the Mojave. It was a surprise that he joined Brendan at the bar, as if he were testing his resolve, while Brendan was half-hoping that he would fail the test. Without a few beers to loosen him up, Paddy was not as easy-going as he used to be. All in all, he was more serious, more shy, and possibly even a little boring.

"There's something in the air here," Paddy said. "Can you feel it?"

"What I'm feeling is stress. Foreclosure. Ruin," Brendan replied. "I'm worried about Martie."

"Don't worry for her. She's addicted to her work, same as you. If you were a girl, Brendan, you'd be her. Not half as pretty, though. Not a tenth. Not a millionth, on your best day."

The eve of the grand opening was not a time to be distracted by revenge. Martie forced her mind to focus on the restaurant, to worry about nothing more than the most important night of her life. She went to check in with Aidan, to see that he was prepared, and found the poor boy overwhelmed with the task of separating invited friends from ordinary patrons. A stylish woman was acting the part of Very Important Person, trying to steer people into the bar while admitting that the bar was too noisy.

April was behind the hostess stand, trying to help, but she was in over her head in dealing with someone who was accustomed to making her own seating arrangements by squashing the little people who got in her way. A friend of the overbearing customer walked in the door and joined in the effort to over-rule Aidan. Martie took charge before things got out of control, only to recognize one of the newly arrived guests as the banker who had promised not to tell Brendan that Martie had saved his sorry ass. "Mr. Wheeler and his party should be on the list," she said to April. "My fault. I knew I would forget someone."

She steered the group to the reserved tables in the dining room, papering over her lapse by describing the evening's protocol. There would be a sampling menu of small plates and the bar was open, featuring craft beer flights and whiskey tastings. A private party would follow the live music performance, where the select few would have a chance to mingle with the musicians in the banquet room on the second floor. The party sat down, but the stranger at the hostess stand was not with them.

"I had no idea that Bonnie was going to be working here," Mrs. Wheeler said to Martie.

"It's a night for surprises," Martie said, but she was not fond of surprises. It was time to find Mr. McKechnie, to have a little talk about who did the hiring and the firing, and who was qualified to be employed at McKechnie's Pub. She found Brendan at the hostess stand, wrapped up in a discussion that suggested Bonnie had hired herself.

"Why shouldn't I be up front?" Bonnie said.

He pulled her away, towards the door, while explaining that she was to greet their friends as they came in, act the part of hostess and not restaurant staff, and let the staff run the place. "You don't work here, and let's not make it look like you do," he said.

"There's nothing wrong with that," Bonnie countered. "Karen works for Brian, she's the hostess at Scampi."

"It's not the same here, honey, okay? Brian cooks and Karen works the front of the room. I don't cook, do I? I work the front of the room."

"Okay, so what do you want me to do?"

Tell her to go home, Martie sent a psychic message to Brendan. She should have guessed from the start that this would happen. Bonnie was entirely too abrasive for a position that required a heavy dose of humility and subtle obsequiousness. What raised Martie's hackles was a sense that Bonnie was intent on interfering, unaware that her incompetence would ruin a carefully crafted atmosphere, disrupting the circus that went with the bread produced by the kitchen. The front of the house was just as important as the back of the house, and Martie had to be fully in charge of both places.

"Just stand here, say hello to people like you did when we hosted the Gordimer Center benefit at the house. Remember?" Brendan said.

The proper analogy was all that was needed to fix Bonnie into a slot where she could fit without causing too much damage. She had only to stand at the door, which Aidan or April would open, shake hands, and pass the guests along to the manager for seating. While she did that, Brendan would circulate and pay attention to every little detail. He was in his element with details. That left Martie to handle the rest, and she was relieved that Brendan had absorbed some of the knowledge she had instilled over the past few days. Behind the scenes, that was where Martie wanted to stay. Hidden away, she had a better chance of cutting Bonnie off at the legs so that she could maintain control of McKechnie's. As long as Bonnie didn't know who was in the running for queen bee, Martie could more easily win the battle that would be fought with stealth, cunning and a head filled with recipes.

The room was filling up nicely with the curious and the hungry, those looking for a new experience in dining and a few who had come for the music. Stopping at each table to say a few words, Martie was surprised to learn that some guests had come from New York City and Boston, praying that the rumor was true. Like desperate penitents seeking absolution, they pleaded with her, asking only if Paddy Dunne was really going to sing tonight. Her heart began to pound. How would they handle the crowds, if people were coming from half way across the country? The kitchen had to perform this weekend, even more smoothly and flawlessly than Paddy and his crew. A bead of nervous sweat tickled the middle of her back.

By force of will she appeared completely in control, unflustered and capable of casual conversation. A diner gushed about her delicious meal and Martie accepted the compliments with humility that was in keeping with her normal self, the one skilled at food preparation. She paused to chat with Ed Wheeler, the banker and accomplice to her scheme, but she could not stop wondering about a conversation she had with Ger O'Hare that afternoon. What did it mean, exactly, that he had left the Irish Republican Army completely and totally? Was he any more distant from the violence than Sal Lardino, who was said to dabble in a little bookmaking from time to time? And could she really avoid running into Paddy for an entire weekend?

"Who in the world is Paddy Dunne and those other two?" Mr. Wheeler's tablemate asked.

"Some buddies of Brendan's from his mom's hometown," the banker said. "This Paddy guy's as red as Karl Marx, but, Brendan says he can sing, so, on with the show. You ever hear of him?"

"Hey, Ed, come to foreclose on my mortgage?" Brendan said, sidling up to Martie and slipping his hands into the pockets of his tailored trousers. Martie shot Ed a quick look, to remind him of their little arrangement.

"Get over it, will you," Ed said, laughing. "We're square for now, okay? My God, did you ever see a man so obsessed with money?"

"So why did you leave Michael's?" Mrs. Wheeler asked Martie.

The question she had dreaded had come up early, and she was not ready with a pat answer. Until a few weeks ago, she was Michael DeCecco's right hand, the executive chef who ran his kingdom while he fucked like a rabbit. "It was time," she said, smiled, and wandered away with Brendan on her heels.

"You don't have to go to Miltown to feel like you're there," Brendan said, a remark that had no context. "So why would you want to? Go there, I mean."

"That's good to remember," she said. "When you're visiting the tables, you can say that to people, put the bug in their heads that this is just like going abroad without leaving the country."

"How's the kitchen? If there's anything you want, just get it. I want you to have whatever you need. I want you to be happy here."

"Brendan, darling, I am over the moon I'm so happy. I'd kiss you, but isn't that your live-in over there?" She gave him a playful nudge, a show of solidarity as if they were best friends, more partners than he and Bonnie could ever be.

A beet red blush spread rapidly across his cheeks, around his ears and on down to his shirt collar. "Full house, huh?" he asked.

Due to the bar being packed solid, Eilis and Josh had to hold their drinks trays aloft as they wove in and out, taking orders and delivering. The Celtic Airs were performing traditional tunes to warm up the crowd while Paddy and the boys had tea and a rest in the office, preparing to go on and amaze their audience. Just as she had been ordered, Bonnie maintained her post near the door, acting the part of gracious hostess to any friends who happened by, all the while enjoying the attention that befell the connected. As long as Martie had the kitchen to herself, all would be well.

At six-thirty, Brendan struggled to get through the mobbed room, politely excusing his way to the stairs. Worrying about every little thing, he made for the banquet room, to be sure that it was ready. The space had been cleared of band equipment and was set up for the post-show party, invitation only, so that the select few could touch a real live icon. He startled the woman who was putting the finishing touches on the buffet table.

"Nearly show time," he said. He could not recall her name.

"Don't that look pretty," she said, wiping her hands on her apron. "First thing Miss Martie taught me. I mean to do her proud tonight."

Taking a closer look, Brendan realized that the shamrock-studded basket of roses that graced the center of the table was not actually crystal and stained glass. He had heard of such artistry, probably seen it on some television cooking show, but he had never expected a pulled sugar creation in his pub. Martie was proving to be even more amazing and accomplished than he had expected. No one would steal her away, not as long as he had breath in his body. He touched his arm, to see if the spot she had brushed with her hand was still warm. Never would he let Martie go.

"You made this?" he asked, studying the sugar sculpture.

"Yes, sir, I sure did. Miss Martie, she designed it, but I made the roses. Head pastry chef has to know how to do spun and pulled sugar. I mean to earn my title, Mr. McKechnie."

As he complimented her remarkable talent, Brendan took note of her name, embroidered on her new uniform coat. Peaches Baker was, in some bizarre way, an eminently suitable name for a pastry chef. All he needed to complete the roster was a cook named Cabbage Boyle or Fisher Fry. The possibilities put a broad smile on his face.

"You have talent," he said.

"God's grace is what I have," Peaches said. "At my church, we pray every Sunday for Miss Martie, that he shines His light on her and brings her into His arms. I pray extra hard for her, that she turns away from wrong. She's a good woman, at heart. It's someone else who led her astray. A bad influence."

He needed no other warning than that of someone who worked in the kitchen and saw more than he did. Until Paddy boarded a plane, Brendan would keep an eye on his rival. Never could Paddy be allowed to have a minute alone with Martie. A bad influence, Peaches had said, leading her astray. Perhaps the damage was done, the seed sown, but it was easy enough to poison the most fertile soil and kill a crop of trouble. The constant surveillance had to begin at once and continue without respite until the threat was gone.

As he passed the office he saw an overjoyed Paddy with the phone to his ear and his feet on the desk. "Aislinn says best of luck to you," Paddy said.

"Willing to give it another try," Liam whispered to Brendan.

They drifted into the hallway, to give Paddy a little private time. "If he can stick to his pledge," Rory said.

"More important that she can trust him," Liam said. "Drunks are the best liars you'll ever find, and it's hard to change their ways. Even now, I don't always know if himself is being honest with me."

"He won't get a drop if I can help it," Brendan said. "He needs Aislinn. More than she needs him, but he's got to get her back."

"What woman needs a man?" Rory said. "They can make do without us, barring the occasional spider assassination. I'll tell you the God's honest truth, if anything happened to my Evie, I'd be dead in a week. Starved, without a clean stitch of clothes and the house a pigsty."

"Keep it a secret," Liam said. "Can't let the wives get word of that, or they'll be making demands."

"Christ, I'm up to my ears in demands," Brendan said with a chuckle.

"Should have married an Irish girl, like your da," Rory said. "We've been poor for so long that we don't know how to spend. Ah, but we're learning fast."

"Go on with you," Liam protested. "I bought the big car to fit all of us in."

"You guys are turning American," Brendan said.

"Never," Liam vowed. "I'm selling the car when I get home. And I'll have the roof thatched for good effect. What else now for the tourists? A few cows? A couple of sheep in the garden?"

"Cows and sheep?" Paddy said, joining the group. "All you want is a *poitìn* still in the shed and they'll beat a path to your door."

"And your old granny sitting at the front door, knitting Aran jumpers," Rory said.

Reverberating through the floorboards, Brendan could feel the pounding of a dozen feet. Ed Wheeler's daughters were into Irish dance and like any proud father he was delighted to help stage a performance of the dance troop. It didn't hurt that he sold the instructor on the free publicity and a chance to promote her studio. The time had come. Brendan led the pack down the stairs.

As the applause for the tribute to Michael Flatley began to fade, Brendan pushed a path through the crowd, with Aidan providing another side of a wedge that parted the waves of people who eagerly anticipated the upcoming show. From the back of the barroom, a chorus arose and washed to the front, becoming a roar by the time that Paddy lifted the strap of his guitar over his head. Uneasy at first, Paddy nodded politely, and still the audience cheered. With tears in his eyes, the singer said, "Thank you very much. Thank you very much indeed."

When Liam took the beater between his fingers, Brendan had a feeling that the lads had changed their opening number at the last minute. Two bodhràns and four guitars drove into an old song that reflected the life that Irishmen once lived, before the Celtic Tiger. It could have been Mac's theme song, the soundtrack of countless days spent on the building sites of London or Berlin, grubbing for work and not certain of payment. Paddy began to beat on his guitar, the lyrics of *Hey Paddy* a whisper that grew louder, stronger and then angry.

Instead of starting straight in on another song, Paddy acknowledged the crowd and segued into a speech, in the manner of some casual banter. He spoke of the men who had emigrated when times were hard and now lay in dirty bed-sits in London, Manchester and Liverpool. Forgotten, unwanted, broken down men who had worked like slaves, sent money home to support the family, the laborers had nothing in their old age but poverty. Taking a swipe at the newly affluent, he criticized Dublin for a lack of support. Most of the people sitting around the stage had no idea what he was talking about, but there were a bunch of workmen at the top of the bar who stomped and whistled their support.

His lecture concluded, Paddy moved effortlessly to a mention of his last trip to Berlin, driving down the Autobahn like Berthold Brecht on *poitìn*. The next song protested urban sprawl, something that everyone, from Berlin to Chicago, could relate to. Brendan built new subdivisions and office parks. He added to the sprawl. The sprawl put food on his table and clothes on his back. Urban sprawl was responsible for Paddy's house at the edge of Miltown Malbay, standing in yesterday's cow pasture. The singer's naiveté was charming in its innocence, the sound of a man who gave his support to the cause without seeing the big picture.

With a master's touch, Paddy warmed up the crowd and set them to blazing. His performer's instincts drove the set list; his ear turned to the mood and the crowd reaction. The selections were largely of one piece: protest songs that came out of The Troubles. In company with Rory's exquisite harmony, they sang of the hunger strike, the prisoners on H-block, interspersing the new with the old. Liam's rendition of *The Bridge at Killaloe* took the listeners back to the Black and Tan era, as if the Rising and The Troubles were a seamless strand that ran through Ireland's history. Every tune was met with wild applause.

Slowing down, Paddy paused to catch his breath. Thinking while his fingers plucked nylon strings, he thanked the crowd again for their warm welcome. He introduced the band, using the noisy interlude to form his monologue. "We'd like to thank the proprietor of this grand establishment for the food and drink," he began. "And now, we'd like to bring him up for a proper thanks. Brendan McKechnie, show yourself, lad. Come up, come up."

On stage, Liam was settling a bodhràn on his knee, the beater skipping quietly over the goatskin, forming a Celtic drum line with the other musicians. Making his way through the audience, Brendan became the center of attention, a most pleasant sensation. Denny of the Celtic Airs gave up his seat, ever so slightly unsteady, and moved towards the back of the stage, stepping out of the lights to play in the background.

"When we were lads," Paddy said. "Which, as you can well imagine, was a long time ago, Mr. Brendan McKechnie spent his summers in our home town, creating havoc and worrying the hens in his granny's coop and being a devil altogether. Not being of a musical nature, he was a wee bit reluctant to play his party piece in public. So, to give the poor Yank our support, we played together. Do you remember your favorite tune, now, Brendan?"

Rory began to giggle, as if the Sunday afternoon performance was still fresh in his mind. A rebellious Brendan was forced by his mother to perform in the pub, and he conspired with the lads to play something that would guarantee the request would never be repeated. With a grin and a laugh, Brendan took the bodhràn from Paddy and tucked the rim under his chin. As if that same summer afternoon became the present, they all began to drum in unison, while Paddy crooned *The Well Below The Valley*. The words described infanticide and incest, lyrics that had scandalized the old biddies in Uncle Donal's pub. Brendan won the contest of wills with his mother, a victory that he never forgot.

"There's two of them by your father, dear." Paddy tapped his foot to the driving beat. They shared so much more than this song; they had a brotherly connection that was stronger than Brendan's links to his brother Robert. A Sunday afternoon in Miltown, and the monsignor had been apoplectic, spluttering and red-faced while Brendan closed his eyes like Paddy did, pouring his heart into his song. "There's two buried 'neath the stable door, at the well below the valley-o." Side by side they stood, Brendan protesting his mother's orders and Paddy protesting the strictures of his life. From that day on, Paddy declared his independence from the small minds of Miltown, encouraged by Brendan to follow his dreams and become a singer. Closer than brothers, but Paddy was still not going to steal Martie away.

The audience whooped at the end, an appropriate response for a song that had a martial air. Shouting to be heard, Paddy thanked them again. "We're all going for a cup of tea now," he said, and the first set ended in a roar, a loud welcome for the new pub that sounded like success.

THIRTEEN

Surrounded by friends, warmed by the stage lights and praise, Brendan circulated through the room while the members of Shift/Move took a well-deserved break in the office. When he saw one of the Belfast fashion plates in pastels standing against the back wall, Brendan groaned. He had forgotten his meeting, a foolish gaffe for one so in need of cash as he was. Pressed by a crowd of well-wishers, Brendan could do little more than wave helplessly, acknowledging the man's presence. At the very least, Mr. Gray could draw some conclusions, gaining confidence that his investment would be well placed in such a busy, crowded bar. So crowded that Brendan had no hope of getting into the back corner, and they could not possibly hear one another if they did try to meet. Gray waved back, smiling and nodding, as if he were thinking along those same lines.

"You're a man of many talents," Harry Wright, CPA, bellowed into Brendan's ear.

"That's the only song I know," Brendan said. "Guess I better keep my day job."

"Did you rob a bank or something? Your sales receipts for the past few days are way over your projections."

"Maybe the chef robbed a bank. The projections were made before I brought her in, and she's been running the show."

"Watch yourself, Brendan. If you've found a sugar mommy, she can bring you down so fast you won't know what happened." Harry took Brendan's arm, the intimacy increasing. "Look what happened at Cafe au Lait. There's a lot of bored women around here, looking for a good time with their husband's money."

"Come on, Harry, I get enough of the third degree from Bonnie. I'm talking about Martie Smurfit. She's a professional chef."

"Quit bullshitting me." Harry chucked Brendan on the shoulder. "How the hell do you expect me to believe that you got her away from DeCecco? See, if it was true, he'd have slit your throat by now. Come on, tell me the truth. You getting a little something on the side?"

"Hey, I get all I need at home," Brendan said. "What do I have to do, take you to the kitchen so you can see Martie in person?"

"I believe you, I believe you. What'd you have to offer? Double salary?"

"Standard rate." Brendan had no idea what he was talking about. Martie could have gouged him royally for all he knew. It had been a matter of taking her at her word.

"No perks? She getting a little bonus from the boss?"

"With the hours she's put in, Harry, I don't think she's got the energy." Brendan was about to make a remark about her husband, but he realized that he didn't know anything about Martie's personal life. He didn't know if she was married, divorced, widowed or single. All he knew was that she had kept some stash of reserve energy, for Paddy at any rate.

"Okay, Mr. Golden Touch. But if you need a stand-in, you know, to put a smile on her face, hey, don't forget your friends."

Brendan was glad of the chance to get away from Harry and his attempts at scandal mongering. The conversation was in danger of approaching the truth, of prying some deeply hidden desires out of Brendan's brain. His relationship with Martie was purely business. He knew nothing about her, her background or her history, and he was satisfied with the arrangement. Contrary to Harry's overblown imagination, not every restaurant owner was a Michael DeCecco. It was not as if Brendan had acted on his impure thoughts. Paddy was the one for that, as Brendan had heard through the office door.

When Bonnie tucked her arm through his elbow, Brendan was startled out of his sexual reverie. Surrounded by the members of her book group, she insisted that he give a presentation on the spot about Ireland, about Paddy and the boys and McKechnie's in Miltown. He was not free to mull over his own thoughts. On command, he was expected to entertain her friends with clever anecdotes that she had long ago grown weary of hearing. One more time, he related the saga of the party piece, the gasps that arose from his family, the loud guffaw from his father, and the thrashing that he got for performing such a dirty song in front of Grandma.

Rather than amuse a bunch of women he scarcely knew, Brendan longed to visit with the lads. He would prefer to reminisce with men who had been there, not tell stories like some itinerant troubadour. Trying to make his way to the stairs, Brendan was blocked by one guest and then another. Everyone and everything conspired against him, as if Bonnie had choreographed the entire party. She needed his physical presence to reflect brightly on her, and she managed to bind him to her side, not unlike a puppy on a leash.

Before anything went further, before Bonnie set the pace, Brendan decided to tell her outright that she was not to insert herself into the pub. For the past three months, she had been dropping hints, offering to help out when the place was busy. She might mean well, but she was demanding in a spoiled brat sort of way. To have Bonnie at the door, looking down her nose at the paying guests because they did not meet her standards, was too frightening a scenario to consider. God help him if someone got edgy over the wait for a table. Bonnie would tell them to go elsewhere in no uncertain terms, and her brand of gracious service was guaranteed to drive people away by the carload. Seeing Aidan at the entrance gave Brendan a brilliant idea. Rather than face her anger, he could put the manager to the task. At least the restaurant manager did not have to wake up to Bonnie's cold shoulder and sour face.

"The hours are a disadvantage," Aidan said to April. His brogue was as thick as the fog off Spanish Point, but Brendan doubted that all the Irish charm in the world would overcome a homely Irish face.

"Parties after closing. We miss some of the fun, I guess," April said. "I don't want to end up just talking shop, you know what I mean?"

"It's just a matter of finding the right spot. Where the nightlife doesn't begin until one or two," Aidan said. "I'm familiar with a few, if you'd like to see what this town has to offer."

With Aidan so thoroughly involved in a flirtation, Brendan had no hope of breaking in without appearing rude. A new idea sprouted in his tired brain, something clever in a devious way. He had no doubt that

Bonnie talked of helping out but really meant watching out, keeping an eye on him because she had an obsession about him cheating on her, a mania that she developed after some past relationship crumbled under the weight of infidelity. If Paddy could be convinced to have a word with her, he might be able to show her that her fears were ridiculous. After all, Paddy had known Brendan since childhood and he could be brutally honest. Sure Bonnie disliked him, but she understood how Paddy's ingrained sense of Catholic guilt would keep him from bearing false witnesses despite a deep friendship.

"There you are," Aidan said, as if he were searching every corner of the globe to find his employer. "Martie's needing you for something."

Pushing through the kitchen door, Brendan felt the energy. He had never entered a restaurant kitchen before, and for the first time he was coming into his own place, running all out. The noise, the heat and the utter chaos were terrifying. Where was the cozy intimacy of Aunt Eleanor's kitchen? No smiles greeted his arrival; indeed, no one noticed that he was standing there, getting in the way of waitresses scurrying to and fro.

"Would you eat this?" Martie bellowed over the exhaust fans. She held a plate, steaming and hot, under a burly chef's nose. "So how the hell could you even think of serving it?"

The rejected entree clattered back onto the metal counter as Martie reached for the strip of paper that was spitting out of the printer. "Fire eight," she called out, and a piece of beef was instantly slapped on the grill behind her.

"Eighty-six the lamb," the chastised chef sang out, turning his attention to the rack that was bathed in the searing flame.

Sliding around him, Martie moved to a burner and shook a pan that clattered against the grate. In a perfectly choreographed dance, she moved back to the counter as another cook swung away, to deposit a piece of chicken on a hot plate. From the pan, Martie drizzled some sauce and then settled a colorful fan of vegetables into a fanciful decoration. Her fingers moved like a musician's, certain and strong, with a rhythmic grace. First one cook and then another and another bent into the scene, plating and saucing and garnishing without once tripping over each other or whacking an unsuspecting arm with a red hot pan. A spoonful of marrow peas danced into position under Martie's fingers as her eyes took the smallest detail of every dish that came from her underlings. Satisfied, she lifted the plates onto the metal shelf and shouted, "Service please. Table Nine. Order up."

The kitchen was a madhouse filled with crazy people running amok, bobbing up and down, shouting, swearing, moving. One strip of paper after another spit out of the printer, and Martie ripped them off as quickly as they appeared. Like a general in the midst of battle she ordered her troops, speaking the language of haute cuisine that Brendan did not comprehend. The slips were posted on the edge of the metal counter, tacked up and then pushed to the side and finally pulled off, always making room for more. He had felt out of his element from the first time that he saw Martie in an apron. Right now he was not even in the same universe.

Backing out of the way, he slithered along the wall until he was next to the dishwashing station. Clouds of steam gushed to the ceiling and drifted away on the currents created by the exhaust fans. On the wall above the racks of dirty glasses, someone had nailed up a picture of Our Lady of Guadalupe. Although protected under glass, the paper print had been steamed into faded ripples that reflected a long journey from Mexico, through many other dishwashing stations in many other restaurants in Moraine Hills. Her beatific face, blurred by exposure to water vapor, looked down upon the men who worked tirelessly in the heat, engaged in a futile battle to get all the dishes washed. More dirty plates arrived with every rack of clean plates they provided in a Sisyphean struggle to make progress while only falling further behind.

"Keep them coming, Eddie," Martie told the blank-faced man who waited awkwardly for some instruction. Another one of her special cases, most likely, as the dishwasher appeared to be mentally handicapped, trained to do this one thing. "I'll tell you when to stop bringing the dishes, okay? You're doing really good for me, honey, you just keep right on going."

An addled grin and a ducking bow was Martie's answer, confirming Brendan's assessment of the childlike man and the chef's charity and patience. The dishwasher was qualified for little else in the working world beyond the repetitive and simple. There would be no thought of promotion, no plan to learn another skill and move ahead. Through Martie, one person was given an opportunity to earn a few bucks and be out of the house, surrounded by people who looked out for him. Hiring the handicapped had never seemed to be as easy as Martie made it look, without much difficulty.

"Yo, Brendan, come on, let's go," Martie said. She appeared magically at his side, tugging at his arm and pulling him along as if she meant to kick him out of her kitchen. Instead, she put two dessert plates in his hands, rearranged a blackberry and gave him a nudge towards the dining room door. "Table six. Kiss ass. Kiss so much ass you need a roll of toilet paper for a napkin."

Leading the way with bread pudding resting on her left forearm and macedoine of summer fruits in her hand, Martie kissed the fingertips of her right hand and applied them to a plastic-coated holy card that was tacked to the door jamb. With a bump of her hip, she opened the door and disappeared into the soft murmur of satisfied diners.

"What does that mean, Mr. McKechnie?" Peaches asked. "Every time she goes out that door she kisses that picture."

Crouching slightly until he was at eye level, Brendan examined the card. A sweet faced maiden gazed heavenward, her halo a sparkling gold crown over blond curls. In her hand was a ladle, a saintly symbol that only a theologian could explain. A set of keys dangled from the woman's waist in a classic Catholic holy card scene. No harm to join the congregation, Brendan supposed, and he touched his lips to the sacred object. Carefully holding the plates level, he pushed the door open.

"Whatever it takes, Peaches," he said. "And I could use a little divine intervention these days."

One table looked pretty much the same as another. For a moment, Brendan stood in place near the door and looked around, trying to guess who might be waiting for dessert and a lingering ass-smooch. With a subtle nod of her head, Martie pointed him in the right direction, to table six, where Emer was filling coffee cups and laying on the sounds of Roscommon with a trowel.

"Wouldn't you know that the food critic for the *Tribune* would turn up on the busiest night," Martie whispered to Brendan as he passed by. "Ha, just see if we don't shine."

The spun sugar 'steam' on the espresso cup filled with chocolate mousse nearly fell off as Brendan's hand shook. He seemed to be confirming her complaint, that it was cruel of the food critic to test the pub when the kitchen and staff were pressed to their limits. No less cruel than throwing the hapless contractor into the lion's den, but this was not the time to quibble over a lack of experience. Plastering an electric smile on his face, Brendan accepted the heavy mantle of responsibility and strolled with confidence to table six. He managed a decent impersonation of a skilled restaurateur, his technique obviously copied from Michael DeCecco's style of grandiose warmth. She hated to see a reminder of Michael because it only reminded her of how he had screwed her around and then screwed her over. Before the night was out, however, she was going to upstage her former employer and he could go cry in his bouillabaisse over her loss.

More concerned with the kitchen than Brendan's possible ineptitude, Martie hurried back to the clanging of the pots and pans. Above the din she picked up a woman's voice, strident, harsh and demanding. She would not tolerate strangers nosing around her workplace, not even one of Brendan's friends. Before she could find the person, she heard the voice again, calling out in a manner that was best described as North Shore entitlement rude. God help the woman if she went a step further and used the phrase 'Boy'. Martie would slap her silly.

At the service entrance, she discovered Bonnie in all her imperious glory, berating the young men who were loading up the back of an ancient Buick station wagon. "What do you think you're doing?" Bonnie said. The workers stopped in their tracks, heads down.

"You got that freezer cleared out, Jabari?" Martie stepped into the fray. Yes, she was on the verge of letting Bonnie have it across the head, to knock some sense into her.

"What's the meaning of this?" Bonnie demanded.

"It's left over from yesterday and the day before." Martie said. Turning to Jabari, she caught the look in his eye, but she felt helpless to change his opinion of Bonnie and her kind. "Manon has some desserts. You should have quite a feast tomorrow."

"Excuse me, but does Brendan know that you're giving away food?"

"As a matter of fact, no, he doesn't." Martie paused, smiling dangerously. "I don't think he has a clue what goes on back here."

"Do you have any idea how much money you're throwing away?" Bonnie said. "I really don't think that we're in a financial position to be so careless."

"Actually, I do know. Down to the penny. It's a tax write off," Martie said. Her temper began to cool. It was not Bonnie's fault that she was so utterly clueless. She lived in a ghetto, as much as Jabari and his cousin Quemont, and they knew as little about Bonnie's life as she knew of theirs. "Look, Bonnie, I've been doing this for years, okay? Say, if you've got an hour free, why don't you go up to Gilead and help them set up the soup kitchen at their church? Or maybe you could stop by and help serve the food tomorrow afternoon?"

As expected, Bonnie was left speechless, feeling like a complete ass, and Martie caught herself slipping into an equally bitchy attitude. Her desire to deflate the overblown ego was delivered too harshly, but what better way to force open Bonnie's eyes, to show her the other part of the world that did not dine out weekly in fine establishments but prayed that those fine establishments had some scraps to hand out so that they could eat a decent meal. They were great ones for fundraising, the Bonnies of the world, but they did not practice their charity in the trenches, in the dirt and the misery of the abject poor.

"And if I didn't give this stuff away," Martie added. "It would end up in the dumpster. Quemont, honey, did you clear out those cases of instant potatoes from the basement?"

"Yes, ma'am," Quemont said, being careful to not look in Bonnie's direction.

"Surely those can't be going bad," Bonnie protested. "I placed the order myself, and they were delivered not more than two weeks ago."

Jabari rolled his eyes and smiled, while Quemont let loose with a hearty laugh. "Miss Martie serving potatoes out of a box?" Quemont said. "No, ma'am, no instant nothing in her kitchen."

The young men bid Martie a farewell, closing with a very shy nod of goodbye in Bonnie's general direction. Returning to her post, Martie was dogged by a woman who had taken umbrage at being mocked. "I suppose it was Brendan who put you up to throwing away what I ordered," Bonnie said. "Everything I say or do is always wrong."

Checking the open orders, Martie pulled two slips off the rack and slid them under two plates that Jay had just set on the counter. She ripped the next order off of the printer, called it out to the meat station, and turned back to Bonnie, who was ducking and bobbing out of the way of the waitresses. The last thing that Martie needed was an meddler, hell bent on inserting a pert nose into matters that did not concern her. "Tim, where's the duxelles? Let's go, let's go."

As if he had sprouted wings, Brendan floated into the kitchen, a man whose head was up in the clouds. Getting one look at Bonnie, his eyes flashed angrily. "I asked you to stay up front by the door. What are you doing in here?"

The knife that Martie wielded glinted in the harsh overhead lights. She chopped a scrap of fat off of a chicken breast, banging the knife handle on the cutting board. Through the racket of pans, flame and exhaust fan, the entire staff was surely hearing every word of an argument, something that was best kept upstairs in the office. Tim burned his finger, intent on listening to the owner battle it out with his girlfriend in the cool and subdued tones of the upper middle class. No one raised a voice or spewed profanities, but the tension was thicker than the vapor of the bain marie.

While Martie owed her allegiance to Brendan, she could not help but feel pity for Bonnie. The crux of the argument could be distilled down to one simple statement. Bonnie had gotten what she wanted, with a grand McMansion, designer clothes and a large engagement ring. What she did not like was the back side of the coin, the fiancé who was never home because he was working long hours to provide all the goodies. Sadly, the days of the proper English gentleman were long gone, when a man had independent means and never lifted a useful finger. Wealthy men were few and far between, and by settling for a working stiff, Bonnie had gained half of her dream and half of her nightmare. Like most men, Brendan could not understand what the problem was, because as far as he was concerned, he was meeting his end of the bargain, and the woman was supposed to deal with it. The two of them could argue until death did them part, and they would never reach a solution. Neither one seemed interested in finding a compromise. Who was she to talk? She wasn't exactly seeking consensus with Manon herself.

FOURTEEN

Back and forth the unhappy couple discussed their issues, while orders came in and food went out. Busboys scurried, Emer and Eilìs flirted with Josh, and the pile of clean plates never disappeared. Peaches plated a poached pear wedge and drizzled caramel sauce in a zigzag line; Brendan told Bonnie that he had hired Martie because she was Michael DeCecco's equal, no, superior. Peaches' assistant sliced the baguettes and pulled a tray of soda bread out of the oven; Bonnie complained that she was being ignored when she wanted to be a part of Brendan's life, which needed to be more than working non-stop. The chicken breast slipped out of the tongs and Jay cursed before kicking the meat under the counter. With a loud sigh, Bonnie accepted her position as hostess to the private party. On her way out the door, she declared that they really should go to Miltown in July, what with Paddy being so much more pleasant now that he had quit drinking, and if Brendan had told her who he had hired, she never would have interfered in the kitchen.

"Sorry," Brendan said, as if he were apologizing to the entire staff before ducking out to the dining room. On cue, Martie rapped a pan against a burner to focus everyone's attention on work. This sort of thing could be risky, if the help took a notion that their positions were on shaky ground. They would need some kind of reassurance, a sense that nothing was going to change, even if the owner was dealing with the pain of a break-up. Maybe the time had come to force the partnership. Martie was the rock upon which the pub was built, and her people had to know that everything was stable.

Just like selling a client on an extra five thousand square feet of warehouse space, Brendan chatted to the local food critic whose word alone could make or break the pub. Friendly without being overbearing, he exhibited concern over the table's pleasure without lapsing into apologies, and generally acted the part of devoted host at an important society get-together. To the best of his ability, Brendan faked his way through an analysis of the various dishes, which were not the boiled to death standards that once characterized Irish cuisine.

A mention of this new trend in cooking that was gaining popularity in modern Ireland merged into a brief story about the evening's entertainment and long ago summers passed in a sleepy and forgotten town. Satisfied that he had presented his Hibernian credentials, Brendan rotated to table nine, eight, and then looked for a way out. Paddy caught up to him at table five.

"Isn't it all grand, so?" Paddy said to a quartet of somewhat stunned guests. "Better than anything we had, wouldn't you say, Brendan?"

Introducing his friend to people who had never heard of Shift/ Move or Paddy Dunne was a drawn-out process, with explanations needed. Polite, the diners complimented the band and expressed their gratitude for the opportunity to discover a new aspect of Irish music. One member of the party promised to buy one of the CDs that were available at the hostess stand, so impressed was he by Paddy's voice and instrumental excellence.

"The new one's not officially released until July, and I've accepted the inevitability of iTunes so the old discs are just me being stubborn," Paddy said. "I've dedicated the album to the memory of Rachel Corrie. A brave woman, to stand and face down the bully boys who were bulldozing those homes in Palestine. Ground into the dirt, she was, side by side with the oppressed people of that troubled land."

On the North Shore, there were clear differences in style and fashion that identified the conservative, mainline Protestant element of Deerhaven. Ladies who favored pearls and summery sundresses were mated to gentlemen who sported khaki pants, topsider shoes, and polo shirts that were often worn when playing polo. The quartet at the table did not fit the bill. In clothes that were more colorful, more trendy, and more expensive, Brendan saw the well-heeled of Port Clinton, home to no less than three synagogues.

"I loved your version of *Masters of War*," the lady in chunky jewelry said.

While it changed the subject from Israel to America, the woman had done little more than give Paddy something else to lecture on. Horrified, Brendan cut off any further discussion and pulled Paddy away. His friend had apparently climbed off the bar stool, only to mount a soapbox. Paddy had given up drinking, but the passion he once put into liquor was now directed at saving the world, and he would run over anyone who got in his way. As selfish as ever, he did not seem to give a single thought to manners, to the sensitivities of those around him. The once gregarious Irishman was becoming insufferable.

"What is with you?" Brendan said, dragging Paddy to the foyer. "Those people are Jewish."

"A man has to be true to his principles," Paddy pontificated. "There's injustice in this world and I'll not stand by. I'll speak openly, to force them to see. We've got the power to change this world, Brendan, can you not appreciate that? The importance of it all."

"But you can't get in a guy's face like that. Use the stage for your pulpit, and speak out to everyone. No one likes to be singled out and picked on. You know that better than anyone."

After his father died, Paddy ceased to be just another one of the lads and became 'the poor boy' who was sighed over by all the neighbors. A teen trying to blend into the scene, he bonded with the boy from the States who treated him with equality, as if the orphan was the same little boy he had always been. Brendan knew where Paddy's convictions came from, arising from a deeply ingrained sense of injustice at being picked on and singled out in a form of discrimination. When they were young, it was Brendan who took it upon himself to guard Paddy's back, to prevent a fistfight or throw the first punch as necessary. Now, he feared that he would have to take up the same position, but the situation was not quite the same as it had been in Miltown. They were adults now, not kids, and a grown man should have a sense of protocol, of what was suitable and what was best left unsaid. Could it have something to do with the loss of Paddy's crutch, the ability to obliterate reality in an alcoholic haze? Sober now, the singer was older but not much wiser than the kid from County Clare.

The diner from table five grabbed Paddy's shoulder and Brendan spun around, ready to defend his friend. "Pleasure talking to you," the man said, shaking hands all around. "You know, I get to Dublin on business and I've been in a pub or twenty. This place, I got to tell you, it's authentic, but this guy, man," he slapped Paddy on the back, "He's got the politics and the arguing down cold. Breath of fresh air. Forget that politically correct bull, you know?"

"You see, Brendan, there's no offense taken," Paddy said.

The guest lowered his voice and leaned closer to Brendan. "I'm all for the Palestinians getting their own country, but, you know, there's some things I can't say out loud around some people."

"Mr. Dunne, if you wouldn't mind." The chunky necklace lady touched Paddy's hand, a newly purchased CD in her hand. She gave him an expensive pen and popped the case open, her large teeth shining behind iridescent red lips. As Paddy signed his distinctive autograph, complete with a guitar caricature to replace the 'y', she added, "But who's this Allende guy we're supposed to kill? Or did we kill him?"

To preserve the mood, Brendan gave Paddy a swift stomp on the foot. "Jesus, Brendan, what are you about?" he hissed.

"Come on, son, they're going to tear my place apart if you don't get back on stage," Brendan said. The time had come to save his own skin, to keep Paddy's newest addiction from driving away the customers. European socialism was fine as a point of discussion, but this was not the place to argue American foreign policy. There were occasions that called for complete neutrality, and if ever there was such an occasion, surely this was it.

"And doesn't that prove it all?" Paddy said, not ready to let go of his Margaret Thatcher and Ronald Reagan-hating diatribe. "Blinded by the pursuit of wealth. Did you hear the woman? Doesn't even know what was done in her name."

Back on stage, Paddy tuned his guitar while he tuned his thoughts. Only then did Brendan realize that the first set had not been typical of the old gigs, lacking the funny stories and silliness. The humor must have come out of the bottom of a glass, because a sober man had performed a rather sober set.

"Did you forget your shovel, Paddy?" an Irish ex-pat called out, and the man on stage broke into a smile. At once, he began to strum and the band followed along behind him, singing a song that praised the Irish working man.

The intimacy of the small room grew as Paddy selected tunes that meant something to him and to his listeners. There were more traditional ballads mixed in with some of Shift/Move's slower airs. Not so much a clap-along, the set developed into a private encounter between a former alcoholic and his fans. Tongue in cheek, he made fun of his experience with delirium tremens. The pictures on the wall that talked to him, the Infant of Prague statue that danced; Brendan recognized objects from Ann's flat above the antique shop where Paddy must have gone to dry out. The audience roared out their approval.

After an exhausting performance, Paddy was a diligent guest at the private party in the banquet room. That was how Brendan reported it to Martie, who was too busy to get away for a minute. With words, he painted her a picture of the singer working the room like a politician, all to promote the pub to the bankers and accountants and vendors who extended credit. Paddy probably would have pressed flesh until dawn if Brendan had not sent him back to the hotel. Rory and Liam were not teenagers anymore, either, and the weekend was going to be a long one. The trio would need their rest.

In the bar, Des called out, "Time, gentlemen," as he stacked glasses for Saturday's lunch rush. The last stragglers settled their tabs and shuffled out the door while Brendan closed up the patio. April and Josh cashed out for the night, with Ger doing the honors at the register. Waving a foreign bank note under Ger's nose, April boasted of her luck that night. Spying the girl's benefactor, Brendan sighed. "God damn, I forgot about Mr. Gray. He's waiting to talk to me. Guess I'm not going home any time soon."

"These are hard to change, you know," Ger said. Martie perched on a stool, her tea steaming under her nose. Pausing to splash a few drops of whiskey into her cup, he showed the money to Martie, an eyebrow raised. Returning to April, he explained how difficult it was to exchange North of Ireland bank notes, which were used only in the Six Counties. When her mouth slid down into a tiny pout, he cheerily offered to buy it from her. "I can use this when I go home, or I can send it in the mail to my sister."

"What's it worth?" she asked.

"One and fifty to a pound or so."

"Just give me even money, Ger, and we'll settle another time. How's that for a tip? One hundred American and one hundred Irish. He's probably some old pervert, but I'll take his money. Hey, Aidan, my treat tonight."

Examining the hundred dollar bill and the two fifty pound notes, Ger congratulated the giddy waitress. He reached into his pocket and pulled two bills from a gold clip. "Fair enough. And I mean to give you a fair exchange rate, miss, and don't let me forget."

Line cooks and busboys drifted out of the kitchen, saying goodbye to Jay, Martie and Peaches, who were enjoying a nightcap after an insane evening. Ger wiped down the bar, putting a shine in the finish at the end of the day, while Des toted wine bottles to the basement storage room under the bar. Aidan and April strolled out, looking suspiciously like a couple. Des popped up from the hole in the floor and for a second the two cousins stood side by side, as if conferring through mind-reading, but Des went back to his work in the lower level without settling anything.

Making a move to join the visitor at his table, Brendan was nearly bowled over by Ger as the bartender pushed past, heading for the same spot. With a noise that echoed like a gunshot, Ger punched the money onto the table and put his face only inches from Gray's nose. In a split second of total silence, the air was sucked out of the bar.

"Don't think I don't know what you're about," Ger snarled.

The chilling silence was broken by the crash of a chair hitting the floor. The stranger pushed past Ger and ran to the door, coming up short when Dessie appeared at the bottom of the bar. In a frightened vault, the man leapt over the bar, trying to escape. It was a moment of madness, the scene playing out in flashes that concluded with a blood-curdling scream and the sickening sound of a body striking slate tiles.

Everyone ran to the bar and looked over the edge, into the open hatchway that led to the storage room. A crumpled mass was sprawled on the floor, a tiny trickle of blood soiling the pristine slate.

"Jesus Christ," Dessie mumbled. "Jesus Christ. Is he dead?"

"Pray God he is, so," Ger said.

"We have to get him out of here." Martie was stunned but a corner of her brain was functioning, the self-preservation lobe that was about to explode.

"Shouldn't we call 911?" Brendan said.

"Are you mad?" Ger said.

A moan drifted up out of the cellar. The man moved a leg, ever so slightly.

"What'll we do with him?" Jay asked. He was a military man, accustomed to following a chain of command. If Martie told him to slit the man's throat, he would jump down into the wine cellar with a knife and ask no questions.

"For God's sake, he's hurt," Brendan protested, seeking an ally for his position. "It was an accident. And what do those three bills on the floor have to do with anything, anyway?"

"He should be left to die like a dog," Ger continued his rant.

"Not in my restaurant," Martie said. Any bad publicity would sink them. The only solution was to make the situation disappear like it never happened. Then she would kill Ger, wring his Sinn Fein neck with her bare hands. "Friend of yours, Ger?"

Replacing the chair in its proper place before picking up the bills, Ger spread the United States currency between his hands, to show everyone something only he had seen. "Counterfeit," he declared. "And do you know where the North bank notes came from?"

"You're not saying your man is a soldier in the IRA, now?" Des stammered.

"Ah, you're like all the rest," Ger grumbled. "Who's always the first to get the blame for every crime in the Six Counties?"

"You owe us an explanation," Martie said. She stood next to Brendan, arms folded across her chest, her face set in a hard stare. In agreement with her simple statement, Brendan also folded his arms across his chest, looking Ger right in the eye.

"If you brought trouble here, Ger," Brendan said. The coldness of his voice was startling in its chill. She had to keep Brendan from over-reacting. They all had to be calm, to think with their heads. There were so many ways that the accident, or whatever it was, could hurt business in ways she could hardly imagine. Martie was not going to let one shady character ruin her dreams.

"The bank robbery was an inside job. Criminal enterprise, pure and simple," Ger said. Without a doubt he was talking about Northern Ireland's crime of the century, in which tens of millions of pounds were lifted out of a bank vault and hauled away in a nondescript van, the cash undoubtedly disappearing into thin air as little of it surfaced after a decade. "The orders were given out, and the consequences handed down for them that weren't on board with the new policy. Every man who tried to launder the money was informed on, so there they are, with twenty-six million dirty pounds and no way to clean it up. Not long ago, a few million were stolen from a hiding place. There's one hundred of it here."

The bank robbery in Belfast was old news that had not received much coverage outside of Europe, and wouldn't have been a news item if not for the enormous amount of money that was taken. She understood what Ger O'Hare was implying. The big problem she had a few minutes ago had suddenly expanded into an enormous problem. A stranger had tried to use McKechnie's to launder stolen money. Ger had put a stop to it, which was good, if they could all solve the dilemma that he had created in the stopping.

"Did you not leave the organization years ago?" Des asked his cousin.

"We laid down our arms," Ger said. "But I'll not stand by and let the Red Hand sully the glorious name or the memory of our brave comrades."

Lovely speech, but Martie was in no mood for bold talk. "Did you know he was here?" she asked. "And if you did, why didn't you go to the police? Or tell us?"

"I'm sorry for the trouble, but to go to the police," Ger said. "The PSNI is just the RUC and Special Branch in fancy dress. Would I trust them, what they might say to the local coppers here? Would you like the FBI probing your arse, so?"

"I know where you can take him," Peaches said.

FIFTEEN

In unison, all eyes turned to the soft-spoken pastry chef. Her jaw tightened, a look that was bold and determined, coming from a woman who led a hard life but pulled herself up from the bottom. Martie looked around at the people who would have to swear to secrecy, who would admit to seeing nothing if anyone should happen to ask. For Dessie and Ger, who had grown up along the border, that line of thought was second nature. They were born into the world at the start of The Troubles and would never trust a policeman until the day they died.

Of Brendan's loyalty, there was no doubt. He was as involved in the situation as she was, his livelihood at stake and his desire to make this criminal disappear even stronger then her own. That left Jay and Peaches, who had nothing invested in the restaurant but their time. This was only their job, and there were plenty of other places looking for experienced help. If Peaches worked out the plan to cover up the crime, she became complicit, and that would mean that Jay was the wild card, the loose cannon who could sink the ship.

"Where we going to?" Jay said.

"Place up in Gilead," Peaches said. She bit her lower lip, contemplating. "He got money on him, Mr. Ger?"

Down in the cellar, Ger and Des rummaged through Gray's pockets, turning up large rolls of Northern bank notes and a clip of counterfeit hundreds. "He's a walking ATM," Ger reported. "And they're good counterfeits. Came out of North Korea, but they're too hot to move in Europe."

"Okay," Peaches said. "He went to buy crack. The drug dealers don't like nobody trying to cheat them with phony money, so they beat him to a pulp. Maybe broke his skull."

At the mention of a drug transaction, another crime, Brendan started hyperventilating. "What the fuck?" he said. "You want to pay cash to illegal workers, fine. You want to bribe the plan commissioner to get the right zoning, I'm right there. But a drug run? A drug run? We could get killed."

"We have a criminal in our restaurant who is injured due to the action of one of our employees and if he gets himself a better lawyer than us, who pays, Brendan?" Martie asked.

"He's not acting on his own," Des said. "And when his associates come looking to even the score? Peaches has the best solution. If your man dies, he dies. We're not the killers. We're not saving him either. Unintended consequences of war."

"Don't let him bleed all over," Martie said, hurrying to the trap door with a tablecloth.

After wrapping the body in the thick white fabric, a bundling process that paused at every moan from the injured gangster, Ger and Des carried the body up the wooden steps, struggling with a heavy load. They dumped him on the floor of the employee locker room while Peaches pulled her car to the exit, a dark and quiet part of the alley that was deserted late at night. The accessories to the crime hovered near the door, not speaking a word. Martie froze when she spotted a figure walking down the alley, whistling *La Vie En Rose*. "Oh, Dear God. Manon," she whispered.

The rusty old minivan idled noisily, or at least it sounded like a jet engine revving in Martie's ears. She stood by, feeling helpless, as Brendan helped the bartenders hoist the body into the back, where a third seat had long ago been removed. When a muffled groan echoed off the dumpsters, everyone froze in place and held their breath. In silence they waited for all movement to stop, a quiet that was broken by the pounding of Martie's heart, pulsating in her ears.

"Did you forget me?" Manon asked, striking a jaunty pose while cradling a bottle of wine. "More food for the soup kitchen? Wait for me. I'll bring wine for everyone."

Before she knew what was happening, Manon was locked in Jay's arms, mouth shut tight by a large hand clamped over his face. "I will remove my hand," Jay said with frightening precision. "You will keep quiet. We on the same page?"

Manon nodded, or as much as she could. "I do not want to know, yes?"

"You do not want to know," Martie said. "I'm going to get my car. We'll move out in a convoy. Peaches, baby, don't lose me."

She pulled up to the door and the bartenders popped into the back seat, with such stealth that she wondered if they had done this sort of thing before, smuggling across the border or operating as IRA soldiers in the quiet of the Irish countryside. They waited for Brendan to lock the back door, with Jay at his side, the soldier who knew how to watch a man's back. Here she was, a chef, riding in a troop carrier, ferrying soldiers to the next battleground. This was madness, granted, but she would have done everything, worse things, to protect her restaurant. It was Brendan who slid into the passenger seat next to her, sending Jay and Manon to ride with Peaches and keep their problem nice and quiet for the last part of his journey across America.

Brendan turned to look at her, and then swiveled around to look at the bartenders slumped in the back seat. "Wait a minute, shouldn't you two," he said, but Ger picked up on his meaning and tumbled out of the car at once. She wanted to giggle at the comic opera that was playing out, nearly forgetting that this was deadly serious, dangerously real. Dessie closed the car door behind him, easing the latch slowly so that it caught without making a sound. They hopped into Peaches' rust bucket while Manon tumbled into Martie's back seat, pulling the door shut with a racket that echoed off the walls. The minivan crept down the alley and Martie followed at what she guessed was a normal and completely unsuspicious distance.

The headlights of the cars swept through wide arcs as each vehicle turned onto the street. Through Moraine Hills, past Deerhaven and then traveling out of Shields, Martie held her gaze to the road and the tail lights of the car in front of her. She was entirely focused on driving when a cell phone buzzed, so loud it sounded like an alarm. Startled, she let out a loud gasp, as if the cops were on to them and they were calling to tell them so.

Coming up with an excuse for Bonnie seemed easy for Brendan, as if he had a trove of handy reasons for being late. Smooth as silk, his voice spoke of concern for employees who lived in dangerous places, taking it upon himself to see them home. Not to worry, though, because he was accompanied by the burly bartenders, bodyguards in a manner of speaking. The lull that followed must have been caused by Bonnie's side of the conversation, possibly berating her significant other for entering risky territory, or maybe she had no idea where Gilead actually was. With a little chuckle, Brendan implied that she was silly to be worried about his safety, he was perfectly safe, he was not alone. If Bonnie only knew exactly who he was with, the woman would probably have an immediate heart attack.

"Oh, yeah, great night," Brendan said. It was amazing, the way he could chat away as if this were a perfectly ordinary evening where business was better than expected and wasn't the haddock especially tasty. From time to time he would grunt some sort of acknowledgment, letting Bonnie ramble on about whatever, but at least they weren't fighting over the incident in the kitchen. A left turn signal pulsated and Martie steered around the corner, tight on Peaches' bumper, to arrive in a part of the state that she had never seen before. Rather hastily, Brendan ended the phone call and switched gears, from casual to full blown edge of his seat tension.

Aimlessly, it seemed, Peaches drove up one street and down another, circling several blocks while Martie followed, giving up on remembering which way she had come so that she could get out again. By the time Peaches guided her car into a dark, garbage strewn alley, Brendan had dug his hands into the dashboard. She stopped behind a garage with a broken door that hung from a single hinge, looking like the entrance to a haunted barn. With headlights out, the two cars sat, as if waiting for a miracle to come down from on high.

A man poked his head out of the gaping opening of the garage, looking from side to side to see if the coast was clear. Brendan had one hand on the door handle and the other waving protectively in front of Martie, as if he was going to barricade the door and shield her with his body, sacrificing his life for hers. He had gone nuts, that was the only explanation she could come up with. Completely crazy, to be worried about a possible mugging when they had a body, quite possibly dead by now, in the back of the car in front of them. As the young man left the garage and walked towards Martie's car, Brendan began to murmur entreaties to the Lord.

"Roll down your window," she said when the man rapped on the passenger side door.

"What?" Brendan hissed. He was staring at the gun in the shoulder holster worn by the gentleman gently rapping.

Cursing him under her breath, she used the button on her door to open the window. As the visitor leaned in, Brendan leaned back, blocking her vision. She had to give him a nudge with her shoulder to move him back. "I'm so sorry, Jabari," she said. "This isn't right, getting you mixed up in this."

"It's cool," Jabari said. "This dude's trouble, huh?"

"Worst kind of trouble," she said. "Passing counterfeit money. And stolen money. He's got pockets full of hot cash."

"No different than the gangbangers I arrest every other day," Jabari said. "They muscle in, they kill a business. I know how they operate. Hey, R-Diddy, they hit your place too?"

"No, I come along for support," Manon said. She asked no questions. She did not want any answers. What she had seen was enough to sabotage more than Martie's career prospects. The possibility made Martie queasy.

"What are you going to do?" Brendan mumbled, searching for his courage. Jabari's eyes appeared nearly yellow in the gloom of a distant streetlight, his skin sparkling from sweat that had little to do with the heat of the June evening. "Do we leave him here?"

In reply, Jabari opened the door and Brendan and Manon got out. When another man popped out of the garage, Martie tried not to laugh at Brendan, who nearly jumped out of his skin. The bartenders came around to the back of the minivan, leaving Jay to guard Peaches while Manon put a protective arm around Martie. The tablecloth-wrapped criminal was brought into the garage, and in a matter of minutes, the men came back out, the tablecloth now bunched up in Brendan's hands. A very brief discussion ensued, something so serious that Brendan and Jabari both wore deep frowns, while Jabari's cohort stood silently, studying the ground at his feet. Nervously, Martie scanned the alley, searching for windows with lights on, where someone might be observing the group of pale faces that did not belong in the dirty back alley in Gilead.

Jabari and the other man melted into Peaches' car while Martie's accomplices in crime returned to her sedan. The shorter of the group, Jay had the honor of riding in the middle of the back seat, squeezed between two Irishmen who had not a word to say. Manon squeezed into the front seat with Brendan riding shotgun, everyone staring straight ahead. Peaches drove off and Martie followed, hoping that her pastry chef would at least get her back to a recognizable main road.

"Mind if I smoke?" Martie had to check the rear view mirror to see who had asked the question. The normally sing-song trill of Ulster was oddly muted, to the point that she had not recognized Ger's voice. With the back window rolled down, he lit up with a very shaky hand. Up ahead, Martie saw a few cars crossing the road she was on. She prayed that it was a way out of Gilead, and then watched as Peaches turned west, her rickety old auto billowing exhaust.

A blast of cool, humid air streamed into the car from the open window. Brendan flipped on the vents and adjusted the outlets so that the air was blowing on his face. Sweat trickled from his hair and beaded on his temples until he wiped it away with the back of his hand. The sound of the streets filtered in, growing louder as Martie came up to the intersection. Police sirens wailed and she slowed to see where the squad cars were. At the corner, just ahead, a group of prostitutes were working, each girl waving one hand in a discreet invitation to pull over and transact business.

"Oh, Jesus," Brendan mumbled.

Like origami, the back seat crew bent and compressed their three bodies into one compact mound, desperate to hide below the headrests and dark upholstery. Martie's eyes shot from side to side, searching the road for oncoming traffic and the fastest means to get away. She had been merely scared before, and now she was genuinely terrified. If the Gilead police showed up, Detective Jabari Baker would deny he knew the six people in the car and they were on their own, without a good alibi.

"Hey baby," a woman called from the curb. Martie had to come to a near complete stop when the car in front of her seemed to respond to the greeting by slowing down to a crawl and weaving slightly to the right. The hooker was attracted to Martie's car, a newer and cleaner model than the one in front. She stepped off the curb and approached Brendan's side of the car, hips swiveling with an exaggerated sway. "I do you, baby. Thirty bucks. Hell, I do you and your whores, thirty bucks."

Finding an opening, Martie stepped on the gas and squealed around the cars that were stopped ahead. Quickly pulling back into the right lane, she exhaled loudly and wiped her palms on her pants. From the back seat, she could hear Jay groan, the result of getting banged around when she veered like a race car driver.

"Wonder what she'd charge for the rest of us," Jay said.

"I can go back and ask," Martie said.

A snort of suppressed laughter broke the tension, but Brendan was at a loss for witty remarks. He rested his hand against his chin, leaning on the door, as if in deep thought. His attention was fixed on the passing scenery, a series of rundown shacks that gave way to old bungalows fronted by weedy yards. "They had a couple of bags of rocks," Brendan said, still obsessing about the evening's caper.

"These were drug dealers?" Manon asked.

"They were nobody," Martie said. "You never saw them. We were all in your kitchen celebrating the grand opening tonight."

"Then we make the scene this way," Manon said, "Back to my place, for breakfast. Like we used to do in Paris, Martie, do you remember?"

Her time in Paris was so far away it might not have actually happened. "I'm sorry. You don't have to do anything if you don't want to get wrapped up in this mess," she said.

"Yes she does," Jay said.

"I do," Manon said. "For you I would do anything. You know that."

"It's a set-up. The cops are going to find him based on a tip and charge him with possession." Brendan was talking as if he had not heard a word of the ongoing conversation.

She did not have to worry about the bastard dying alone in an abandoned garage, which troubled her. At least he would get medical care. Her grip on the steering wheel loosened. "What about the money? What did they do with that?" she asked.

"I guess they're going to plant some of it around the neighborhood and hope someone tries to use it. Bring in the Secret Service without having to call them," Brendan said.

"He takes one step out of that garage and he won't exactly blend in with the neighbors," Jay said.

"And if he says he was at McKechnie's, it's all of us here to say he wasn't," Dessie said.

"Yeah, and how did he get up to Gilead without a car?" Jay said. "And where did the crack come from? No, where he started his night isn't going to matter. It's where he ended up that the cops will be interested in. Bet he won't even remember half of it. Happens, with a concussion, you get amnesia. Like me, I can't remember anything after the bomb went off until I woke up in the hospital, and my buddies said I was talking to them the whole time."

"We've got to clean up the cellar," Ger said.

"Before the cleaners come in," Manon said.

"The luck of the Irish," Brendan said under his breath. "I'm sorry I ever listened to my father."

The pub was unchanged when they returned, the trap door still hanging open and the table in the back corner still out of place. With bar rags and buckets of hot water, Ger and Des attacked the small pool of blood that had coagulated at the foot of the stairs. Brendan took on the most important job in the cover-up operation. He went up to the office and erased the security video. All he would have to say, if asked, was that he had meant to arm the system after stopping by La Grenouille for a little party but he forgot.

Already up to her neck, Manon stuffed the stained tablecloth into a large black trash bag that she stowed in the trunk of her car before opening La Grenouille's back door and welcoming her guests. They ate omelets and tried to carry on some semblance of lighthearted chatter, but silence kept intruding. Brendan checked the time on his phone and sighed with a deep weariness. "I've got to get home before Bonnie gets worried and calls the cops," he said.

"Maybe I should call Peaches," Martie said. "I'm worried about her."

"You can't call," Manon said. "No calls for the police to ask about why you call so late."

First Ger and Des left, soon followed by Brendan and finally Jay. Like old times, Martie fell into the pattern and bussed the table in the kitchen while Manon gathered up the pans and rinsed them in the sink before loading everything into the dishwasher. The gravity of her actions hit her at last and Martie slumped to the floor.

"So stupid," she said. There would be no sleep that night, or any other night. "What was I thinking? That I was throwing out the garbage? Just dump it and go?"

"You did what you thought you had to do," Manon said. Her embrace was a shelter but Martie feared that it was no longer safe.

"Would you have done the same?" Martie asked. The question that throbbed in her skull could not be given voice.

Manon ran a hand through her short brown hair and sighed, deep in thought. "I don't know, chere. But it is done. Like in Paris, when you were sacked. I thought and thought, should I protest or is it better that I keep a job in case you needed help. So I thought and thought and then it was too late. I am too cautious sometimes."

"Who made up those lies, back then?"

"Does it matter? You survived. You moved ahead."

"Would you go behind my back if you thought what you did was for my benefit?"

"What I think I say to your face." Manon got to her feet and offered Martie a hand. "Stay with me tonight. You should not be alone."

Brid's Soda Bread

White flour 500 gms
Bread soda 1 tsp
Buttermilk 425 ml.
 salt

Don't be adding nonsense

Don't take any nonsense either.

SIXTEEN

The bar room was full of soldiers, a sea of crisp beige and green fatigues. Near the kitchen, Jay was holding forth with a group of reservists, one of whom was proudly demonstrating the wonders of his prosthetic leg. The air was scented with a slight odor of beer mixed with the aroma of pork and beef. Brendan strode quickly to the kitchen, his eyes shifting as if he was hunting for blood spatter evidence, but there was nothing out of place. The staff was going about their regular routine, and Peaches was making rhubarb crisps with her usual efficiency. Nothing happened the night before. There was nothing to suggest otherwise.

He waved to Martie and she joined him in the employee locker room. "He was trying to use me to launder the money," Brendan said. "I couldn't figure it out before, but I'm thinking that he would have given me the bank notes to exchange for him, you know, use my good standing at the bank. Then after a while he would have asked me to buy him out or something, but he'd get clean money back. By the time the hot money was traced, he'd be gone and I'd be screwed."

"I always wondered how they did it," Martie said. She was thinking of Sal, of the cash that he waved around like so much green paper. How would anyone know where it came from? She shuddered, even though the room was not that cold. There had been a couple of times when Sal

121

had offered to back her, if she needed financing to open up her own place. Thank God she had been smart enough to see the thorns on that Italian rose before she was snagged. Better to pull a fast one on Brendan than be tied to Sal for all eternity. Some debts could never be repaid.

"Jesus Christ, that would have been the end of everything," he said. "If I wasn't hurting for money so bad I never would have given him the time of day."

"You're doing fine. You don't need any other investors."

"No, you don't understand. When I told you I was in over my head, I didn't fill in the details."

"I know where we're at, Brendan," she said. In a way, all this mess was Ger O'Hare's fault, and since Brendan hired him, the burden of guilt was on his Irish-American shoulders. She shook her head. All the fault lay with the money-laundering bastard who tried to use the pub for his criminal purposes, and if not for Ger's astute observations, they would be in worse shape. The bartender had actually saved McKechnie's. And yes, she was to be blamed for the half-baked plan to hide everything.

"I can't hold off my creditors forever," he said.

"They're fine," she said.

"We'll make it, won't we?"

"Yes, we will. We will."

"I wonder what happened to the other guy who came in with that asshole."

"What? What other guy?" she spluttered. The printer spit out a string of orders and the line cook called for her. "Why didn't you say something about another guy?"

"It makes no difference," Brendan said as he headed towards the front of the house. "Would you have done anything different?"

Too soon to pick up the band, Brendan sat at the bar and tried to read the newspaper but he couldn't focus on the words. His eyes kept wandering to the trap door. Did Dessie's feet sound heavier when he walked over it, or was it an illusion? The bartender delivered a pint, steps weary, mouth too tired to speak, and then Des went back to the top of the bar to shoot soft drinks into glasses full of ice. Someone new took the tray, an older man who looked somewhat familiar.

"Another one of your relatives?" Brendan called over to Des.

"Do you not remember Eddie's da?" Des said. Brendan could not even recall Eddie. "Your lad doing the washing up, his father. Used to be a waiter at Les Nomades. Can you believe your luck, so, to find that kind of experience without looking?"

"Oh, yeah, I'm a regular lucky charm," Brendan said. "Everything's roses, isn't it?"

"From this side of the bar, 'tis indeed all roses."

"Where's Ger?"

"Scheduled for four. Had a bit of a shock last night. Flashback sort of thing, like that traumatic stress business, it was, like a bad dream."

"Well, I didn't sleep last night either."

"Who'd expect it, after all? Grand opening, full house, your man performing. Who could sleep after that? And me, ran my feet to bits last night, and there's more to come tonight."

By any measure, Dessie was profoundly sincere, that the only thing that happened last night was opening night. Either he was insane or a champion at denying the truth. Returning to the local section of the daily paper, Brendan found nothing at all about bodies being discovered in abandoned garages in Gilead or foreigners being picked up on drugs charges. He peered over the top of the paper and watched Des take inventory of the bottled beer. Without a doubt, the man had mastered the art of knowing nothing and seeing nothing. Brendan could learn a thing or two from the bartender who put his head down and went to work as if nothing had happened out of the ordinary. Of course, what constituted ordinary in Lifford was a little different than the ordinary of Moraine Hills.

Roaming through the pub, Brendan poked his head into the dining room, where the afternoon sun was twinkling on the fishing floats. If only they were crystal balls, ready to foretell his future. Where did he stand with Martie? Was he going to lose her just when things were getting started? He was beginning to understand that he had lost Paddy Dunne. The man who sang last night was a stranger, remotely connected to the lad from Miltown and the raucous balladeer who entertained the crowds in Uncle Donal's pub on the other side of the water, but it was not the same. The room, the decor, the music was reproduced, but the people were all different and only Brendan remained unchanged.

"No way she's gay," a soldier said. The reserves were like frat boys, discussing sex in subdued voices.

"She's not the dyke," another said.

"So she's the wife, then. Fucking waste."

The squad spotted Brendan and the discussion came to an abrupt halt. As a unit, the soldiers came towards him before he could escape up the stairs to his office. The uniforms brought to mind the scene that could yet occur, police officer blue replacing camouflage. Head bowed in shame, he would be led out the front door, cuffed, surrounded by FBI agents or U.S. Marshalls. One day soon, he would be sitting in a cell and Bonnie would leave him and his family would deny all knowledge of his shameful existence. And all because he had let himself get wrapped up in his father's dreams of public house grandeur.

"We'd like to thank you for your hospitality," the man with the bionic leg said, extending a right hand that was webbed with thick white scars.

One compliment led to another, and the officer mentioned Ms. Smurfit and her kind interest in a wounded vet's case. Jay Elizalde, the sous chef, had no direction until he met Martie at a career fair. A vague interest in the restaurant business was developed into a vocation, with two years of college fully funded under the G.I. Bill, followed by a promised job and some very rapid promotions. Under the plaudits, Brendan found the actions of a very clever woman, someone who had essentially done what any smart executive would do to create a core group of loyal employees who stayed by her side through the lows and the highs. There was some truth to Paddy's observation that Martie was Brendan McKechnie in a skirt.

"I've been to Ireland a few times myself," the lieutenant said.

"Really? Ever get to the west coast?" Brendan asked.

"Sort of. Shannon stopover."

"Hear you're a friend of this Dunne dude," another reservist said. There was a strong undertone of snide sarcasm in his voice.

Before Brendan could reply, a man with oak leaf clusters on his shirt collar piped up. "He's a piece of work. But he sure can sing pretty."

The televisions blared soccer and baseball and golf, providing amusement for those with nothing better to do than hang around a bar on a Saturday afternoon. A couple of parties were eating a late lunch in the corner once occupied by Mr. Gray, his presence essentially erased with the ease of turning over a table. A cover. That's what Martie called it. How many covers they did was her gauge for a successful night. A screech of reverb from the speakers shocked Brendan off the stool.

Louis was back at his board, getting ready for the upcoming show. On stage was a teenager with a unruly mop of curly hair, strumming a guitar. Following directions, the kid strolled across the stage, chanting "Test. Test. One, two, three" into each microphone. For a minute, Brendan felt as if he was sitting in the local high school auditorium, waiting for his nephews to perform in the talent show. They would be at the pub later for the big night, the gathering of the McKechnie clan missing their matriarch because she had gone back to Miltown to be with her sister as she mourned her loss. Picturing her face when she learned of her youngest son's arrest for assault, battery, conspiracy or whatever else he was guilty off, Brendan leaned on the bar, his head hidden behind his hands.

"You might consider opening on Sunday afternoons for sessions," Des said.

"We used to do that at my uncle's pub," Brendan said. He recalled with fondness those long ago Sundays in Miltown when families came and local musicians performed for their neighbors. He listened to the young man perform with teenage intensity, his voice soft and then growing stronger as he expressed the emotion of the tune. One day Brendan wanted a son who played the guitar. Would that day ever come, or had he deposited his future in an empty garage in the dead of night?

His phone buzzed with a reminder and Brendan was glad to have a chore that would require his attention. Anything to keep from dwelling on Mr. Gray and the whereabouts of his associate. When he reached the hotel, Liam informed him that Paddy had decided to walk it again. Brendan could not have been happier. He could worry about someone else and forget his troubles.

The exuberance of two musicians riding a crest of joy was infectious. Rory and Liam traded snippets of anecdotes from the Friday night performance, stories that weren't completed due to one man hurriedly interrupting the other to put in his opinion. All in all, the night had been a success, a few hours of pure musical bliss that would fuel the next show. Wrapped up in the chatter, Brendan veered off on a different route and Rory asked him where they were.

"This is the real high rent district," Brendan said, his hand sweeping across a vista of old trees and old stone walls. He must have come here on purpose, some subliminal suggestion from an unknown source, to demonstrate the adoration for Victorian British culture that had driven the founders of Deerhaven to create these elaborate estates. They were the

American version of the British landlord in Ireland, the robber barons who built their houses on the backs of Irish laborers. "What do you think? The big houses in Ireland don't look any different to me."

"High society," Rory said.

"The kind that you never hear about," Brendan added. "Old money, very discreet. Never see a name in the paper unless they've gotten married or died. Alcoholics, drug users, kids in trouble, but you'd never know it."

"How does it happen that they all build their houses alike?" Liam asked. "It's like a mold that they passed around."

"No one's improved on the castle style of architecture," Brendan said. He caught Liam's glance, a slight raise of an eyebrow that reminded Brendan of his own mansion, a castle in miniature. It was not his dream home, and he hoped that the lads understood that, even if he could look back now and realize that he hadn't put up all that much of a fight when Bonnie's vision of her ideal residence was rendered in a blue line print.

Rory rolled down the window and shouted out to someone walking along. "Pull over, will you," he said to Brendan, thumping him in the back of the head. As if waking from a dream, Brendan turned to see Paddy, perspiring and flushed, climb into the car.

"This heat is killing me," he said. Using the sleeve of his shirt, he wiped the sweat from his face. "We'll do *The City of Chicago* tonight and I'll be thinking of all the Irishmen who came to live in this oven. How did your mammy stand it, Brendan?"

"We went to Miltown for the summer," Brendan said, chuckling at the memory. His mother hated Chicago summers. There was a time when she took her children to Ireland for the month of July and part of August, but this year she left at the end of March, in part to avoid the roasting climate but also to avoid the loneliness. She had a daughter in San Francisco but California did not suit. She had a son in New York but a condo in Midtown held no charm. Living with sons Robert or Brendan was rejected. What drew her was the familiar, the soil from which she arose. Brendan expected her to one day dig up her husband's corpse and plant him in the auld sod so that she could rest eternally with her husband, but in her choice of locations.

"Mingling with the swells, were you?" Rory teased Paddy.

"Sure and I'm one of them myself," he said. "The gardai drove past and never gave me a second look, so well do I fit in."

"Figured you for a brickie in search of his hod," Liam said.

The old slag was refreshing, the very thing that Brendan needed. Here was a Miltown summer, trading good-natured insults and making jokes. He had begun to feel that he could not get it back, but he was discovering it again, filling his car as he motored through the leafy shade of a perfectly smooth road. For now, at least, Paddy was with him as of old, replacing the windbag who rattled on the stage last night. For a brief moment, Brendan didn't have to wonder where Mr. Gray was.

Laughter eased away as the group entered the bar where Denny of the Celtic Airs was singing in sweet harmony with the curly-haired microphone tester. Man and boy, their voices blended as the guitar laid down the rhythm for the concertina to follow. Framed by the stage proscenium, the duo was an image taken from Miltown's Willie Week festival, two musicians merging notes to create a work of beauty. Even their faces were in harmony, sharing light brown waves of hair and full lips that formed perfect notes.

Spontaneous applause met the song's conclusion, with Rory adding a loud whoop of appreciation for Denny's dexterity. The performer grinned, caught off-guard by an audience that was not expected. The boy put the guitar back on its stand, as if he was embarrassed to have handled Paddy's instrument without permission. He offered a sheepish bow before turning to his fellow artist. Denny only laughed and lifted a bottle of Evian to his lips. "Well done, Ryan," he said after taking a sip. "Didn't I tell you practice is the key?"

Ryan snatched the bottle from Denny's hand in a swift move that sent a tin whistle clattering to the floor. "Fuck you," he said.

"Give me that," Denny growled.

Ryan held the bottle to his nose and inhaled deeply. "Liar," he said. "What else are you lying about? Did you make up the part about my mother too?"

"Gentlemen, shall we start, so?" Paddy said, breaking an awkward silence.

The cap was in Denny's hand and he screwed the bottle closed, moving it to a spot behind his seat, not saying a word. "Don't make a scene," he said in a stage whisper. "I can explain. Later."

For a tense moment, the musician busied himself with his uilleann pipes, filling the bellows and adjusting the strap on his arm. He looked up from his chores and caught Ryan's eye, flames of blue anger meant to immolate the piper. Denny cast his vision to the floor, a slight flush spreading up his neck to his ears. Paddy tuned, plucked and generally made noise to fill the vacuum.

"Sit in with us, son," he said, overflowing with ebullience and good cheer. "Didn't I see you play last year? At McAuley House, it was. Sure, I never forget a voice. As for a face? Aren't the old eyes not what they once were?"

A humbled, bleary-eyed musician seemed to plead with the young man, his entreaty expressed by the slump of his shoulders and the lowering of his eyes. Brendan turned to Ryan, to gauge the boy's response, and then he saw it. The hair, the sharp angle of the nose, the shape of the chin; father and son were butting heads over the drink. Father and son, but there was a distance between them, as if they had only just met. Something felt very odd. Brendan took a step backwards to regain his balance.

"Go on, lad, we've enough guitars here for an orchestra," Rory said.

Ignoring his father, assuming it was his father, Ryan took a seat on the edge of the stage and gladly accepted the offer of Paddy's nylon-stringed guitar. He fingered a chord, the pupil in awe to be touching the master's instrument, under the master's guidance and care. The rest of the musicians followed Ryan's lead. After the opening notes faded into the chorus, Brendan recognized the song he had half-heard at the high school talent show two months ago. At the time, he had not realized that it was one of Shift/Move's standards, being too preoccupied to hear anything beyond his own voice worrying about the pub and the ever growing costs.

The harmony flowed between Ryan and Paddy, even though Denny and Rory were adding their voices to the mix. Full sound, guitars, pipes, fiddle, mandolin, and Brendan was carried back to another age, when the music was lush but Paddy's voice was weakened by alcohol. Never before had his notes sounded so strong, his heart on display in the emotion expressed through a subtle lift in volume. Paddy could wring a tear or raise a laugh, just in the modulation of his voice. There had been a time when he was learning the power of that art, when he could draw girls to his side like buzzing bees to honey. It was a skill that Brendan had always envied, but not everyone was born with the gift.

Without pausing, Ryan started in on a second number, a ballad of alcoholism and abandonment. At first, Brendan assumed it was the boy's own composition, the lyrics so perfectly suited to the situation, but Paddy and Rory sang the chorus. The words took on a new meaning, a greater significance, as if Paddy were confessing his sins and seeking Ryan's forgiveness. Or was Paddy asking his mates for mercy, seeking clemency from Brendan for affronts that were forgotten in a haze of gin and beer? The muscles in Denny's jaw tightened, but he never lost the beat.

Des proclaimed the young man's brilliance while applauding with vigor. It was a compliment that Paddy reiterated, expanded to enormous proportions with an avalanche of kind words. Brendan found himself on his favorite stool, taking in the scene before him. There was more than mere praise here. Paddy was ingratiating himself with the boy, but why? Could it have anything to do with Martie, in which case, what did she have to do with Denny? It was not hard to imagine that she was Ryan's aunt, and that made Denny her brother-in-law. Of course she would try to find work for the alcoholic, to help out the sister's family, and it was almost a certainty that there was some estrangement between parent and child. The drink did that to families, tore them up, and there was something that Paddy knew first hand.

Nothing definite was settled when Ryan returned the guitar. He might sit in tonight, he was not sure if he could make it, he would see, he would try. The way that he turned his back to Denny spoke clearly, telling of his shame to be connected to the drunken piper, while longing for the pleasure of playing a set with Shift/Move. The teen's dilemma was painful, everyone was trying to help, but all they did was add to his burden. When Ryan walked past on his way out, Brendan felt that he was watching a child grow into a man.

The rehearsal went forward, but there was now an invisible barrier between Denny and the rest of the group. He had been exposed, his secret revealed, and a cloud of discomfort enveloped him. Once caught, he couldn't return to his disguised beverage. Before the night was out, Brendan feared that he would have to send drinks around to the band so that Denny could get through the evening, put on a good show and please the customers. Let the man turn to sobriety tomorrow, outside of McKechnie's. Tonight of all nights was not the time to preach to a drunk about the evils of liquor.

"Okay, I'm set," Louis said. Brendan jumped in his seat, forgetting that the sound man had been there all along, fiddling with his equipment while the storm blew through the bar.

"We'll never sound better," Rory agreed.

They retreated to the back table where Mr. Gray had been outed less than twenty-four hours earlier. The group ordered lunch, but Brendan could not sit still. He picked at the corned beef sandwich, nibbled on a chip, and finally gave up. Any minute, he could be arrested. Any minute. Unless Graham Brown turned up, looking for his partner in crime. Any minute, Brendan could be gunned down. Any minute.

SEVENTEEN

The list of contacts stored in his phone was long, but organized. He scrolled from the bottom up until he found the name he was looking for. Listening to the ringing in his ear, he stretched out on the sofa and put his feet on the armrest, until he pictured Martie in a similar position, or would it have been Paddy on the bottom? He hopped up and retreated to the desk as his brother Robert answered.

"Hey," he said. That was all that was needed. Just a hey. "What time are you coming tonight?"

"Are we a little worried about filling the seats, kid?" Robert asked.

"We were packed last night," Brendan said. "Just want to make sure you're here, that's all."

"Didn't I say I would come, and bring the family? What's up? You sound a little odd."

Brendan sat in the chair, the air escaping from his lungs like a punctured balloon. "Stress, the usual. Anyway, Paddy and the guys are going on at seven. I was thinking if you got here by six we can sit down to dinner."

Brendan picked up on the sound of voices in the background. "Taylor wants to know if it's true that, wait, who am I asking about, Taylor?

Excuse me, Taylor and Kelsey both want to know if Ryan Hartnett is going to sit in on a couple of songs."

The pieces of the personal life puzzle fell into place. Martie was from one of those big Irish families, where the oldest kids had kids while their siblings were still little. Martie was thirty-one, thirty-three tops, and probably did most of the babysitting. She was likely to be especially close to her nephew, and maybe she never married or had kids because she had her fill of babies from taking care of her nieces and nephews. It wasn't too late for her, if she wanted to change her mind. But who would she change her mind for, him or Paddy? "He is, yes. They rehearsed. Just finished."

Teen girl squealing in the background told him that Ryan was the chick magnet that Paddy has once been, seducing the ladies with a warbling voice and instrumental virtuosity. While he had not been listening to the boy's performance at the talent show, he had been startled back to reality when the girls in the audience went wild at the conclusion of the set. An older man was not the best judge of appearances, he realized, especially when trying to determine why pretty girls would swoon over a gawky boy with a spotty face.

After a short scuffle, Taylor snatched the phone, not trusting her father to manage the critical interrogation required. "No one said anything about it in the cafeteria yesterday," she said. "Are you sure?"

"It was last minute. He happened to be here during the sound check, and Paddy takes an interest in young musicians. What difference does it make, anyway? Aren't you excited to see your old uncle?"

"We see you all the time," Taylor said.

"Do you remember Paddy? It's been a long time since you saw him," Brendan said. In truth, Robert had kept his children away from Paddy because Paddy was an unstable drunk.

"So Ryan's going to be there," she said. "For sure?"

"I can't make any guarantees, *mo stor*, but he'd be stupid to pass up the chance," Brendan said. "So, is this Ryan dude stupid or is he smart?"

"Like, straight A's, Uncle Brendan," Taylor said with dramatic impatience.

"Very smart. Sounds like he'll be there, all right."

With the grace of a dancer, Brendan skipped down the stairs, victory within his grasp. While he probably would not have time to actually sit and eat a complete meal with his relatives, he could at least have a drink with them, until Martie needed him to deliver plates to the important diners or glad hand new arrivals at the front door. A restaurateur was a busy man during normal dinner hours, especially one who shared the chef's desire to excel. No, to out-do the competition. With a start, he remembered that Bonnie was coming again. They had yet to reach a compromise about the hours he would have to put in, and she was not thrilled about his suggestion to shift Saturday date night to a ten o'clock start instead of seven. In his mind, it was a perfectly reasonable solution to her latest complaint, and one that made sense. Martie understood the thinking. She wouldn't complain about late dinners.

Stepping into the middle of a conversation, Brendan learned that Rory and Louis were making plans to record the performance. The two of them chattered away, trading techno-geek terms about equipment or wires or computers, for all that Brendan understood. A picture flashed in his imagination, cover art that featured a photograph of his pub on the front side and a black and white image of Uncle Donal's place on the back. "Live from McKechnie's" would be emblazoned across the image, and on the back would be a note that the album had been recorded at a live performance in Moraine Hills. Looking at his watch, he wondered if there was time to call the local photographer, to run over and snap pictures for the liner notes.

Such thoughts evaporated when Ger strolled in, calling out a greeting while donning an apron. Looking sleep-deprived, the bartender's grey patina brought back all that had happened the night before. The dark rings under his eyes suggested a troubled mind, the post-traumatic stress of a flashback to some other perilous time. Ger picked up a towel and went about polishing a glass, and in that instant he transformed into the other man who was at the bar earlier in the week, holding court with a quick joke and a sly wink. Brendan noticed a slight change in Ger's stride when he crossed the trap door, or at least he thought that the bartender was almost jumping over the spot rather than stepping on the area. The door creaked and he disappeared down the rickety stairs, possibly to check for stray splatters or some speck of dust that was out of place in the storage room below. The reminder set Brendan's stomach to churning and he got himself a cup of tea to soothe his nerves. Ger returned with a case of wine, just a normal chore, a typical action on a typical Saturday. To the clink of wine bottles being slotted into the cooler, Brendan went back to the tea, already growing cold.

"Now, Sunday tea," Rory said, easing on to the stool at Brendan's left. "I've always been fond of a fry."

"Aislinn rarely serves fried anything," Paddy said. "Watches the cholesterol and the fatty acids and God knows what all. What are we teaching our children, when our ancestors once starved?"

"The ancestors weren't too worried about what they ate, as long as they ate," Liam said. "I don't care to go back to a diet of spuds and buttermilk myself."

"Let me see what I can arrange with Martie," Brendan said. He was too restless. He needed to talk to her, to hear her tell him that everything was going to be fine.

He did not like the look that Denny flashed at him, a glare or maybe just a curious stare at the yellowing bruise on the back of his hand that remained from an encounter with a wayward compressor. Not a glare, but something more like a sneer or a smirk twitched on Denny's face. Maybe the musician was just suffering a lack of alcohol, which he did not seem to have sampled since the water bottle incident. What was Martie's relationship to Denny, anyway? They never talked about their lives, or at any rate, she had never said much of anything about her past or present. Considering how much of his guts he had spilled, he was entitled to a little of her story, at the very least, to make things more fair.

Because nothing had happened, Peaches did not talk to her cousin the cop and so Martie could not ask even one of the million questions that crowded into her head. She had to talk to Brendan, to explain what she had done with her life savings and get him to agree to her plan. Not that it was the best time to have such a serious discussion, but when would there ever be a good time again after the previous night? She just about smacked his head with the kitchen door as she went out while he, apparently, was coming in.

"Let's go upstairs for a minute," she said. "We should talk. In private."

They did not get far. A gang of policemen walked in the door and Brendan gasped so loud that Martie thought he was going to faint. "Fuck, fuck, fuck," he whispered, his lips not moving.

"Chuck, what brings you here?" Martie said. Her voice was a little too loud, her cheer a little too strained. Deny, deny, deny. It would become her litany, her prayer.

"You, darling," Chuck said. He swept his hat off his head to reveal a shining bald pate. "And the food. Before you file a sexual harassment suit against me."

"What woman could resist you," Martie said. "Stopping for lunch or dinner?"

Brendan's knees were shaking, nearly knocking together, while Martie bantered with the local police chief. His arms shifted until his clenched fists were nearly touching, as if the handcuffs were already on his wrists. Taking his elbow, she steered his right hand toward Chuck's invitation to shake hands as she made introductions, but it was debatable if Brendan was listening or was too busy panicking to respond. Would he buckle, if it came down to it, would he turn on her and let her take all the blame? Aware that Chuck was fascinated by Brendan's bruised hand, she launched into an anecdote that she prayed would come out of her mouth in a normal tone.

A smile appeared, a bit unsteady, as Brendan added a few words to the story he had already told countless times. Martie put her arm on his back in a gesture of solidarity and felt his coiled spine unwind. He was no doubt worried about her loyalty, and who could blame a man when he was in cahoots with a near stranger. A gentle rub, then, to indicate they were united and of a single mind. Her mind.

"There's men who ask for the overnight beat, just for the food," Chuck said. "Past what, close to ten years? Gourmet meals, not any of that fast food shit. It's been French, then Italian, and now this Continental cuisine."

"New Irish," one of the officers piped up. He rested his hand on his holstered gun, sending a ripple of fear through Martie's gut. Black pants tucked into black combat boots told her he was a member of the drug enforcement crew.

"We're having a meeting, and I was hoping we could use the dining room," Chuck said. Had he scouted the location, searching for exits that a frightened and cornered criminal might take to escape capture? Were officers posted at every door?

"Excuse me for a minute," Brendan said. His dash to the men's room was so swift that he almost tripped over the bar stools before nearly colliding with a table. If he thought he could make an escape through the jacks he would soon discover that there was not a single window in the rest room.

"You're welcome to use the place whenever you want," Martie said. What else could she say? When she caught Chuck gazing with starstruck longing at the musicians rehearsing, she did not hesitate to make introductions, avoiding any eye contact with Paddy. If she could not keep her distance from him physically, she would stay far away mentally, and hope to fade into the shadows before some glimmer of recognition fired in his head. By bringing the police and the band together, she created an opening to retreat back to the safety of the kitchen and the comfort of a back door to an alley that would bring her to Manon. She would not go to jail without saying good-bye.

Until Chuck and his colleagues left, Martie could not rest. She drifted towards the dining room, to peek around the corner and see if the boys in blue were still there. Chuck looked up and caught her eye, then wagged a finger at her to come join them. His smile terrified her. When he asked her to bring Brendan over, she knew that the game was over. There was nothing to do but go quietly, without making a scene. She knew lawyers, dozens of lawyers, very good lawyers. It wasn't the end of her world. Bad publicity would sink her, and the pub, and all the money she had invested. She couldn't think of that. She had to concentrate on her alibi, on denying. Deny, deny, deny. Amen.

At the bar, Ger was filling an order for the dining room, soft drinks all around. Emer leaned against the bar, waiting, chatting away as if all was well in the world, while Des greeted the first arrival of the afternoon, a young couple who were annoyed at being carded. Liam's distinctive chuckle, a tenor to Paddy's deeper baritone, reminded her of last July and how foolish she had been. Denny threatened her after she denied his request to meet their son, swore that he would tell the adoptive parents that Martie was a lesbian whore who should be kept away from Ryan. So what did she do? Jumped into bed with Paddy Dunne to prove she was normal, a woman who had sex with men. Why did she let Denny become her judge and jury, as if he could be made the victim of her anger? He felt nothing because he never cared about her or their son, and only used Ryan as a club to beat her down. The decision to reunite with the boy, the pressure to set up a time to meet, it was all a game to inflict as much damage on her as he could because he could. Stupid, to even consider it, to give in to the curiosity of what became of the little bundle she handed off to a nun in a hospital.

She had wondered, though. Every day for over sixteen years she had wondered if the baby was happy, if the parents were indulgent or severe, if the child was normal emotionally or if she should have kept him after all. A letter from an attorney, forwarded by Denny, had answered those questions but then she began to wonder what Ryan looked like. In the end, she agreed, without thinking things through. How was she to break the news about Manon without alienating people she had never met? Was it a mistake, to allow contact, or was it a bigger mistake to not be up-front about her lover? Martie had yet to figure out how to present Manon, and could only hope that some initial interaction could give her some guidance on the best way to proceed. There were no recipes for success when it came to creating positive relationships out of tangled beginnings. And how would incarceration on some felony charges add to the difficulty?

"Brendan, sorry to interrupt, but Chuck needs to see us," she said. Dust motes sparkled in the shafts of sunlight that streamed through the windows, an image of peace, quiet and contentment. The room took on a hazy quality, as if it were no longer in focus. For a moment, she made time stop so she could savor the pleasure of a dream realized, but it was only for that moment.

She had no hint as to the purpose of the meeting, no reassurance to keep Brendan from stumbling over his feet as he turned the corner, bumped his shoulder against the corner of the snug, and rebounded into a chair. The clatter echoed around the empty dining room. Martie could not keep her eyes from wandering towards the front door, waiting for a battered Irish mobster to bound into the room, waving an accusing finger, shouting abuse and demanding justice. Deny, deny, deny. She had never seen him. No one had ever seen him, just ask Des or Ger or Detective Jabari Baker of the Gilead Police Department. The man with the cracked skull was a complete stranger, spewing nonsense because of brain damage and who would Chuck trust, an Ulsterman in a pink cardigan sweater or his favorite chef?

Using his foot, Chuck pushed a chair away from the table, inviting Brendan to sit. A river of sweat poured down Martie's back and soaked her armpits. She offered desert, if only to have something to say, or maybe in the back of her mind she was planning to make a run for it, getting a few minutes head start. No, she couldn't leave Brendan to face the worst. They were partners, and she wasn't walking away from a quarter of a million dollars.

"We really appreciate your hospitality," Chuck said. "But we have to watch our girlish figures."

"Last night was a little bit of a headache for us," the one labelled Roehmer said.

"We'll get to that in a minute," Chuck said. "What we wanted to ask, and I know it's not right to ask the same businesses over and over every year, but it's not like everyone jumped at the opportunity to feed a bunch of cops for free."

"You can count on Michael DeCecco to complain the loudest about the lost business when the carnival's in town," Roehmer said.

"What carnival?" Brendan asked.

"The Chamber of Commerce carnival," Martie said. She held in a laugh, a loud guffaw of utter relief. "I've always been happy to entertain the security detail and you don't have to feel guilty asking me again. Most of the regulars stay away. Don't like the crowds and the noise. Just give me people to cook for and I'm happy."

"Oh, right. Moraine Hills Founders Day," Brendan said. He giggled instead of laughed, a dead giveaway to his state of mind. "Slipped my mind completely. Been so busy getting the place opened, and, yeah, come on over any time you like."

Guilty men behaved like Brendan, with a shrug of the shoulders, a grin and overblown enthusiasm. To accentuate his mistake, he scrubbed the smile from his face and tried to adopt a serious look but that only served to call attention to his artificiality. A guilty woman would kick him in the shins to bring him around, so Martie tried a softer approach. She rested a hand on Brendan's thigh, thinking it might calm him down. He turned to her with an odd look in his eye and she pulled her hand away.

"So Officer Rodriguez here," Chuck said, indicating his black-booted guest, "will be working with the gang crimes unit. Crowds attract the drug trade and we won't let that happen in our nice little town.'

Brendan nodded like a bobble-head doll, acting like he understood, but the mention of drugs sent Martie's head reeling. She had been so sure, just a minute ago, that they were safe, but now she had a drug enforcement officer giving her the eye. Had the whole thing with the bank robber been some kind of elaborate set-up, a sting operation gone wrong or a plot by Michael DeCecco to bring her down? The plant had been planted, so to speak, and if only she had been sensible enough to call the police in the first place but when had there been a chance before the game was up?

"Now, let's talk about something else. Why didn't you call us last night?" Chuck asked. He was reading her mind, which meant her face was utterly transparent. Deny, deny, deny.

She cleared her throat to gain time, to think of the right response. "You need an engraved invitation?" she asked.

"What, you think we just show up?" Chuck began to chuckle. "You know, if it's a question of paying the guys, we could have worked it out."

Stunned did not begin to describe Martie's state of mind. She had considered asking Sal Lardino for help, only considered, and here was the Chief of Police making an offer with the casual air of the ordinary transaction. But this was not the best way out, either, not paying off a blackmailer who would be free to keep coming back for more until she was flat broke. There was no money to bribe anyone, that much was true, but if Chuck would set up a payment plan she could avoid prison, even if it meant compounding the crimes. For the rest of her life, monthly installments. The nightmare grew worse, a lifetime of servitude with no guarantee of a fixed fee.

"Took some digging, to I.D. those dudes," Roehmer said. His grin was pure evil, malicious, and Martie felt her skin crawl.

"What did you find?" Brendan located his tongue and stammered out a dumb question. Bargaining with corruption was more of a man's job, especially a man in the building trades. He knew a thing or two about pay-offs, and if he could buy their freedom, Martie would let him negotiate.

"With the internet, you can't hide anything," Chuck said. He was about to go on when a party taking the table behind him asked him to scoot in to make room. An older couple then followed right behind the foursome, weaving around and distracting the men from their discussion. Suddenly, the private meeting was not so private anymore.

"Well, we'd better go," Chuck said. He counted out several bills and dropped the tip onto the table. "You're getting busy. We got plenty of time to iron out all the details. Good to meet you, Mr. McKechnie. Martie, darling, all the best, huh? Glad you're in your own place. You deserve it."

With her legs like jelly, Martie followed them to the door. The police knew something that was available on the internet, but what happened the night before could not possibly be posted anywhere, not in any chat room or forum or website. They had public information, then, which did not include what Ger knew or could find out though his contacts in Strabane. The quiet men never shared their knowledge with the authorities, but they would have passed along a tip to one of their own. So Ger was acting on that tip when he caught the criminal trying to pass hot currency. Which meant Ger would have to pressure his contacts to locate the creep and his creepy associate. And then what? Whack them? Better would be an anonymous tip to the police, and then the staff of McKechnie's Pub would deny, deny, deny until the end of time.

By the time Martie had a free minute to speak to Ger, the band had gone up to the office to relax before the show. She cornered the bartender while he stood on the trap door, feet planted as if he were a tree. "I swore an oath to leave it all behind," he said after Martie described her plot.

"Then you'd better un-swear," Martie said.

"With my hand on the Bible," Ger added.

"I'm granting absolution. Ger, we have to find out where the other guy is before he comes back looking for his buddy."

"I swore an oath."

"To do what? To let the UVF or the UDA burn us out? The cops are sniffing around already. Don't leave me hanging out to dry."

Torn between a promise and a thirst for revenge against the loyalist gangs, Ger walked away with the gait of a broken man. Silently, he filled an order at the top of the bar, a purely mechanical process that did not disguise the turmoil in his head. He wore his hatred for unionist thugs in the creases of his face. Vow or no vow, he would eventually realize that there was no other choice but to make a call, use his former associates for good by whispering in the right ear. Something as innocuous as a phone call was hardly akin to breaking a vow to lay down the guns and abandon the armed struggle. All Martie had to do was convince Ger of the same.

A tide of people washed in and it was not long before the bar was packed two or three deep. Irish brogues mingled with the sounds of New York City and Boston, grumbling about open tables being held for guests who were not yet there while others were forced to stand. The big night had begun. The grand opening. Martie hurried back to the kitchen before it lapsed into chaos, and came face to face with her former mentor, the restaurant king of Moraine Hills. It was Michael DeCecco himself.

"I'm sorry," he said. He held her in place with his beautiful brown eyes, filled with longing. "I was wrong. So very wrong. Will you come back to me?"

EIGHTEEN

The police were on their tails, two dangerous criminals were on the loose, and there was nothing to smile about, nothing to be happy about, but Martie was ready to explode with joy. Fears that had been put aside were resurrected, every doubt about the chef and DeCecco's intentions came rushing back to the front of Brendan's brain. An urge enveloped him, an intense desire to beat Michael and his shit-eating grin to a bloody pulp.

"Well, I guess I'm in the way," Michael said. He began to back out, slithering towards the service entrance.

"Stop in later," Martie said.

"We'll see." He took a few more steps backwards as Brendan mirrored his every move. "I'm short in my kitchen these days. I can't always get away."

A brief flash of steel glinted under bright lights, and Brendan could almost feel the line cook's knife in his own hand, thrusting effortlessly into Michael's back. Multiple stab wounds, the autopsy would read, a crime of passion, justifiable homicide. Furious, to the point of near insanity, Brendan followed DeCecco to the back door.

"Okay, okay, I admit it," Michael said.

Red-faced, blood pressure rising, Brendan could do little more than raise a clenched fist and point a finger, waving in a futile gesture of crazed impotence. Aware that his arm was shaking with rage, he folded his arms across his chest, tucking his hands under his armpits to hold them steady. Before things proceeded, he was going to get a full confession out of DeCecco. Brendan had to hear the full story from the man's lips, to be shown exactly where he had stumbled into the tiger pit and which pointed sticks had lethally impaled him.

"Why?" Brendan said.

"Because she's the best chef around here, why else?" Michael said. "Hey, it's me who should be pissed. You put a dent in my staff."

The muscles in Brendan's jaw clenched, but the tightness began to ease in his shoulders. There was a slight aroma of victory in the air, but it was drifting out of McKechnie's kitchen, and not from the yet to open bistro down the street. For a second, Michael examined his shoes, shook his head, and faced Brendan with his trademark smile.

"Maybe she's pissed at me, you think?" Michael said. He laughed. "I'm the asshole who introduced her to that piece of work."

Even though Brendan had no idea what exactly Michael was talking about, he nodded his head as if he agreed with the assessment. Whether the piece of work was Sal Lardino or any member of the restaurant staff, it had little to do with Brendan's current predicament.

"What can I say?" Michael continued when Brendan failed to speak. "I've known him since high school, and Christ I was jealous of his way with the ladies. A few notes and he melts all resistance while I'm Mr. Charming and getting jack shit. I don't know, I guess I believed him because he could have any girl he wanted, so he must have some secret knowledge, right?

"Here's a lesson for you, Brendan. Don't believe what a drunk tells you, because they lie. They lie better than anyone else. Listen, I really got to go, okay, one last thing. You make her happy, you understand? I owe her that much at least, to make sure she's happy. Cooking is her life. Her passion. When it comes sex, though, well, she's pretty fucked up in my opinion. Anyway, don't forget the Restaurant Association meeting next Wednesday. You're joining, aren't you? Dude, you've got to join."

The man who was once his arch-enemy was now inviting him to the elite club, and Brendan was as dazed as a man who had gone without sleep for forty-eight hours. He took Michael's hand, accepted the invitation, and returned the pleasant smile. Make Martie happy meant so many things, but coming from DeCecco, it might mean the one thing that Brendan was not so sure he could do. Not that he didn't want her sexually, but there was Bonnie, plus the stupidity of sleeping with an employee and the possibility of losing her skills in the kitchen when the affair ended.

And how might the affair end? With him being hauled away to serve time. If the police uncovered Brown or Gray, the entire pub would be ended, and Martie would suffer. There was one thing that he could do to make her happy, or at least make her more secure. He would have to make her a partner, set things up so that she had first rights to buy out his half if he ended up in jail. With no time to lose, he would have his lawyer draw up the papers, that night in fact.

The dishwasher banged shut as Eddie went about his routine, mechanical labor that made man and machine one unit. Overhead, La Virgen De Guadalupe watched over the crew, compassion for the hard-working immigrants in her soft, water-rippled eyes. As bins came in full and went out empty, Our Lady radiated protection over all who toiled to the blare of ranchero music. Eddie and his colleagues emptied each tub in exactly the same way, never wavering from a set program of sorting cutlery from crockery. In a way, Brendan envied the simple-minded rigidity, the structured tasks that had no room for variations that led to trouble. Here were three men who lived rich, full lives, carefree, simple, while the boss was being crushed by worry.

"You can't get through to serve the back tables," Josh was saying to Martie as he loaded up his tray.

"Can you believe it?" April said. "I've got a table from Baltimore. Drove all this way just to hear some Irish singer. And they're sleeping in their car tonight because they couldn't find a room."

"Your man from the Consular Office is here," Eilìs said. "Wanting to speak to himself, welcome him to America, but I don't know what to say to him."

"Hey, Brendan," Martie shouted over the deafening racket. "Got a job for you."

"What was that all about?" Brendan asked, gesturing towards the door that DeCecco had used a few minutes ago.

Her bright smile returned as Martie plated pork medallions and drizzled sauce over the meat. "He apologized. How about that. Ate some of his own shit."

143

"Apologized for what?"

"Tim, let's have that other tray of cod up here. Cut more chips. We're going to run out, I swear. Let's push the burgers in the bar."

"Martie," he pressed.

"Screwing me over," she said.

Reticence was a feature of the Irish, and Martie was proving her Irish roots. She was not going to explain further, that much was clear, at least not in front of her staff. All Brendan needed was a little bit more, enough to assure his heart that Martie was here to stay. "I'm offering you a partnership," he blurted out.

There was a definite sparkle in her eyes when she looked up and met his gaze, a suggestion of tears perhaps. Her response was pure business as usual, a plate deposited on the rack and a shout out to April.

"You're cool with it?" April asked.

"As long as you understand that if you two fall out, you're the one I'd let go. The manager is more important, less replaceable. Are you cool with that?"

"Why would I have to lose my job?" April asked.

"Because none of us could put up with the drama," the sous chef said, dancing a culinary two-step with Martie. "Shit, I'd throw the both of you out if it was up to me."

Fish and chips made an appearance on the rack and Eilìs was off, heading to the dining room while April returned to the bar. Given an opening, Brendan tried again.

"Full partner," he said.

"I'm not in half," she said. She pulled a slip of paper out of the clattering printer. Eddie's father Carl squeezed in next to Brendan, looking for the appetizers. "Fire eight. Two volailles. Service, please. Carl, table three."

"You're half," Brendan said. More than half, but more he could not give. She was the heart of the operation, while he was only the builder. Any other contractor could have put up the building, but if Martie had not turned up, he would not have a line of people out the front door and every seat taken.

She came around from the burners, unbuttoned her coat and fastened it again on the other side, covering up the splatters and stains. Without ceremony, she put plates into Brendan's hands, rested another on her forearm and picked up the fourth. "Come on. Let's go kiss some consular behind."

Martie paused at the door to the dining room, to touch a kiss to the holy card.

"What are you doing?" Brendan asked.

"Divine intervention," she said. "Saint Martha. Patron saint of cooks and housekeepers."

"You believe in that?"

"Am I a full partner in McKechnie's Pub?"

"Are you happy?"

"By the way, I talked to Ger. He understands the situation. He'll make a call before the night is over."

"You look happy."

She leaned over, dishes balanced on her left forearm, and planted a kiss on his cheek. "Why don't you invite the consul's table to the party tonight. They can talk to Paddy all they want, and he can give it to them with both barrels. Don't you just love politics?"

Holding the door open with his hip, he let Martie enter the room in triumph. They were family, more than partners. The way that Martie kissed him was the way that his sister kissed him, affection that was flavored with teasing. He missed his sister and the way that she could call his bluff when he ranted about some petty injustice or other. Through chance or his Irish luck, he had acquired Martie, a sort of stepsister who would be more loyal than a mere partner with only a financial interest. In the back of his mind, he sensed a fleeting wave of loss, as if he had almost had his hands on something that he wanted but it evaporated or drifted away like a cloud.

"Hey, Mackie," the voice boomed out in the subdued buzzing of dining chatter. Looking around, Brendan noticed a man waving, the finger snapping gesture of Sal Lardino forever frozen in his mind. Acknowledging his presence, Brendan gave an exaggerated nod and a shrug to show that he was on a delivery. A few facial gestures promised a visit as soon as humanly possible, and off he went, to speak to a real, live consular official, a humble servant of the Irish government who could do wonders for the restaurant if he recommended it as authentic, good value for money, and better than anything you'd find in Dublin. Maybe not better, but the consul would think so, even if political expediency forced him to hold his tongue.

It was fine for Martie to circulate, pausing at each table, chatting with her apron draped over her arms, hands in pockets. Brendan was going to make sure that Lardino had whatever he wanted, special attention or a free drink, in the off chance that the pub would need Lardino's particular talent. Always thinking ahead, Brendan was prepared for failure on Ger's end. It was possible that the Irish connections could not help, that no one knew anything about Brown and Gray. At risk of retribution from the gang who attempted to launder money through McKechnie's, Brendan would have to turn to someone for protection, and the local police were not an option.

Sal made introductions in a manner that was gracious while overblown in a melodramatic style. Greeting each guest in turn, Brendan saw old black-and-white snapshots come to life. Chunky blocks of women, columns of solid flesh without curves, handbags safely slung over forearms, and now he knew where such thick-waisted females came from. Mrs. Lardino, daughters Maria and Laura, and mother-in-law Mrs. DiStefano, could all have stepped out of the photographs decorating the wall of the local Italian eatery. Always a gentleman, Brendan smiled cordially and shook each woman's hand, noting the firm grip of the farm wife in every one. These four ladies alone could intimidate a man with nothing more than the heft of their arms and the tough look on every face. How Sal got past Mrs. DiStefano to court his spouse was a wonder, and he couldn't imagine what sort of man would have the guts to so much as think about dating Maria or Laura.

"How do they make the sugar like steam on the mousse?" Maria said.

"The pastry chef has some tricks up her sleeve," Brendan said. In truth, he didn't know how Peaches did it. "You wouldn't believe the flowers she made out of sugar."

"You got a party room, Martie told me," Sal said.

"Yes, yes, we do, but, um, it's, the singers tonight, they're old friends of mine," Brendan stammered. There was room for five more, if he had to court Sal even further. "It's set up now, for tonight, for after."

"Sal, I can make an appointment with Martie to see it," Mrs. Lardino said. "They're busy tonight with a party."

"You want to have a party here?" Brendan offered.

"Maria's engaged," Sal said, his chest puffing to the point of near explosion. "My sister's throwing a shower, and I want my girl to have the best. The best everything. That Broad Bridge Cafe over in Deerhaven is okay, you know, and there's not many places that do banquets around here."

"Well, if it's the best you want, you can't do better then McKechnie's," Brendan said.

"Daddy, can we have the mousse in the espresso cups for dessert?" Maria asked. "Annamarie'll die. She thought her petit fours were so classy."

"Showing up her cousin," Sal said with a laugh. Clearly, he would bend over backwards and twist into a pretzel to upstage his relations. The man lived for the big show. "So, my wife'll call and the girls can take care of things. Oh, say, the reason I called you over. Got a tip from a friend, and thought I'd pass it on. There's a story going around, about some counterfeit hundreds in circulation."

The smile on Brendan's face could not hold up, but he was able to recover just enough to arrange his features into a concerned frown. His heart pounded in his ears, nearly deafening, when he longed to hear every word with complete clarity. "Really? Around here?"

"Here and there," Sal lowered his voice slightly. "Good ones, too, from North Korea, or at least that's the story. Better tell your people to watch out for them, check the hundreds that come in."

From an engraved gold money clip, Sal extracted a hundred from a small stack of large bills. He held it up to Brendan's eyes, pointed out the security strip and then put the cash on the table. He elaborated a little more about the paper turning up in Port Clinton, supposedly, and it might have been passed up north, in the *melanzane* towns. A friend of a friend had heard that the Secret Service was on the trail, and the Secret Service had someone in mind who might have been seen at the airport a day or so ago. Every word was taken in, digested and absorbed into Brendan's brain. Sal had inside knowledge, he had connections, and he might be Brendan's last resort to save his bumbling hide. Or, the Secret Service would find Brown and Gray and that would be the end of their threat. Let them claim that they had been at McKechnie's. A respected contractor's word had more weight than that of an Irish gangster. Whatever option, there was a way out that did not end in a jail cell. Unless something had happened to Jim Gray in the abandoned garage.

Following Martie back to the kitchen, Brendan waited while she washed her hands and switched the front of her coat to the working, dirty side. She chatted with the cooks, telling them about the diplomat's party and the adjoining table that received a brief overview of Irish music and Paddy Dunne's place in the firmament. Brendan contributed his bit, accepting the openings that Martie created in the flow so that he was almost one of them, the important people who ran things. They discussed the idea of a table in the kitchen, reservation only, two sittings. and Martie had the crew in stitches with her observations about the hired help eating in the kitchen while the wealthy dined in quiet peace, among the attractive furnishings of the dining room. What a world, she said, where the rich wanted to live like the poor and pay extra for the privilege. As exciting as watching the assembly line at a Ford plant, she added, a comment that drew complete agreement from the cooks. Brendan laughed along with the rest. He could finally laugh, knowing that he had an exit strategy.

"Here, Brendan, in the bar, front of the stage," Martie said, pushing some plates around on the rack. "April, let Brendan give you a hand with this order."

Jaunty steps took him out of the kitchen, but progress came to a halt just past the door. Aidan was doing his best to confine the drinkers to the area close to the bar, to give the seated patrons enough room to bend an elbow and lift a fork without stabbing someone, but people wanted to see the stage. The Celtic Airs were filling the room with soft music, although they could barely be heard above the din. With Josh running interference and April close behind, they snaked their way to the tables in front of the stage, where a very jovial publican took two plates off the tray, turned to ask who had ordered the shepherd's pie, and came face to face with his family.

He had forgotten all about them, that they were coming, that they would sit up front, that they existed. Robert broke the tension by laughing at his kid brother who was striking a pretty ridiculous pose with two hot plates scorching his fingertips.

"What did I tell you," Bonnie said with a laugh. "Oblivious."

"I guess this one's yours," April said. She set the last dish in front of the empty chair, as if reminding Brendan that he was expected to sit there and eat like an ordinary diner.

Automatically, he glanced at Bonnie, to gauge her reaction while hoping that she didn't notice the way April winked at her addle-headed boss. A woman whose vision could best an eagle took note of the voluptuous bosom and accused him of infidelity through one glare from her narrowed eyes. Ignoring Bonnie, weary of her petty jealousies, Brendan gave his brother a manly nudge and a lecherous grin.

"You know, I'm getting to like this place," Robert said. To Bonnie's great annoyance, the brothers snickered as Robert admired the retreating figure in snug black trousers. Brendan made a point of tucking into the fish as if nothing more attractive could be found within the boundaries of the pub's four walls, while Taylor and Kelsey rolled their eyes and expressed their disgust. Robert's wife Didi slapped him upside the head.

"Did you notice, how she put all the plates down in a certain way?" Brendan said. It was a matter of catching Bonnie off-guard, to put her mind to a different task and escape further interrogation. "Always puts the protein right under the customer's nose. That's presentation. Pretty cool stuff that I never thought about. Very professional staff."

Taylor picked at the chicken breast as if she was afraid to be seen actually eating. With her fork, she scraped off some of the sauce, but put it back after tasting it. He wondered if her tongue detected calories with some internal sensor while normal people picked up on flavor and texture. As for Kelsey, the incoming high school freshman, she pretended to only nibble at the buttered bread while devouring every crumb, a rookie at the eating disorder game. She examined a spoonful of cold potage of summer vegetables, her arm like a scale that weighed portions to scientific precision, before gracefully sucking down the creamy puree. The girls' heads swiveled in unison, checking out the crowd, watching the Celtic Airs, and then turned back to the conversation.

"Wow, this is like, really good," Kelsey said. Didi winced, as if stung by the comparison to her own culinary achievements, which Brendan had tasted and then tried to avoid. Thanksgiving dinner was an annual trial.

All around the table, plates were shifted across and sideways with an admonishment to taste this, try that, it's heaven, it's fabulous. The evidence of everyone's enjoyment was gradually taking shape on plates growing empty, while Bonnie poked and prodded through the vegetables on her plate as if in search of a flaw to criticize. The victory was Martie's, an indisputable fact.

"You said Ryan Hartnett was going to play." Taylor pouted, her distress evident by the way she twirled a strand of hair. Her life would be ruined, apparently, if Ryan failed to show.

The head swiveling began anew, with Kelsey craning her neck to peer around a crowd that was too thick to see beyond the first layer. "I don't even think he's here," she said, challenging her uncle to prove her wrong.

The Celtic Airs concluded a slip jig with a strong flourish, garnering a loud rumble of applause and cheers. "And now, without further ado," Kevin said, and the noise rose twenty decibels.

Detecting movement, Brendan turned his head towards the lobby, where the crowd seemed to be parting. The police chief, with two other uniformed officers on either side, was working his way through, creating an aisle, and coming straight towards Brendan. He wanted to stand, but he could not. He wanted to swallow, but the beer was stuck in his throat. His wrists began to ache; he looked for a sweater or jacket to throw over his hands after the cuffs were on, to hide the shackles from the public eye. How could Chuck be so vicious as to arrest him here, in front of his family and friends? Steadily, step by step, the three policemen came on, the people surging around in their wake. So many witnesses to his humiliation, Brendan knew almost every one, but Paddy was safely hidden in the office, well away from the degrading scene that was about to unfold. What small mercies could be found, Brendan searched for every one.

His eyes locked onto the holstered guns, dark and heavy pistols that bulged with menace and a threat of death to those who did not cooperate. He saw Chuck's hand move, aimed at his head, ready to grab him by the collar and lift him to his feet. The chief put a hand on Brendan's shoulder, a gentle touch when he expected a strong grip. The wedge opened, and Paddy, Liam and Rory pushed ahead, taking the stage amidst a deafening roar. With his legs shaking, Brendan sat in stunned silence, while Chuck patted his back. "You need a little security when you've got a star playing," the chief said, shouting into Brendan's ear.

Air sucked into Brendan's lungs and took the beer along. He began to choke, fumbling with his napkin so that he did not spew over the table, while Chuck slapped him hard between the shoulder blades. Overwhelmed by adrenalin, Brendan could do little more than smile foolishly and nod. He reached for his glass and swallowed in an attempt to clear his airway.

"Are you getting up to make an introduction, Brendan?" Paddy said. "I think they all know that we're here. Go back to your dinner."

His throat now raw, Brendan squeezed around the table and reached up for the nearest microphone. Smiling with mischief, Paddy called for quiet, so that all could hear the words of wisdom that Brendan McKechnie was about to impart. Every time Brendan started to say something, Paddy cut in, making jokes, while the band tuned their instruments. "I'd like to thank everyone who came from near and far," Brendan said. A bead of sweat tickled his scalp.

"That's a weak welcome," Paddy said. Bellowing, he shouted, "You're very welcome from Boston and New York. And you're very welcome from Ireland."

The opening number was a traditional ballad, with Liam on mandolin and Rory on tin whistle, a fast paced tune that was greeted with wild cheering. Satisfied that everyone appeared happy, Brendan took his seat, but he could not shake the feeling that Chuck and the other two policemen were keeping an eye on him. Chuck was positioned near the patio door, where he maintained a clear access corridor for reasons known only to him. The other cops stood near the stage, right hand on holster and left hand on flashlight, a standard police pose of vigilance, but what were they on guard against? Trying to be subtle, Brendan pretended to scan the crowd as he imagined an impresario would, and he was certain that Officer Roehmer was parked near the bar. Fearing that time was running out, he slipped slowly through the throng around the bar, heading for the kitchen.

NINETEEN

Her head was focused on timing, the orders coming in and going out, the cooking and serving, everything precise. Little nagging thoughts crept in, some whiny voice that asked why Denny had turned up after so many years, hell-bent on destroying her. What was the point, if not to bring her down because he resented her accomplishments. That was how it was with Denny, as Michael DeCecco confirmed earlier. There was something about Denny that garnered sympathy, especially among those who know what sort of dysfunctional family he came from. People did things for him out of charity but in time he always repaid the favors with cruelty.

It was Denny who assured DeCecco that Martie was retiring from the kitchen to teach cooking, a lie that had the slightest basis in truth. At some time or other, Martie probably had mentioned an interest in teaching when she was too old to meet the demands of a professional kitchen. With Denny, a fact could be distorted into a fabrication that served his purpose, and it had served his purpose to sabotage her career. She had recovered, only to sabotage it herself by hiding a crime. What was done was done, and now she had to do a little digging to find out what the police knew. There were no guarantees that Ger would make a call.

Martie scanned the rack of orders and tried to mentally calculate a short break in the action, but once again she would miss the music. Any successful career required trade-offs, and entertainment was her sacrifice. The restaurant was more important than listening to a few tunes, and in truth, she did not want to hear Denny. He had captivated her with his talent all those years ago, when she was working her first job at DeCecco's brand new Italian eatery. Fifteen years old, terrified by her attraction to other women, and vulnerable to a man who offered her the opportunity to prove to her parents that she could be straight if she tried really hard. The world was a better place with Ryan in it, she thought. It was not all bad. But that did not change her disgust with all things Denny.

Food opened many doors, and so Martie personally delivered her signature McKechnie burgers to the security detail that was killing time in the staff locker room. She knew Cliff from the day shift of the Moraine Hills police department, but it was Doug who would have the information that she wanted. A policeman in Gilead, he moonlighted as a rent-a-cop, and she sincerely hoped that she could lull him into a stupor with meat and then grill him for information.

"Say, Cliff, can I ask you something?" she began, pulling up a chair. "If there was something going on in town, like some con artists trying to pull a fast one, or someone passing bad checks, would you tell us, or would it be confidential?"

Balancing the plate on his knee, Cliff sliced the sandwich in half while he listened and thought. "Well, if it didn't interfere with operations, sure, I'd let you know."

"Getting the word out can be good for us," Doug said. "Jesus God, this is the best fuckin' burger I've ever eaten. What was I saying? Yeah, crimes. It's worse for the citizens if they don't know. Say for instance, you're spending counterfeit cash. Now, if the store owners are made aware, they look for it, and they can help I.D. the perp."

"You get much of that?" she asked.

Cliff snickered as he dipped a french fry into a ramekin of catsup. "They got another kind of justice up in Gilead, huh, Doug?"

"Very funny, smartass. Don't tell me that one of your Outfit boys wouldn't do the same to someone who tried to pass bad currency on them," Doug said. "How stupid can you be, to buy rocks with phony bills?"

Alarmed, upset, and sorry that she had agreed to Peaches' idea, Martie hurried back to the burners where she belonged, the only place on earth where she was confident that she was doing the right thing and doing it well. She concentrated on the orders that came up, put her mind to directing the staff, but she could not erase the image that Doug had created in her mind. Granted, what the Irish gangster had done was wrong and he deserved to be dumped in an alley, but beyond that, she couldn't justify further punishment. All she had wanted to do was dispose of some bad publicity, get rid of a pile of garbage in pastels. She could see that things could get worse, especially if the police made an attempt to retrace the man's steps. And what of his partner; she suddenly recalled that Brendan had seen the guy with another man who might even now be lurking in the crowd, hiding behind the dumpster and ready to leap out and kill someone in revenge.

"Yo, Chef, I'll handle the line if you want to work the front," Jay said.

Martie looked up from the pan she was shaking and wondered how long she had been standing there. A few minutes ago, she had been over the moon because the house was at capacity and running smoothly. Now she could think of nothing but drive-by shootings and random violence. And what about the retribution she feared? Every one of her employees could be in danger for all she knew. That was it. Ger was making that call, immediately, whether he liked it or not.

The chef's coat was unbuttoned and then re-buttoned, clean side out. Before Martie's hand touched the kitchen door, Brendan flew in, looking very pale. "I think they're on to us," he said, modulating his voice to be heard over the fans.

Martie's heart began to race. "Did you see them?" she asked.

"Four of them," he said. "Look, if it all comes down, I've got my lawyer drawing up the documents for the partnership."

"Wait a minute," she said. "How do you know there's more than the two you met?"

"The cops," Brendan said, his voice cracking with nerves.

As if they were responding to a call, Cliff and Doug stepped out from the dishwasher's station and casually strolled towards Peaches. Brendan was mesmerized by the men in navy blue, so much so that Martie could not get his attention. Orders were still spilling out of the printer and Jay looked a little overwhelmed. With no time to shake Brendan out of his stupor, she hurried back to the line and assigned the entrees and appetizers. More information. She needed more information, and she would pry it out of the policemen with sweets. As if he were chained to her, Brendan followed on her heels.

"There's champagne in that," Martie warned as Doug salivated over the mint-sprigged glass bowl of macerated fruit. "No alcohol on duty, right?"

"Miss Baker here tells me there's nothing that doesn't have alcohol in it," Cliff said.

"Well, consider where you're at," Martie said.

After a bit of a chuckle, Martie took hold of the conversation and directed it back north, to Gilead, pretending to be concerned over Peaches' welfare and suggesting that the pastry chef should relocate, to get away from the drug and crime infested neighborhood. Between bites of bread pudding without the whiskey sauce, Doug put his knowledge of crime statistics on display, breaking down the town block by block, while Martie listened carefully for the first mention of one particular street. Given an opening, she pounced, and through clever phrases and guile she concluded that her nemesis had not been spotted, arrested, or otherwise turned up where he had been left. With equal deft, she took the discussion to another tangent, covering her tracks in the event that the Ulsterman re-appeared.

No names or descriptions were mentioned, but she managed to tease out the story of the unfortunate drug addict who was beaten to a pulp for buying crack with bad money. When Quemont dropped the counterfeit bills around, no one had thought that the person who happened to find one would suffer such a fate as to end up in the hospital. Martie's anger mushroomed, with all the blame for a junkie's beating falling on the thug's head. If it would not be so costly to her personally, she would turn to Sal Lardino and his connections to extract retribution from the Ulster criminal, payback for his dirty tricks.

Peaches performed admirably, plating apple tarts and dusting them with powdered sugar while flirting with Cliff. She was inviting him to her church before long, taking the thread of the discussion as far from criminals and beatings as it could get. There was nothing more to be gained by wasting time in chatter. Martie returned to her spot, while Brendan walked two steps behind her. Clearly, he wanted to say something, or ask for a direction to turn.

"I've been thinking," Martie said. She wiped the edges of six plates, one by one, set them on the rack, and called out that the order was up. "They know we're on to them. Why would they come back here?"

"Because they're stupid?" Brendan said.

"No, Brendan, they're not that dumb. I think they've been pushed to the brink to unload the goods. They're in strange territory, without their network."

"How do you know they don't have connections?" Brendan picked up a fan of carrots and nibbled, nervous and unthinking. "How did Sal know that there's, uh, goods, around?"

"He told you that?" Martie asked.

"Do you think our Irish friends might like to play cards? A little private game with friends of Mr. Lardino?"

"Christ, they'd get killed. No, no, that's not right to do that."

"No?" Brendan asked, not so much a question as a statement.

"What I mean, Brendan, is that Sal knows about things because he protects his business interests. He did you a favor to warn you, and you're going to give him a big fat discount on his daughter's bridal shower in return," Martie said. "That's how he does things. Not just him, either, most of the businessmen who eat here would do the same."

Turning over control to Jay, Martie went to turn her coat, only to realize she had done it already and there was no clean side anymore. She steered Brendan to the door. "The more I think about it, the more I'm convinced that those two wouldn't come back to cause more trouble. Criminals like that, they work in packs. You know, safety in numbers."

"I don't know. Maybe," Brendan said. "A pub full of Irish-Catholic immigrants isn't exactly friendly territory."

"All I want is to see them put away where they can't hurt us," Martie said. "There is no way Ger is not making a call, or a hundred calls if he needs to. Some poor junkie is in the hospital because of that Ulster asshole and I'll be damned if I'll let that slide."

Scanning the crowd in the bar, aware that it was impossible to pass through, Martie sighed with relief. She had pulled off a miracle. The kitchen was humming, the staff was on top of it, and she was at the peak of her career. Until Denny opened his mouth, she would have had all this at DeCecco's new bistro, with Michael practically handing the place over to her to run without his interference. She smiled with the gratification that came from getting Michael to grovel, to admit that he needed her far more than she needed him. What a glorious day it had been, to hear Michael admit to making a huge mistake in not talking to her about the option to buy into his planned restaurant, instead of relying on the inebriated ramblings of an old friend who was not to be trusted. She bought into McKechnie's instead, and would shine with her own light rather than reflect the dazzle of Michael DeCecco.

Hearing that Denny had sabotaged her efforts to advance in DeCecco's empire had absolutely put an end to any further attempts to be civil, forever into infinity, and from here on in, she was moving along, cutting Denny out of her life like he didn't exist. Serenity to accept the things that she could not change, that was her achievement for the day. She wished that she could share her triumph with Manon, but she understood the demands of the industry. The time for sharing was always after everyone else had gone home, bellies full and palates tingling.

People pounded on tables, stomped their feet, and raised enough racket to lift the roof off its beams. They had come to hear Shift/Move, but what they were getting was a very personal performance, not unlike the casual groupings that sprung up in pubs when local people turned up with whatever instrument they played, sat together, and made music. If all these people could have crowded into Paddy's living room on a Saturday night, they would have heard the songs in the same way, just a group of talented musicians who were hanging out, jamming, trading licks. That was as much as she could savor of the evening. There was still a line waiting to eat in the dining room, and orders were coming in without respite.

"Thank you very much," Paddy said. He paused, waiting for the noise to ease up. "We'll be starting up the jukebox later tonight. Right now, we're doing our dedications, so keep your requests to yourself. A melody from the great Phil Cunningham, which I admit is a request but when it's the gardai asking you don't ask questions."

From the first notes of the pipes, Martie recognized one of her favorite tunes, a waltz that Denny once played for her. Kevin touched his bow to the strings of the fiddle and *Miss Rowan Davies* began to blossom, the sound growing more complex and full as Paddy added a guitar. She could feel it within her, the reeds of the uilleann pipes vibrating haunting notes and the mandolin adding a tone of distant admiration. At the door to the patio, the police chief spun his wife in a small circle, using the space that he had kept open for safety reasons as his personal dance floor. Years of hard work, struggle and frustration drifted away from Martie as she shut her eyes and lived in the most perfect of moments.

Just as the song ended and the last notes of the pipes faded, Paddy jumped into another classic, *The Raggle-Taggle Gypsy*, and the set was off and running at high speed. The new song broke through reveries and Martie turned to go, pausing just long enough to catch Ger's eye. He twitched, an indication of the pressure he was under. It was the middle of the night in Strabane, an outrageous hour to make a phone call, and Martie didn't truly expect Ger to call immediately. She only wanted to reinforce the urgency, to prompt the man to ring his contacts at first light and see what could be done to help the despised police service in the north of Ireland locate a couple of wanted men.

The music from the bar was piped into the kitchen, but the usual racket of a restaurant blotted out any pleasant sounds. A call went out to eighty-six the sea bass, with another hour to go before the dining room was scheduled to close. Martie had to monitor the prep station, where two line cooks were garnishing trays of salmon appetizers with caviar in a style that resembled an assembly line manned by robotic arms. She made a swing through the dining room, offering a silent prayer of thanks to St. Martha for favors granted, and attempted to thread her way through the packed foyer to look in on Aidan. Just outside the front door, a police car sat parked in one of the valet spots, the inside lights on. A man was sitting in the back seat, arms in a position that implied handcuffs and arrest.

"Aidan," Martie called out. "Aidan, what's up? How's it going?"

"Grand, grand," the young man said. His smile forced his eyes to disappear behind narrow slits, as if his cheeks were too large to contain his happiness. He had April on the brain.

"I meant out there, the cops."

"Not happy that he couldn't get in," Aidan said. "The police have been brilliant. Very discreet altogether."

Not knowing what the second Ulsterman looked like, Martie saw no point in going out to gawk, and draw even more negative attention. As it was, she could tell easily that there was a line out the door, all people patiently waiting for a table to open up in the dining room. Turnover was slow, with the seats taken up by those who settled for the better-than-nothing that was the dining room, out of sight of the stage but within the boundaries of the sound system. The more determined fans had staked out standing room in front of the windows, where they could watch the performance on the outside and listen to the less than perfect acoustics of the front sidewalk, where the sound of cars drowned out the softer notes.

"I've got an idea," Martie said. Good public relations was as much a part of her business as sautéing and slicing. "Let's get some baskets of chips out here, pass them around. Those folks aren't going to get in before we shut down. Take Brendan with you. Maybe he knows that guy in the squad car. Have him get a good luck, just in case."

A very disgruntled proprietor popped into the kitchen, grumbling about having to make happy faces at customers at the worst possible times. Ignoring the rant, Martie slapped a paper cone of hot chips into Brendan's hand. "Here, take these out there and check that man in the squad car," Martie said, pushing Brendan through the door before the police left for the local jail.

"You think it's one of them?" Brendan said, his eyes growing wide with fear.

"I don't know the other one, the one with his skull intact," Martie said. "Go, go, go."

Credit Brendan with being subtle, but he couldn't determine who was in the car before it pulled away, no lights flashing to draw attention to a fracas at McKechnie's. He swore that he exuded good cheer while strolling through the mob, dispensing a taste of traditional cooking to entice potential new diners. Talked away, and managed to sneak a few peeks over his shoulder at the same time, until the patrol car made a U-turn in the middle of the street. Just then, Martie's heart began to beat a little faster. What if the police searched the man's pockets and found wads of bills, counterfeit and stolen? That would lead to questions, and questions brought answers, and answers would mean an investigation and a detective spraying Luminal around the basement stairs. The chief of Moraine Hills police department was dancing with his wife in the restaurant, and they were all safe, as long as Chuck didn't believe the word of a foreigner. Unfortunately, like so many other things in this world, there were no guarantees.

"No luck, I couldn't get a good look at him," Brendan said. "Ger's going to make some calls, that's it. I can't keep going like this. I'm getting an ulcer."

"Have faith, Brendan," Martie said.

On stage, Paddy fielded a request from a fellow Irishman. Martie looked at her watch, shocked to discover that the group had been playing for the past three hours without taking a break. The after party would be getting under way shortly, and she didn't know where the kitchen stood with preparations, if they were on time or running behind. Given the placement of the stage and the distance to the stairs, it would be impossible for the guys to leave and come back for an encore. Even now, Paddy was sounding like the end of the evening, his voice growing hoarse as he thanked everyone for coming, winding up what he called Shift/Move's whirlwind tour of the Midwest.

"You better get up there," she nodded towards the stage. "Get Chuck; the security detail."

The audience stomped and whistled, cheered and called out for more. Paddy protested, saying it was time for him to go home, the family was missing him. As if in response, Liam plucked out the opening notes of another song, the slide on his left hand making the metal strings of the guitar whine. This would be the last song, a lament for all the Irish who had left home and gone elsewhere to find a job, and had sent everything back home to support the family while they were trapped, unable to afford the trip back home for a visit. It was a mournful tune, filled with the loneliness of the emigrant, the missing of loved ones.

"Paul's got the partnership agreement," Brendan said. This was hardly the time to discuss their personal business, with all that had to be done before the night was over, but Martie was getting used to Brendan's unexpected pronouncements. "Don't leave without signing it. We've got to get things settled before it's too late."

"Yeah, okay, later though, not now. What about Bonnie? Listen, is there going to be a problem with this partnership?"

"Martie, the only problem with Bonnie is that she thinks any partnership between a man and a woman is a sexual one." Brendan sighed his weary, exasperated, highly put upon sigh. "Can I ask you a personal question? Is there anything between you and Paddy?"

"Hurry up, get out there and keep control on the situation," Martie said. She gave Brendan's arm a hug and hurried off to the dining room. Deny, deny, deny. Amen.

TWENTY

They were a good natured group, even if they didn't believe that Shift/Move had left the stage for the last time and were not coming back. If someone needed proof, they had only to look at Louis, who had turned off the small lamp over his sound board and begun to unplug and coil wires. Brendan could think of nothing else to say, short of thanking everyone for coming and asking that they remember their servers. The bar was open until two, all were welcome to stay and enjoy the pub, and please come back again. That was it, the end of the grand opening that Brendan had dreaded back in the dark ages, when his dreams were falling apart before Martie saved him. Now he had to keep Paddy and Martie as far apart as possible until Aer Lingus put an ocean between them.

Aidan was doing an outstanding job at the foot of the stairs, checking names against a master list that had been amended several times. The private party was not publicized, but who couldn't notice that some people were going up the same stairs that Paddy had ascended? A uniformed policeman stood next to Aidan, arms crossed over his chest, eyes hard, the embodiment of no trespassing.

"Great show," Cliff said, extending a hand to Brendan.

"Thanks. Say, that guy that got arrested," Brendan said. "Was he causing trouble outside?"

161

"Someone got arrested? Here?"

"Well, maybe, I don't know. I thought he was."

"Brendan, come on, everyone's waiting for you," Bonnie called down from the top of the stairs. "Can you stop talking and get moving?"

He certainly could not come out and ask if the man in the back of the squad car was named Graham Brown, and did he have a roll of stolen Northern Ireland Bank notes in his pocket. As much in the dark as he had been since Thursday, Brendan scrambled up to the banquet room, where Paddy was waiting at the door, to announce a grand entrance and start up a wild round of applause.

The centerpiece of the buffet table was decorated to perfection, to the point where Bonnie heaped praise on Martie's eye for detail. Her ebullience was a sign that she was in a good mood, relishing her role as hostess of something that was important within her circle. As if she were royalty at a garden party, she worked the room with Brendan in tow, pausing to say a few words to the guests before moving to the next in line. It was a relief when Paddy pulled him over to meet the Irish consular official's party, giving Brendan an opportunity to scan the banquet room in search of his attorney. He was not going to enjoy this party at all until business was taken care of and Martie's position was made secure and legal.

"Paul, did you get the papers drawn up?" Brendan asked, pulling at the lawyer's arm to bring him closer. He hated conducting this in public, but time might run out and Martie could be out on the street.

"Left the file in your office, " Paul said. "Connie dropped it off. Say, what's the rush? Why couldn't you come by on Monday?"

With the grace of a dancer, Brendan performed a mental pirouette. "Hey, can you pick a better time for my announcement?"

"Oh, oh, sure," Paul said. "Always the showman. You could be that Paddy guy's twin."

"If you ever heard me sing, you'd never say that," Brendan said.

There truly was no better time than here and now to tell the world that Brendan McKechnie was going into partnership with Martie Smurfit, a merger of construction mogul and culinary queen. A match made in heaven, the trade papers might call it, a brilliant union of two titans with complimentary skills. All that was needed was Martie's signature and Brendan could rest easy, to focus his thoughts on the thugs who could come back to kill him before the night was over.

In spite of the show's conclusion over thirty minutes ago, the bar was still full, as if the patrons expected Paddy and the lads to change their minds. There had been a time when Paddy would have joined his fans at the bar, a company of drunkards who held greater appeal than Aislinn waiting at home. With Paddy off the drink, Brendan saw the barflies in a different light, a harsh glare that stripped away the patina of bonhomie and harmless fun that was, in reality, nothing more than an alcoholic's disguise.

The dining room was dimly lit, closed for the night. The fishing floats on the mantle reflected their colors onto the wall and ceiling, a tricolor rainbow that suggested the serenity of the water's edge at Spanish Point. Come winter, a turf fire would burn on the hearth, but he had no assurances that he would be sitting in one of the armchairs, relaxing at the end of a hectic Saturday night. Martie on the right, Brendan on the left, with a pot of tea on the table between them; he could envision such a scene if he closed his eyes and prayed that it came to pass. In Miltown, Father McIlhennie had an unspoken reservation for the left hand chair, and Dermot McKechnie loved nothing more than beating the priest to the seat, with Uncle Donal to the right and a bottle of top shelf whiskey on the table between them.

"Is the party that boring?" Martie said, startling him.

She stood waiting, her chef's coat unbuttoned with neither side clean.

"Need you to sign something," he said. "If it all comes down tonight, I want you covered."

"What's coming down?" she asked.

"For God's sake, Martie. Obstruction of justice, battery, attempted murder. Pick one."

"Will you stop," she said.

"I'll stop when those two are put away, or," he paused. "Or dead."

"Jesus Christ," Martie hissed. "Will you listen to yourself?"

"Are you listening? Pretend everything's fine, go on, and come visit me in Stateville."

She pulled off her jacket, stripped the scarf from her head and shook out her hair. "You're friggin' nuts."

"How am I nuts? Explain it to me. I'd love to be enlightened."

"Here's how, genius boy. The cops are on our side, okay? We didn't do anything wrong."

"Nothing wrong?" He was getting so enraged that he was struggling to keep from screaming. "We had a man fall down the stairs, and we took him, not to a hospital, but we dumped him in some alley."

"So? Didn't he deserve it?"

"That's not the point." Somehow, he wanted to make her understand, but they were not connecting, as if they spoke different languages.

"Okay, here's the point," she said. "The idiot that the cops hauled off tonight? Not the first time he's spent a night in jail."

"Why didn't you tell me before?" He was going to make her his partner, yet she was not treating him as a partner, sharing any and all information. Her secrecy had been a problem from the beginning and it could be the problem that would doom their arrangement. "God damn it, Martie, I'm sweating blood here, worrying about one of them coming back here, and you keep your mouth shut?"

"Hey, I'm a little busy back there. While you're sitting on your fat ass, having a fine old time, I'm in the kitchen busting my butt to run this place. You want to come talk to me about something, come on in. The door swings both ways, Brendan."

"What the fuck do you think I'm doing up front? Think that's easy, kissing ass for four hours straight? Looking over my shoulder every minute?"

Martie was on her way back to the kitchen before he could finish the sentence, as if she was choosing to ignore him, just like Bonnie did. "God damn it," he repeated, pounding his fist against the fireplace.

"Brendan," she said from across the room. "You don't have a fat ass. You have a very nice ass."

Disarmed, he was rendered speechless by a brief, utterly charming and extremely suggestive comment. He felt that she handled stress in a different way than he did, not obsessing over the details, but perhaps compartmentalizing issues so that she could manage the chaos of the kitchen without interference from the thug conundrum. Then again, what she said had a ring of truth to it; she was handling more than her fair share, and he had no right to dump more on her without taking a hefty portion of the responsibilities. "If you want a piece, you're welcome to it," he blurted out.

"Save it for Bonnie," she said, laughing.

"You coming up?" he said to the closing door. Staring at the empty space that Martie left behind, he sighed. "That went well."

He slumped into the chair on the left of the fireplace, deflated. How did she manage to blow hot and cold, and trick him once again into blabbering out his deeply hidden desire? Now he had done it, come right out and said something that made his lust completely obvious. As soon as she pushed through the door, he leapt to his feet, drowning in discomfort and awkward embarrassment.

"Stop in the office," he mumbled. Somehow he had to find his footing once again, to resume dealing with a business partner, rather than thinking of her in terms of sex and what exactly did she do with Paddy on the sofa.

"What a night," she said.

The door to the office was cracked open and Brendan barged in, the owner who had right of access, no matter what the tacked-up star claimed. Bonnie was busy stuffing clothes into a canvas sack, picking up discarded and sweat-damp shirts for the laundry. She planned to wash the clothes so the group wouldn't have to lug mildew-sprouting cotton across the ocean. "Not that I'm doing a favor," she said. "It's the wives who appreciate it. The ones who have to unpack."

Martie lifted a soiled T-shirt from the desk, using her thumb and forefinger to ferry the garment into the bag. She took a seat and rifled through the stacks of sheet music, searching for the partnership agreement. With gravity, she opened the large envelope and extracted the pages, tapping the forms on the desk until each page was neatly aligned. Squirming in the chair as if it were covered with burrs, she took her time in reading over what she undoubtedly could not understand. Paul was a champion at writing in the most obscure legalese imaginable.

"You know, I don't have a lawyer to check this over for me," Martie said, turning to page two. "Can I trust you?"

"I wouldn't," Bonnie said. Her smile reminded him of their first year together, a mix of teasing and lust. She hadn't smile at him like that for a long, long time.

"A vote of no confidence," Martie declared.

"This is the same man who swore we would see whatever musical I liked, but have we been to the theatre yet this year?" Bonnie said.

The third page of the partnership agreement became a fan as Martie sat at the desk, waving the sheet. Eyebrow raised, she put the paper down and turned to the side, where she propped up an iPad. A touch here and a slide there and she opened a page. "Sunday matinee? Tuesday night? Plenty of good seats available," she said.

"I don't know if I can get away," he said. "This place doesn't run itself."

"Tuesday night," Martie said, her finger touching the screen in places that demanded commitment. "Perfect, this place will be a ghost town. Put you down for, how many seats, Bonnie? I'm sure you could find another couple or two who would enjoy this one."

His earlier sexual innuendo hung in the air, resting between them with the oil-painted visage of the late Dermot McKechnie looking down, observing. The woman he thought was his partner was working for the opposition, as if Bonnie had gained yet another ally in her quest to rein in Brendan. Why had Martie abandoned him when he was giving her half the business? Had Bonnie gotten to her, turned her like a double agent? There was some kind of power struggle going on, and if he did not find a way to wiggle out, Martie could take over the whole place and he would be the one out on the street, as welcome as any other paying customer and with the same level of input.

"Six?" Martie said. "Nothing available in the center. How about right center?"

From the minute that she walked in the door, Martie had taken control and he had let her run free. In the kitchen, she would call the shots; he was willing to concede that aspect of their joint venture, but he could not allow her to insert her nose into his private affairs. Bad enough that he had to deal with Bonnie's demands. She didn't need another foot soldier, but he sure did, and he would find a way to drag Martie back into his camp, one hundred percent behind him.

In the blink of Martie's pretty blue eye, Brendan was scheduled for a Tuesday night in the city. He did not understand how she did it, how she made him utterly powerless. She didn't seem like a force to be reckoned with, not a woman whose smile wrapped around him like a tender embrace. Before he could protest or insert his studied reasons to decline the tickets, Martie was up and out of the door, moving on to the next item on her agenda.

"This is the best night of my life," Taylor rushed in, gushing with the overblown emotion of a teen girl. "Ryan actually talked to me."

"What did he do before, run the other way when he saw you coming?" He checked the partnership agreement, just to be sure that it was signed. They were united at last, legally bound, and it would be a little easier for him to wrest control from an overbearing chef. With a trick or two of his own to use, he felt confident as he inserted the document into the envelope.

"It's like he didn't even know that I existed," Taylor said. "He didn't know, actually. We never had classes together or anything."

"Martie is a sweetheart," Bonnie said.

He scrunched down the laundry bag and tugged the drawstring. "Not always," he said.

"She just paid for our tickets," Bonnie said. "I suppose you don't want to go after all."

Reverse, his brain screamed, reverse, reverse. The glow was fading; Bonnie was turning on him and her influence over Martie could spell disaster. On the one hand, if he and Martie ever became more than business associates, it would be a good thing if Bonnie eased herself out of his life. He was insane to think of such things, to chuck what he had for another woman with a penchant for folk singers. The stress of the past week was warping his mind. "You haven't seen her in the kitchen, screaming at the cooks," he said, deftly maneuvering around a potential pitfall. "In general, yes, she's very nice and she looks out for people."

He dropped the bag next to the door, hoping not to forget it later when it was time to go home. Bonnie stood there, waiting for him to either follow or lead. Like a true gentleman, he offered his arm and she slipped her hand in the crook of his elbow. He was one of Martie's causes, a man playing house, in danger of losing someone who meant the world to him, a man who put work first because it was easier than making a firm commitment and getting married and making babies and having sex with only Bonnie for the rest of his life. Martie was looking out for him, as much as she was looking out for homeless and battered women and wounded veterans. "I'm lucky she's working with me," he said. It was up to him to look out for Martie, to prevent her from running away to Miltown with Paddy.

"We should go to Ireland this summer," Bonnie said. "And you should be supportive of Paddy, to help him stay sober."

A waiter passed by with a tray of champagne. Brendan picked up two glasses and gave one to Bonnie before offering up a toast to the future. Sipping from the flute, she chatted about musical comedies and Tony awards without pausing for breath. Brendan could not recall the last time that he had actually stopped whatever he was doing and listened to her. When had he last given her time to say what she had to say? Clearly, it was not such a great sacrifice to give up a Tuesday evening, to sit in an uncomfortable seat and try not to fall asleep. Martie was right, he could get away from time to time. As for Friday or Saturday, he was sure that she would put her foot down about abandoning her on the busiest nights. He was starting to get the hang of this restaurant business.

"Just one glass is enough," Bonnie said, reading Brendan's face. "I can't believe this. Everything's so perfect."

"The pub's up and running, I've got an incredible team to manage it," he said. "Tuesdays will be quiet around here. No reason not to get away a little."

"The Midlife Crisis Bar and Grill," Bonnie said. "I hope you don't have a resurgence when you reach the doddering old age of forty."

"This," he said, waving his arm to indicate the scope of his dream, "is not a midlife crisis. It's an investment. Jesus Christ, if I built an office complex and didn't sell it you'd say the same thing. Where do you think the money comes from for the house and the cars?"

"I know where money comes from," she said. "And I know where stress-induced heart attacks come from. So what good is the money when you're dead? Take time to smell the roses that you're always planting."

He could not argue with the truth in her observation, nor would he try. Her concern for his health shook something loose in his mind, an old memory of a little boy wishing his father would come watch him play soccer just once. Work always stood in the way. "Once a week, at least," he said. "We'll smell all the roses you like."

Putting pressure on Ger, Martie stood next to the service bar at the back of the banquet room, making idle conversation with Chuck. The summer carnival preparations were foremost on the police chief's mind, with constant mention of MEG officers and gangs crime units bringing a bead of sweat to Ger's temple. The bartender opened a bottle of champagne, but he never stopped listening, and that was exactly what Martie wanted. After a few more minutes of Chuck's diatribe on drug pushers attempting to set up shop near the local high school, Martie took advantage of a passing guest to hand Chuck over to Brendan's attorney, to discuss prosecution and judges until the sun rose again.

"Ger," she said softly. "What if someone called the Ombudsman's office up there in Belfast? From a public phone? Just to mention that some stolen money was seen in Chicago?"

"Not the police?" he said.

"What police?" she said. "Catholics can't go to the police in the north of Ireland. But someone could pass a tip to the Ombudsman's office, now, couldn't they?"

"That's been done, I've heard." There was a very clear sigh of relief that punctuated his statement. She waited for him to swallow the bait. "And after the call's made, when your man with the phone's been found dead in the laneway, the guards can't find anyone who saw or heard a thing."

"Listen, Ger, I'm definitely not asking you to make a call like that. There's ways to get justice that don't involve guns. See, you know that there's a couple of criminals in Chicago, and if someone else knew who could let the police here know, then maybe they'll get picked up and that's it. Jail or whatever, but your hands are clean and you haven't broken a vow."

"I'd prefer the other solution," Ger said. The champagne cork popped loudly, making Martie jump. The bartender smiled and winked at her.

"So who did you promise to go straight? Who made you swear to give up violence?"

"Ah, sure and you know yourself," he said. "What man wouldn't do whatever for his girl?"

"Girls come and go," Martie said. "When you break up with this one, does that negate the vow?"

"Nothing of the sort," he said. "She's my life partner, and I'm planning to bring her here as soon as I can."

"Living in sin? Gerald O'Hare, shame on you," she said.

"Living in sin? Jesus, I'm living with my cousin and his brood. There's no sin there, I promise you." Without spilling a drop, he filled the empty champagne glasses on the tray. "But once we're settled, there'll be more than enough sin for anyone's liking."

Asking Ger to help the Northern Ireland police service was akin to asking him to commit treason, but suggesting a back door option, and assuring him that no one was asking him to put his neck in the noose, worked wonders. So ingrained was his distrust of the police that he never once thought to give them the information that would lead to a couple of gangsters. One call to a friend overseas and he would keep McKechnie's far off the radar in case of an investigation. In part, the problem was solved. The final solution rested on the ability of some anonymous tipster in the north of Ireland making clear to the authorities what had to be kept obscure. Maybe her troubles were over. Maybe they weren't. She went back to the kitchen to inspect and then mounted the back stairs to the party.

Paddy was certainly the king of the evening, surrounded by admirers. Martie hesitated to enter the room, afraid that Denny would appear and make a scene. A step into the room and she thought better of joining the party. She had managed to avoid Paddy and last year's Willie Week fiasco. A few more hours and she would be clear of it, to put her mind to preparing for a fateful meeting. The Hartnett family that had adopted Ryan had accepted her invitation and there was no going back.

After discussing scenarios with Manon, she had come up with a way to put some distance between the reunion and Moraine Hills, in the event that things went very badly. Martie had decided to be honest and include Manon, and if the Hartnett family was horrified they could jump in their car and go back to Deerhaven. If they could accept Martie for what and who she was, then they would all enjoy a fabulous dinner at the little farm that Martie and Manon had purchased several years earlier to provide their kitchens with fresh, local produce. She was worried sick about what might happen, and the last thing she needed was to put herself into a position where Paddy would recall things. There was more than enough to deal with without adding more stress.

Back in the kitchen, Martie pulled on her chef's coat, rearranged her head scarf, and started on the last few orders out of the bar. Trays of canapés and samples of menu items were still going up in the dumbwaiter, as if the partygoers upstairs were a pack of starving beggars determined to fill their bellies. With things under control, she left Jay in charge once again and headed down to the food lockers, to take inventory before filling out Sunday night's order sheets. Whatever was to be offered on Sunday, before the delivery trucks could roll in, would depend on what was left over after Saturday night, and she feared that there wouldn't be much.

Counting up the remaining meat, poultry, and potatoes, she was amazed at the quantity of food that had passed through the kitchen in two days. Without question, this had been one of her most successful evenings, with the added bonus of being the star of her own show. If only Aunt Brid could see her now. Dear Aunt Brid, who defied her brother and welcomed Martie into her home, who seemed unfazed by the stupidity of youth that her niece demonstrated. Her aunt had been a saint, giving Martie all the room she needed to discover a simple truth about herself.

From Dublin to Rome, Aunt Brid stood ready to offer advice as Martie trained and fell in love, fell out of love, slept around and vowed celibacy. From Rome to Paris, Aunt Brid was a pillar of support, quietly encouraging Martie to follow her dream wherever it led. Aunt Brid was suspicious of Manon, not sure of the big farm girl's intentions and very protective of her niece, but she came to love the French chef. When Aunt Brid finally met Denny, she hated him and never changed her opinion of the raging alcoholic who had surrendered to his demons. Aunt Brid was more than a saint. She was wise.

"I made it. Everything I worked for, all those years. I'm here," Martie said. Her life savings had been invested wisely, and she was going to reap the rewards that were denied her when Denny set out to ruin her life. She climbed. He tumbled. He could rot at the bottom where he fell. It was not her concern. She had more than enough to worry about. He could still ruin one more thing.

Beef

Grilled Sirloin with shallot sauce

    8 oz meat

    garlic, oil = walnut?

    serve with pomme mousseline

        potatoes

        butter

        heavy cream

        salt, white pepper

Shallot sauce: ~~Whalebone Bob Wire~~

Chateau de Cruzeau

Merci Manon, oui?

172

TWENTY-ONE

Groggy from a lack of sleep, Brendan almost got lost on his way to the hotel and then could not quite remember where he wanted to take his friends on a last-minute sightseeing excursion. Paddy was in no better shape, complaining of a sleepless night filled with bizarre dreams of a woman in a white coat, face blurred and not coming into focus no matter how often he rubbed his eyes. In talking over the significance of the image, Brendan realized that Martie had not been anywhere near Paddy since they hooked up in the office. Was he worried that she was going to run off with the singer when she was just a groupie looking to put a notch in the bedpost? She was a great one for keeping herself to herself, however, and avoiding Paddy could have been a ruse. So where did Aislinn fit in? Was that a ruse concocted by a couple planning to decamp for the Emerald Isle? Did the signed partnership agreement mean nothing?

The isolation of a tour boat on the Chicago River was the perfect place to pin Paddy down, without an easy means of escape short of jumping in the water. Loyalty was in question, and Brendan had to have an answer before he found himself without an old friend and a new partner. He had more to offer Martie, if it came to that. Bonnie would just have to understand. Or be kept in the dark. A successful contractor juggled several jobs at once. Juggling two women couldn't be much different.

Cruising up the Chicago River, Brendan paid little attention to the docent's spiel. His mind was elsewhere, back in the pub, trying to figure out where Martie's mind was. In spite of Friday night's terrors, she was remarkably calm about the whole thing, and she had stuck around for the rest of the weekend when she could have disappeared. In fact, she had not taken any time off yet, except for the occasional nap here and there, so the money-laundering issue that he created was a non-starter. On the other hand, she might have been sticking around because Paddy was there, the main attraction who was leaving Sunday night. But if she was lingering because of Paddy, she hadn't made any kind of display over his departure, as if it were no big deal, or was Paddy's leaving not going to be a separation? Brendan leaned forward, his head falling into his hands as he sighed with exasperation.

"How's the head this morning?" Paddy asked. "That I don't miss at all, at all."

"It's work, not beer," Brendan said. "If Martie quits, I'm through. I'm dead meat."

"Is she thinking of leaving?" Liam said. " Sure it's the PMS talking."

They snickered like schoolboys, as they had snickered in Miltown all those years ago at the mention of any word associated with women. The tour guide pointed out the condominium complex on the left, a makeover of an old cold storage facility with walls that were stuffed with horsehair. Rory noted the lack of quays along the river, as if the waterway was nothing more than another type of road to transport goods for all the warehouses that lined the banks. With that, Paddy launched into a diatribe about commercialization, utilization of natural resources and beauty spots, and the greed of the entrepreneur. Glad of a distraction from his worries, Brendan took the bait and fired back, criticizing the pollution of the Liffey and lauding Chicago's attempts to clean up the river.

By the time that the tour was gliding out on the lake to show off the skyline, the group had settled into a quieter mode, relaxing as they enjoyed the ride and the cool breeze. Bonnie had Paddy's ear, telling him about her plans for the summer. It was the first that Brendan had heard of it.

"Don't expect much, now," Paddy said. "Irish women flock to New York City for the shopping, and Dundrum is left for those without the price of a ticket."

"I just want a little shopping bag that says 'Brown Thomas' on it," Bonnie said.

"Sweet Jesus, they're shopping for the paper sack now," Rory said with a laugh.

"I just don't know about getting away." Brendan squirmed inside, unsure if there would be anything left once he took whatever income he had and used it to stave off the pub's creditors, who would be pounding on the door after he lost his cook and the restaurant became a ghost town. Assuming he would be there for a foreclosure, rather than in jail doing time for obstruction of justice or attempted murder.

"Well, you didn't have to wire my sister the money, you know," Paddy said. "Ann called me this morning. She'd hold the bills for a year if it meant you'd be over for Willie Week. Isn't that just like a McKechnie, to pay their debts before they're due?"

In the distance, the Ferris Wheel at Navy Pier spun so slowly that it did not seem to move. Brendan didn't recall cutting any checks for any payments that related to the pub. He hadn't even seen the payroll checks that would have been issued on Saturday, a fact that he had completely forgotten until now. While it was possible that his accountant had issued payments based on some overly rosy income projections, he didn't picture Harry actually kiting checks. With only a few days available to make up the shortfall, Brendan was under pressure again, worse pressure than before, to come up with the cash. Just when he thought his troubles were easing, things were getting worse. He wanted to call Martie, to ask her if her paycheck bounced, and if it did, could he make it up to her? Would she please not go to Ireland with Paddy?

"Sun's hot," Paddy said.

Brendan mopped his sweating forehead with the sleeve of his shirt. This notion that things were looking up was a pipe dream, a flight of fancy by a desperate man. He never should have bought into his father's suggestion of building a bigger and better pub than Uncle Donal's, and only because Uncle Donal had no interest in expanding or changing, no matter how much Dermot tried to convince him. Donal had his own ideas of success, and making more money was not part of his plans.

He walked back to the boat's bar to buy water all around, with Paddy tagging along to help carry. Away from the crowd, Brendan saw his only chance to pose the questions that plagued him. "Is there something between you and Martie?" he asked.

"Did she say something?" Paddy replied, a note of panic in his voice. "It's driving me mad, all the things I can't quite remember. There's so much I did under the influence that I can't recall. Things I never told you."

"If you can't remember something from a couple of days ago," Brendan said, only to be cut off.

"No, no, not recent things. No. Since I gave up the drink I've more aware than ever of the hurt I caused. At the end, at the bottom there. After Aislinn left, and I thought I was a free man, I played that role to the hilt. Having it off with any female willing. I'd rather not talk about it if you don't mind."

"You and Aislinn are good now, right?"

"If you define 'good' as willing to try it again, yes. There'll be counseling to help us over the rough patches, but I'm not afraid to do what needs doing. It's asking a lot of a woman to take you back after you've proven untrustworthy."

"Building back trust takes some effort," Brendan said. Martie was his woman. Maybe. She had been in the office with somebody, and he knew he was not mistaken in what he heard. Michael DeCecco, then? There was a man who couldn't keep his trousers zipped. And Brendan wouldn't trust DeCecco if the man took an oath on pain of death.

"What's been troubling me so is that I have a sense that I met Martie before, but I can't be sure. She'd have said something, I'm sure. Women don't like it when you fuck and run, and I did plenty of that last summer." Paddy twisted the cap off his water and tapped Brendan's bottle. "Here's to your success."

"Here's to yours. Can't wait to see you in July, old son. Like old times, right?"

There was no sight as spectacular as Chicago's skyline when seen from the deck of a boat on the lake. The group fell into a comfortable silence, too busy taking pictures to talk. While Bonnie ordered the four friends into position along the rail, South Michigan Avenue for a backdrop, Brendan went back to Miltown, to all the poses that his mother and Aunt Eleanor had arranged and snapped for posterity. He had not actually lost his old friend after all. The boy who taught Brendan how to dribble a soccer ball was still there in Paddy, who was now the man he would have become if he had not succumbed to alcoholism. In a way, they were getting together again after a span of nearly twenty years, the drink-besotted interval a reflection of what should not have been. As children, Paddy had always been inclined to be passionate about something, whether it was music or girls, and he was true to form as a sober adult with a burning desire to make the world a better place. Taking his place in the group, Brendan wrapped an arm in a half-Nelson around Paddy's thick neck as Bonnie took another photograph.

"This summer's going to be the best," Brendan said as the boat pulled into the dock. "The ladies can go off shopping for the week and we'll find something to occupy our time."

"We'll say the rosary daily," Liam said to Bonnie. "Benediction every afternoon."

"Sure and we'll be all day in the church," Rory said, rolling his eyes. "Praying for money to fall from heaven to pay for Evie's shopping."

The next stop on the tour was the Ferris Wheel, a long, slow climb into the sky that provided a spectacular view of the city, although Liam was quick to note that the heights of the Hancock Building were impressive, and much more frightening to a country lad who had never been more than twenty feet off the ground. Brendan did the proud construction magnate routine and pointed out the condominium tower near the river that his company had built a few years ago. Several units were bought by friends for their children to call home after college, part of the traditional right of passage that wound through downtown Chicago before looping back to the suburbs when it was time to grow up and raise a family. He was thirty-eight, and running out of time if he was to ever see one of his own on that well-worn path.

"By the way," Bonnie whispered in his ear when everyone else was engrossed in the view of the lake. "I talked to Aislinn."

"Why? I don't understand," Brendan said.

"That's because you don't know women."

"Bonnie, when it comes to women, I am one stupid man," he said.

"Oh, I think I figured that out," she said. With affection, she squeezed his arm and then slid her arm through his.

"You didn't have to agree with me," he said. "That was really nice of you, though, to go to bat for Paddy."

"I feel bad for him. He's so lonely."

Sometimes, Bonnie would make a comment that made no sense to him, and this was another example. For the past two nights, the man had been surrounded by people, fans who were more than happy to see him, and Paddy was as overjoyed as could be to accept the applause and the approval. He was traveling with Rory and Liam, a couple of very old friends, and there was no room for solitude with them keeping watch, making sure that Paddy stuck to his pledge. Brendan believed that Bonnie was picking up on the sobriety, the more mellow and serious tone that defined the Irishman, as compared to his former boisterous self. If she had known Paddy as a boy, she could have seen the change in personality as a reversal to normal, rather than some pathetic circumstance. After all, this was the boy who was orphaned at an early age and singled out in the close-knit community as an object of pity, and had grown a thick skin to compensate. Paddy had plenty of company and plenty of friends. He couldn't be lonely in such a crowd.

No trip abroad was complete without an exploration of the souvenir shops that dotted the Pier. With the trip coming to an end, the visitors picked through the selections, hoping to find an item that was uniquely Chicago. The Irishmen settled for mugs emblazoned with the city skyline, practical items that would find years of use. They had just enough time left for an early lunch, to fill up on better food than anything likely to be served on Aer Lingus.

"This trip, I've been tested," Paddy said. He rubbed the lime wedge on the rim of his glass before dropping it into the Perrier. "I had to find out if I could do it, live in the real world where the drink abounds but I can't touch a drop."

"No one thinks twice these days if someone orders water," Bonnie said. "It's almost trendy not to drink. We're so into health, it's sickening."

"There's a bit of desire there yet," Paddy said. "I can't pretend otherwise. It's a fact. But I've been able to conquer the urge, and accept what I am."

"Never surrender," Rory said.

They began to make plans for July, when they would be together again. Bonnie was far more excited about going than she had ever been, asking Liam about Spanish Point and the beach, walking paths and horse riding. Brendan hoped that she was organizing activities for the children and the wives, so that he could hang around the pubs as he usually did, visiting what family remained in Miltown. Somewhere in all her scheduling, he would have to insert a slot for his mother, who would never forgive him if he did not go to church with her on Sunday morning and then eat dinner with the family on Sunday afternoon. In past years, there had been squabbles that caught him in the middle, with his mother complaining and Bonnie fuming on separate floors of the pub, putting on happy smiling faces when they met in the same room, in public. Bonnie has so many expensive clothes for a week's trip, your mother's always playing the martyr; he couldn't stand to hear it all again. Let them work it out between them. He was going to pal around with the lads, and the rest could make their own fun or go back home. Life was too short, Paddy had a bad heart, and there might not be a next year.

The best seats at the trendiest brunch spot were along the windows, offering a view of the city skyline that Liam compared to the image on his tea mugs. It was worth the long wait, in Brendan's opinion, to send his pals off with a final culinary flourish. In a nod to Paddy's commitment to sobriety, they opted for tea, to give him a break from the ordeal of doing battle with an addiction.

Bonnie's phone rattled over the muted sounds of Frank Sinatra that filled the dining room. She checked the caller ID and shook her head. "Another one. I swear, this thing has not stopped ringing all morning. Who knew that Martie Smurfit was such an incredible get? Brendan, I forgot to tell you. Elisa Crane, you remember her from the Gortimer party? The one who bid some astronomical sum to have a chef come to her house and teach a half hour class?" Bonnie sat up a little straighter and shook her hair away from her face. "She bid thirty thousand dollars for Martie Smurfit's time because Martie Smurfit trained with Guy Savoy, among others. Flies under the radar, Elisa told me, a very private person."

Private. Martie was that, and more. Her past was as blank as if she was in the witness protection program. It was like she was dropped into Moraine Hills from an unknown location. "Elisa Crane has more money than she knows what to do with," Brendan said. "You wouldn't believe the changes she ordered on her summer cottage. Money was no object with her."

"The bid was for charity," Bonnie said.

"Bet she'd be the type to pay double for the same food if she got to sit in the hot kitchen instead of the comfortable dining room," Brendan said. Just because Martie made fun of the concept did not mean that he would have to ignore an idea that could bring in a decent return on the investment. He could rearrange a few things in the kitchen and fit in a table

179

for four. There were more than enough hungry people who would be happy to say they ate in McKechnie's kitchen and watched a professional at work. He didn't see the attraction, but then again, he had spent his life watching carpenters pound nails and drywallers slap mud. Observing work was not particularly interesting in his mind.

"Let's see, who else? Someone asked if Martie would keep doing the weekly cooking class that she did at DeCecco's. You should talk to her about that, Brendan. There's a demand."

In his mind, Brendan pictured a cooking show on television, like the many programs he had watched when he first decided to open a restaurant. The investment could be small, relatively speaking, but the potential for profit was beyond counting. Martie doing a weekly class, but broadcast on a cable network with a national audience would expand their pool of customers. The food tourists would come, and a boost in publicity after the initial rush of novelty died down would be welcome. A live audience would add some excitement to things. He would select the audience carefully, of course. Make a ticket the hottest commodity on the North Shore.

A glance at his watch and he knew that the time had come for goodbyes. Sedated by the heavy meal, they walked slowly back to the parking garage, their chatter focused on their next meeting in Miltown. For a few hours, Brendan had escaped from his worries, but they were there still in the back of his head, ready to bloom anew. Not a word about Brown or Gray. Not a word about drugs or counterfeit money attached to McKechnie's. Was it coming later? Would it be waiting for him on Monday morning?

Bonnie slid into the driver's seat of her Lexus crossover SUV, a vehicle too small to comfortably contain four grown men. "Everyone buckled in?" she chirped, flashing a smile for the members of Shift/Move who could neither shift nor move, so compressed were they. She adjusted her rear view mirror and turned the key in the ignition. Nothing happened. She turned it again.

"When I told you to take it in for a new battery, did you take it in?" Brendan asked.

"Not yet," Bonnie said. "Obviously."

He checked his watch again, a slight twinge of panic tightening the muscles of his neck. How long would it take to get a jump, or worse, what if the battery was shot and the car had to be towed in? He could get a cab for the group, but someone had to stay with the car and he would never leave Bonnie alone to deal with a tow truck driver. At the same time, he didn't want to send his friends to the airport alone, and sending Bonnie would cause another headache because she would need a ride home. With finger flying, he scrolled through the names in his contact list, getting nothing but voice mails on a Sunday afternoon. He landed on Martie's emergency contact number. Martie, at least, was someone he could trust to look after the trio and see them safely on their way.

TWENTY-TWO

The cell phone sailed across the room, to land on sofa cushions that had just been plumped. How could Brendan call, asking for favors, at such a time? "What part of family time does he not understand?" Martie asked.

She had just finished a call from Mrs. Hartnett, who wanted to warn her about Ryan's depressed mood. The young man had spent some time with his birth father, apparently, and discovered that Denny was not the reformed drinker he claimed to be. He was afraid that his birth mother might prove to be a disappointment as well, and all that Martie could do was assure Mrs. Hartnett that she indeed a successful restaurant owner and chef. She cited news articles that Ryan could look up if he wished, only to realize that she had never told anyone she had a baby she had given up for adoption. The whole world would find out eventually, and how was she supposed to handle that kind of publicity?

Manon retrieved the phone, laughing at the outburst that was more emotional than usual. "A friend asks for help, and you would say no? After the, what was it, the incident? Manon asked.

"Four hours from now I am going to meet my son for the first time since he was born, and instead of getting ready, I have to drive from Bristol all the way to Navy Pier and then all the way to the airport because someone didn't replace a car battery," Martie said. All the way to the airport with Paddy Dunne and the chance that a memory would be recovered, in a car with Manon who insisted on going along to be company. Secrets were falling away, toppling like a house of cards, but could she keep just one?

Five acres of peaceful farmland provided organic vegetables and herbs for their restaurant kitchens, while the cozy farmhouse was their refuge from the stress of work. The setting was suitably bucolic, with the chickens across the road and the dairy farm just west of their driveway. It was quiet on the farm, and Martie thought it was the best place to be when she came out to her son and his adoptive parents, three strangers who otherwise would never know, or need to know, that she was a lesbian. Brendan could not have called at a worse time, but how could she say no? As Manon pointed out, they would be back long before the Hartnett clan arrived, and there was nothing to do until then.

The sous chef from Le Grenouille had been hired for the day, and had everything under control. The pot au feu was simmering, the peas were shelled and ready for blanching, and the cheeses were out on the serving board, seeking room temperature. The table was set, napkins folded into fans, and the silverware gleamed in the mid-day sun that streamed through the large windows. All that remained was fretting, which Martie could manage quite well in a car on the way to the airport.

The traffic was light and they reached the city in under an hour, less time than it took a mechanic to show up at the parking garage where the dead SUV sat. Martie found Brendan standing behind the car, hood up in an international sign of distress. Suitcases were transferred, manly embraces exchanged, and in no time the back seat of Manon's car was packed with bodies in a way that reminded Martie very much of the Friday night drive through Gilead. She slid behind the wheel of the glorified truck, a task she usually disliked, but it was better to handle the Suburban than ride shotgun and be expected to converse with the trio in the back seat.

"Did we pull you away from anything?" Liam asked.

"Nothing important," Manon said. "We visit our farm on Sundays, like a working holiday. We cook, try new recipes."

"We're grateful to you," Rory said. "We have a gig in two days time and we could use a day to get our heads back on Greenwich mean time."

"Some people have more than they need and don't even know it," Paddy said. "Were your ears burning, Martie? We were talking about you."

Her hands slipped on the steering wheel, too wet with sweat to get a grip. "And?" she asked.

"You were sold into slavery, we were told. Made to toil for a woman of means," Liam said.

"The charity," Manon said. "Where those who adore Chef Smurfit pay homage with offerings of large checks. They give what they have, money. We give what we have. Our time. Business is not what it was ten years ago."

Martie watched the road signs with full concentration, on the hunt for one that would direct her to the parking lot nearest the International Terminal. She had forgotten to tell Brendan that Ger had called her in the middle of the night, to let her know that the Police Service of Northern Ireland had a new lead on an old bank robbery. Interpol had been on it for at least a week, he had learned. The announcement slipped her mind, which was busy wrapping itself around Manon's proposal. She was giving the idea some serious thought when Brendan barged in with his dead battery, and she was in no position to chatter away on the Bluetooth connection in a car filled with people who had no business hearing what she would be saying. Besides, she was terrified that Paddy would recognize her voice if she talked too much, and if she couldn't disappear, she would do all she could to become invisible.

Part of that effort required her to run off in search of a luggage cart as soon as the car was parked, to leave the men to handle the cases of instruments and carry-on bags. She could see the end of her ordeal at the check-in, where she would turn Shift/Move over to the care of their homeland's official air carrier. Already the line for security was growing, and Martie was not so sure that the odd shape of uilleann pipes and tin whistles might not set off alarms that would delay things further. The last thing she wanted was to have to drive Paddy back to Moraine Hills if the plane left without him, giving him that much more time to bring his fuzzy memory into focus.

The loudspeaker announced something about a flight, but it was unintelligible garble. On the alert for every opportunity to avoid Paddy, Martie offered to hunt down a departure screen to be sure that Aer Lingus was still on time and leaving from the gate marked on the tickets. A small suitcase banged into her calf and she turned to see who was so clumsy. She came face to face with the man she had last seen in an abandoned garage.

"Hey," she shouted. He was not more than twenty feet away, still clad in the same outfit he had been wearing a few nights ago. His shifty-eyed companion looked equally the worse for wear, as if he too had slept in the clothes he was wearing. For seconds that felt like hours, they traded stares, but it was the man who was the first to flinch, his look changing from one of surprise to that of a deer in headlights. He was disheveled, his jacket dirty and flecked with what must surely be his own blood. When he turned, Martie saw the cut on the side of his head, livid and red, traces of blood matted in his hair. The loyalist thug was no longer so artfully dressed or so nauseatingly cocky.

"Hey," Martie shouted, but a rush of adrenalin tightened her throat and the word came out like a squeak. "Hey, you. You fucking thief."

They were afraid of her, these two toughs from Belfast. scared out of their wits by a woman half their size. Together, they turned to run, to bolt, to get lost in the throng of travelers because they were chickenshit hoodlums and they were terrified of an unarmed female. Louder this time, Martie barked out a demand that they stop, the thieves, and then she took off after them. She wanted to get her hands on him, to pound him to a pulp like that junkie in Gilead was pounded for using one of the counterfeit bills. Tackle him from behind, knock him down, then wring his neck. She would use her fists and her feet, scratch his eyes out, rip out his blond-tipped hair by the roots. Every minute of stress she had endured because of him would find release. Every second that had been spoiled because she had to keep looking over her shoulder was going to be repaid in blood and broken bones. She had not slept soundly for days, worrying about the safety of her employees. The son of a bitch would pay with his life, his worthless, miserable life.

In her mind she was running, but Martie realized she was not moving when she noticed that swarms of policemen were pouring in from all sides. Security was tight as a noose at every airport, and all it took to get such a response was two men running like they were being chased, rather than jogging to catch a flight. Her breath caught in her throat when she thought she saw guns pulled, imagining a hail of bullets like some Wild West gunfight. She had not come this far in her climb to the top to be gunned down by the clouted cops who won the cushy airport beat because they were somebody's somebody. The scene dissolved into a blur of dark blue uniforms, with splashes of pastel color moving from the upright to the prone position.

Her heart said flee while her head said stay, to listen and learn her own fate. The criminal pair in handcuffs might just start singing about McKechnie's Pub and attempted murder. She had to know, as much as she could know, if her involvement spilled out on the concourse with international travelers gawking at the scene. Northern Ireland bank notes floated through her imagination and she put her hand on her purse to protect it from being invaded by evidence.

"Purse snatchers?" a police officer asked. "Miss? Are you okay? Did they try to steal your purse?"

"Robbery," Martie spluttered. So many words crowded onto her tongue, pushed along by a brain overflowing with fear and outrage.

Another officer frisked the suspects, rummaging through pockets with the deft touch of a practiced master. His face broke into a grin of absolute delight as he displayed a cluster of small plastic bags, filled with what looked like rock candy.

"What is that?" Martie asked. She had a good idea, but she needed a minute to collect herself before deciding what she could safely say to a man who could arrest her if he found cause.

The injured man was somewhat combative, loudly exclaiming that the packets were not his and someone had planted the drugs on him, a reverse pickpocketing. His associate, on the other hand, remained stoic as a roll of money was extracted from the inside pocket of his suit coat and handed to a plainclothes officer. He finally flinched when a second wad of cash left his pants pocket, and he was visibly shaken when the officer examined one of the bills in the harsh overhead light of the terminal. Judging by the way the cop patted down the man's legs, he must have found some lumps not natural to the human body. A story spilled out, and Martie breathed deeply with relief. The criminal's partner launched into a story about a prize fight won by his colleague; they themselves were the victims of a crime if the money was not legal. They had a flight to catch, it was injustice, a mistake, a double cross and he was innocent. Never once did either either man point a finger at her and demand that she be arrested for assault and battery and attempted murder. The luck of the Irish was with her. She would push it, just a little.

"You'd better check with Interpol, in case they're wanted in Europe," she said.

"Not every foreign visitor is a criminal, ma'am," the policeman said. "Now, would you care to lodge a complaint? You have that right, but

I have to warn you, the prosecutor isn't going to spend much time on a simple robbery when we've got possession."

"I'm fine," she lied. "A little shaken, but nothing was taken."

"I'll need your name, for the record," he said.

"My name?"

He held a pencil over a pad of paper, waiting. "Place of employment and a number to reach you in case we have further questions."

"McKechnie's," she said. "I work there. In Moraine Hills."

"Not Brendan McKechnie?" he asked. "My brother-in-law is an electrician who works for him. Ran all the wires for some restaurant he built. Says the food's good, but pretty la-di-da for the likes of us. You a waitress?"

"No. I'm in the kitchen," she said.

"That's the way to a man's heart," the cop said. "Not that you need the extra help."

The crowd was dispersed in no time, pushed along by police who were wary of gathered crowds in an age of terrorism. Manon pushed through the clot of gawkers who lingered, wondering what had happened when it was already over. "Martie, tout va bien?" She touched Martie's cheek with a comforting hand.

«Ce n'est rien,» she said. "Two men were just arrested."

"We will say good-bye to our friends and go home." Manon wrapped her arm around her, claiming her, protecting her from whatever might crop up.

"Make sure someone calls the British consul. Don't let them get off on a technicality," she said to the policeman.

"We've been watching for those two for days," the policeman said, his voice low as he shared a confidence. "Big deal, us nabbing them. You don't want to get involved in this, ma'am. Just go on home and forget you were here."

"Good advice. Come on, Martie. The pot au feu will be meat paste if we don't get back soon," Manon said.

"What was that all about?" Rory asked when Martie found them still standing in line to check in.

"A little excitement. The police caught a couple of drug smugglers," she said.

"Lucky for us they did not evacuate the terminal," Manon said.

"And just when we're making progress," Liam said. "We've moved all of eight paces since you went off."

There was no need for the women to remain, and in Martie's mind, it was best to get out while the getting was good. She brushed against Manon's hand, as if she would take it and they would walk into the sunset together.

"Bon voyage," Manon said. She strolled away in her usual, unhurried pace until they reached an elevator, where she collapsed against the far wall as soon as the door closed. "So?"

"So?" Martie said. "So nothing. The police caught two criminals who are wanted in Europe. Nothing to do with us."

Her secrets were safe, tucked away until they expired from age and inattention. She let Manon take her in her arms and kiss her, an embrace that grew too passionate for an elevator with a security camera. "We love each other," Manon said. "Why not get married? Maybe Ryan will give you away."

"Slow down," Martie said. Raised in a strict Catholic home flooded with rules, she had drowned. After learning how to swim, she was not ready to tackle the equivalent of a Channel crossing.

"Slow? We have been together for years. Why not get married?"

"I'm already married to my restaurant." Martie rested her head on Manon's broad shoulder. "I can't give myself to you completely."

"And I'm married to La Grenouille. All this time, we are being very French, yes, and having an affair. Nothing would change between us. Just to make the law happy we get our paper to say we are one. I am not asking you to be the little wife at home, like our mothers."

"Don't even mention affairs," Martie said. "You know I cheated on you."

"Long ago, before you would admit you loved women. You were more dishonest with yourself than with me."

"You did put together a very impressive collection of sex toys," Martie said. "I appreciate the effort you put in to maintain our relationship when I was distracted."

A history of bed-hopping could be overcome, but Martie was less than confident that two big culinary egos could co-exist on a daily basis, under one roof. She had gone to Miltown last summer to discuss Ryan's request to meet his birth parents, but she could have spoken to Denny anywhere. Going to Ireland was a way to escape Manon's interference in a very personal decision, a sign that Martie was not ready to commit to one person for the rest of her life.

Hand in hand they walked back to the car, oblivious to the travelers who hurried past them. As Martie latched her seat belt, Manon fiddled with the radio until she found some jazz, never asking if Martie minded or if she wanted to listen to what Manon wanted to listen to. "I have a new goal. To buy out McKechnie," Manon said. "I don't like the way he looks at you."

"What are you talking about? Are you jealous?"

"Always jealous. But with DeCecco, you were safe. He was afraid of you."

"Brendan doesn't know a thing about me. Not a single thing."

She knew about Brendan, or at least the way he thought. A line of frozen sauces or soups had been floated during one of their brief conversations. Brendan had hinted at franchises or an expansion program that would compete with DeCecco's little empire, none of which interested her any longer. She was thirty-two, already feeling the fatigue of age settling into her legs, and what she wanted as a new mother at sixteen was what she had achieved. Maintaining her position would take all her energy. There was no point in proving something more. Her family had cut her off, so who was she showing off to besides herself? Manon did not care if she was a household name or a complete unknown, loving Martie for who she was as a human being. Getting bigger than DeCecco did have a certain charm, however. Buying him out would be the ultimate revenge fantasy.

All nice to dream about, but she had to control Brendan before she could feel secure. His attempt to help out had put them all in a dangerous situation, and she had to find a way to push him aside before he helped her into something equally disastrous. In a few months, he would leave for Ireland. She could ease him out slowly, so slowly that when he came back from his trip he would never realize that he was on the outside looking in. As for Manon investing in the pub, it was a dream on her part. The restaurant business had been on a downward slide for the past few years and margins were painfully thin. Besides, Martie didn't want to get rid of Brendan completely. He could be useful, with his contacts and his skills.

"He would marry his lover if he was serious about their future," Manon said. "Instead, he leaves the door open to other women. Always looking for something better than what he has. One day he might find you. So I put a stop to it now."

Martie had been wrong about Bonnie, seeing her as an interloper when the poor woman was just trying to secure her position. If she could help Bonnie to the altar, she could gain an ally in their joint desire to keep Brendan at home more. "I think there's a wedding in his future," she said. "Sooner rather than later."

"So, tomorrow?" Manon asked.

By tradition, the restaurants in Moraine Hills were closed on Mondays, giving some chefs a day off and others an extra day to toy with recipes or experiment with new ingredients. It was a day to handle personal business. The pressure from Manon was relentless, wearing a woman down. "I can't cook with a ring on my finger."

"It's time you learned."

"Don't start telling me how to cook," Martie said.

"If I hadn't told you in Paris you would be still on the line chopping onions."

"So it's all been thanks to you."

"Of course. You may thank me tonight."

Manon kissed her on the cheek, making allowances for the fact that she was driving seventy miles an hour on a busy highway. Marriage was one of many options, but they would be wise to make their arrangement more stable while deciding on the next step. That much she was willing to do, to secure their shared finances and property. And yet. If Ryan was accepting. If his parents did not flee the farm in terror, or lecture her on sin. Was she looking for a sign? Did she need a demonstration of open-mindedness from a couple who were expected to be repulsed by her upcoming confession? And what if Mr. and Mrs. Hartnett did not care? All well and good, but Martie had to think of the reaction of her staff, and the opinions of her clients. There was risk in coming out in so public a way as getting married.

She did not realize she was driving too slow until the semi road up on her back bumper and blasted the horn. Martie floored it, getting back up to speed while Manon squawked about the strain on the engine. It was hard to believe that there had been a time when she was a fifteen-year-old from a small town visiting a cousin in Moraine Hills and lying about her age to get a job in a restaurant kitchen. If she hadn't gone off-course, she wouldn't have a kitchen of her own, in spite of the obstacles in her way.

She wouldn't know who she was or what she was, and never would have imagined back then that she would be happy with herself. You couldn't make something cook faster by turning up the heat, she realized. The best chefs understood the value of patience.

About The Author

Sean Gleason has worked in the culinary industry for several years, and has used his experiences, both front of the house and back, to create this delightful novel. He lives in Chicago.

He can be reached at Newcastlewest Books.

www.newcastlewestbooks.com

Lightning Source UK Ltd.
Milton Keynes UK
UKOW07f0736011215

263879UK00013B/83/P